D1046695

UNDOING I DO

THOMAS DUNNE BOOKS
ST. MARTIN'S PRESS
NEW YORK

unDoing I Do

ANASTASIA ROYAL

This is a work of fiction. All of the characters, organizations, and events portrayed in this novel are either products of the author's imagination or are used fictitiously.

THOMAS DUNNE BOOKS.
An imprint of St. Martin's Press.

www.thomasdunnebooks.com
www.stmartins.com

Design by Susan Walsh

Library of Congress Cataloging-in-Publication Data

Royal, Anastasia.
Undoing I do / Anastasia Royal.—1st ed.
p. cm.
ISBN-13: 978-0-312-36965-1
ISBN-10: 0-312-36965-4
1. Divorced women—Fiction. 2. Single mothers—Fiction. I. Title.

PS3618.O8927U53 2007
813'.6—dc22 2007031466

First Edition: November 2007

10 9 8 7 6 5 4 3 2 1

For Dorothée and Hans, who are full of love

*And for Bruce, my brilliant star, whose love dazzles, protects,
and gives comfort and joy beyond telling*

ACKNOWLEDGMENTS

To my mother: Your tireless love, enthusiasm, and astute editing skills encouraged me to try harder. To my father: You never give up, and I love you for it.

To my remarkable siblings and in-laws: Deep thanks for standing vigil, now go home.

I am especially grateful for the nurturing five weeks I spent at the Ragdale Foundation. The prairie, residents, and staff there provided the sanctuary I needed to write and the miracle of meeting an incomparable friend, the poet Brian Komei Dempster. Thank you, Brian, for the many weeks—over the years—of your expert and generous editing of this book.

To the late Lili and Miklos Simon, who taught me everything I needed to know about everything.

Eloise Fink, thank you for taking me seriously.

Noreen Edwards and Mark Metz, your long-term friendship has taken many forms. Thanks for letting me use your computer, so many years ago.

Hugs to John Callaway, the best and the brightest. I feel as if I can accomplish anything after talking to you.

David Fivecoate, your brilliant ideas and the sound of your saxophone could get anyone through the worst.

Tuto Newman, your unique style gave me hope.

Kevin Collins, student extraordinaire, your support was crucial.

My special thanks to Steven Popich. Your humor and ingenious nature rescued me.

Ann Callaway, your letters and music are better than chocolate.

Kisses to the scintillating and original Dan Tucker.

Peter Miller, you taught me that some doors are open, some closed, and some have money behind them.

Jay and Jeanne Bonansinga, your sophisticated and sweet enthusiasm is a rare combination. Jay, thanks for the spark that started all of this.

Ted O'Neill, the epitome of charm, generosity, and brilliance—your support has been key.

Marge Roche, everyone could use a mentor as courageous as you.

Marlys and Greg Jorjorian, you saved my life too many times. Thank you for your true friendship.

To the late Michael Lefkow, who knew how to listen, and to Joan Lefkow, whose smile made me feel welcome.

Mark Boyer—your deep understanding of the first version of this book was a miracle. You are too young to be wise, but thank God you are.

Susan Holzer, beautiful and brilliant: Your insightful reading of my book was invaluable.

Ursula von Walterskirchen, *schön und schlau,* and the best of friends: Many thanks for being at my beck and call about German usage.

Maya Romanoff, astonishing and elegant: After meeting you, life made more sense.

And to my other friends—having just one of you in my life would be a blessing: Jawad and his sister Mekhala and their father, the late Ibrahim Abu-Lughod, Tina Rose Avendano, all the "Bad Boys" (you know who you are), Karen Beatha, Red Star Berglund, Dan Bryant, John and Sarabess Cahill, Alexander Childers, Grace Chow, Susan Chorba, the late Del Close, Drs. Polly and Roger Collins, Dan Coma, Jackie and Lisa Comforty, Brian Cox, Walburga Domann, David (Chainsaw) and Norma DuPont, Mr. and Mrs. John Dyrud, Jeffrey Epstein, Mark Epton, Ron Falzone, Jeff and Marie FitzGerald, Heather Florence, Virginia and Gary Gerst, Andrea Gronvall, Lawrence Gyenes, Karen Hagnell and Ted Kommers, Harriet Harvey, Curtis and Zita Hayward, Werner Herterich, Ginny Holbert and Chris Allen, Scott Holzer, Jack and Eileen Johnson, Tim and Marcia Kazurinsky, Francine Lahaye, Sheryl Larson and Hank Kinzie, Christopher Laughlin, Dee Lawson, Jane and John Lionberger, Jeff and Betsy Lupetin, Brighid Malone, Mr. and Mrs. Manouhar and Prahba Manchanda, Michael Martin, Nancy McKearn, Jim McPhedran, Bert Menco, Michael and Laura Montenegro, Jan Muller, Audrey Niffenegger, Joy Ogden, Michael and Suzie Ohrenstein, the sparkly Olivia, Catherine Popowitz, Danny Postel, Kevin Pritchett, Allyn Rawling, Jim Reeves, Tom and Phyllis Robb, Dean and Susan Rolando, Joyce Romanoff, Nancy Shaer, Tom Shaer, Dean Shavit, Saro Solis, George and Kati Spaniak, Mike and Judy Stein, Gail Sturm, Margaret Sullivan, Sandie Swanson, Laura Takuma, Margaret Tucker, Jennifer Waldvogel, Martin von Walterskirchen, Michael Warr, the late Billie Webster, Richard Webster, Heather Woodbury, and Ziggy Dyrkacz from Chopin Theatre.

A special thanks to my editor, Erin Brown, who made completing this book a joy.

Men and women should meet in beautiful rooms,
stroke each other for hours, and then go back to their separate lives.

PART ONE

Ending Beginning

OVERTURE TO A BURN

He lights three candles on her naked body. One between the shoulder blades, another on the small of her back—a flicker above the slight curve—and the last on her thigh, where her bum begins its swell.

She says, "Don't burn me," while thinking, "Here are my burns." The secret, invisible ones, shown to no one. Touch them, she means. Heal me.

But it's far too early to say such a thing to a person she has known twenty-eight days. And nights.

She imagines he is thinking, "She looks holy, too sacred to touch." Most likely he's thinking, "I hope I don't burn her."

Balancing candles, she tries to turn her face toward him.

The points of light sputter on her back. She thinks, "Don't make me into a figure in Madame Tussaud's gallery," but since he's foreign, he may not understand. She doesn't fully understand.

Their thoughts, like wisps of smoke, hover above them. In silence, they slip free of past and future.

All she knows is that they are engaged. Though new to each other, they are all-consumed, yet unconsummated.

As she slept, she felt him like a shadow, or a dream. But he's real, in her room, in her life, now in her bed, the cool liquid of his mouth on the nape of her neck. "I've been up all night, thinking, reading, drinking wine," he says, his rich voice registering an octave below her navel.

She turns her head and his warm tongue sizzles in her mouth.

"Are the candles dripping?" she asks, craning her neck—not the most graceful of gestures—to see herself in the candlelight. Her skin is translucent, flammable.

"Trust me," he says as a droplet of wax sears the back of her thigh.

She winces.

He blows them out like birthday candles, all in one gust, and licks away the vanilla wax.

In the dark, something hot coils in both of them. A flicker on his skin lights the way, and as she pulls him inside, she whispers in his ear, "Make a wish."

I — Final Chord, 1992

"Mom, the moving van is here!" yells my daughter, Elender, as she runs up the stairs to me.

"It's here!" echoes my son, Marcus, downstairs.

Elender tries to catch my eye as I look in the mirror, brushing my hair, unable to untangle words or anything else.

To disguise my silence, she continues. "Daddy says we'll love his new place."

Chatterbox, oh beautiful little chatterbox. Blending into the blue of her eight-year-old eyes, I see the trust she has in me, and I dig the bristles deep into my scalp. She almost smiles, a pouty lip flutter, until my jagged panic snags her.

For a second, we are caught in the glass, our eyes locked, unable to blink.

Then, as if by a flipped switch, the connection is broken and her eyes dodge mine, her mouth sets in a thin line. She swirls around, long hair flying, and runs fast down the stairs.

A madwoman couldn't have a saner daughter.

I need a habit. The cool drag of a menthol, some froth on a mug of Guinness, or sweet cream swirling into Kahlúa would feel right just now. But I don't take potions for solace. I can't count one that truly works.

I had warned my husband, Tobin. "If we move to the States, we'll get divorced."

"Ach ne," he said. "It could never happen."

But here we are, in Evanston, Illinois, border of the Windy City, and today's gusts are blowing him away.

I put the brush down, wood on wood, apply four or five lipsticks—the perfect shade *is* attainable—and walk like a windup mannequin downstairs to the living room.

Someone's watching as I approach the Bösendorfer grand. Tobin? No, I'm wrong.

Nothing is here but the light of a March afternoon. I sit at the piano, and my hands summon Bach. The ordered partita calms my breathing.

From nowhere, Tobin's head appears at the end of the concert piano's sweeping curve. Tall and looking decidedly Aryan today, he bows a soldierly adieu. Ironic. This is his first overture to me in six months.

My fingers glide across the ivory; my foot flattens the brass pedal, then my hands bang wildly. He turns his back, walks out the front door.

From the piano bench, I strain to reach the phone and call my lover of six months.

"Come over," Christopher whispers in my ear.

I hang up the phone, and as I run to my car, Tobin shouts from the dark of the van, "I'll be gone in an hour."

Like little Santa Clauses bumping Tobin's stuffed bags down the front steps, Elen and Marc are helping their daddy. "I'll be right back," I tell them.

As I speed off into the bright street, scenes of Tobin jump out at me.

In the kitchen years ago: boiling a pig's head in a pan so small, its snout is sticking out.

I'm vegetarian.

More recently in the bedroom: throwing back the curtains, jettisoning my clothes out the window onto the muddy lawn.

On our ninth anniversary: tossing a bag of gifts from me out the sunroof of our Mercedes as we drive home from a tapas restaurant—scattering the tie and book and CD on the road, narrowly missing a child on a bike.

Just today: grabbing a jar of peanut butter with only enough left for a teaspoonful and handing it to our seven-year-old son, Marcus. "I bought this; pack it in the van."

The images reflux like lava until I arrive, fully lipsticked, at Christopher's apartment.

Christopher, legal, but still too young, opens the door in boxers.

We kiss into a large leather chair, fall to the floor.

I have thirty-six minutes until I have to be back home.

When I return, the moving van is panting in front of our town house. We were safe there: four secure walls with a tiny yard and one evergreen tree.

I look into the van's cavernous interior, notice my personal things mixed in with Tobin's: paintings from artist friends, cookware, a science book with an inscription to me from my dad, even my robe.

I stevedore a ceramic bowl, made by my best friend, Nina, and run into the house.

The walls are shaking; I hold on to chairs and shelves to go from one room to the other, looking for the children. They are tired and whimpering.

Tobin is balancing the last solid wood bookshelf on his back; he leaves us the sagging, pressboard variety. He is Atlas and we could be squashed under his feet.

Slice the air. Wait. I still love him.

I scan the living room. Books are scattered like tiles on the floor. In the corners, dirt streaks the walls. And this from a man who would make a better hausfrau than I.

I wander the house. The kitchen: spoons and forks scattered across countertops, a veil of sugar over my cookbooks, and a pristine square, like a pulsating Mondrian, where he took the phone off the wall. My bedroom: clothes on the floor in orgiastic twists, tangled sheets stained with oil and his footprints from where he unscrewed the bulb from the ceiling light.

I rush to the children's room, afraid to open the door. Exhalation. This one room is spared. Against the lavender walls, their two small beds—with sheets flat and white—make peace.

I drift downstairs again, find a chair upside down, a desk half in the hallway. '*Spass Tag' für Möbel.* "Fun Day for Furniture." Could this be a hallucination?

I grab a box of pastels, hand it to Elen, who, followed by a silent Marc, flees to the basement for paper and an easel.

I stand in the front door and watch Tobin climb into the cab of the loaded van.

The plaster statue of Bach, an engagement gift from him, is in my hands. I hurl it at the door of the van as it pulls away from the curb. Fugal blow, final chord. It shatters with a percussive thud as my body would have, had I tried to stop him.

Before dinner, the children and I sit outside on the cold front steps. As the sun is setting on our broken home, Elen and Marc take bits of plaster from the statue, use it as chalk on the sidewalk. They write:

I LOVE MOMMY
I LOVE DADDY
I LOVE OUR FAMILY

Sometimes the worst is just the beginning.

2 Fault Lines

This is soulquake, cracks of the spirit. No fault in the land of the Past is dormant. *Gemütlichkeit* gone.

I sit at the kitchen table and feel tremors beneath my feet—each fissure's slow rending of the earth.

Could this disaster please wait?

We didn't cheat on each other. He didn't drink. I haven't lost my figure: "Now where did I put those shapely legs and waist?" He wasn't a drug addict. But no matter where I stand, the earth threatens to swallow me whole.

Female friends say, "How can you divorce him? He's so gorgeous."

"He's yours for free," I tell them.

Nine years and two continents later, there are miles of ground—rubble now—we didn't cover, places we didn't stop or even linger, things we'll never do. Things like staying together.

Crushed by the weight of what could have been, I claw at the dirt. I love, loved—oh, the past tense hurts mighty bad—Tobin for loving me and my music and my art and my peculiar Native American obsession. I loved him for his accent when he spoke English and the way he held my head and called it *"einen musikalischen Hinterkopf."* An Indian would have said, "Head round like moon, makes music." I loved him most of all for the children he caused in me. We should have made it work, for our Elender and Marcus. We could have made it work for ourselves.

Instead, we have a catastrophe in our hands, forcing me to my knees. My head, once round and musical, is flattened by collapsing walls. I try to surface, am stuck, isotopic: half-lived, half-dead. But the children crawl out, looking barely harmed—the best boy, the best girl—amid a world of ash, and their lives take root. With a mother who can't find an inch of unshaking ground.

From the kitchen window, where I'm trying to make a breakfast, I watch them messing about in the yard. Elen starts to climb the towering evergreen tree, but Marcus pulls on her shirt, stretching it until it almost comes off her spare frame. She yells something at him and they both laugh. She jumps down to help him with a hole he has been digging.

A few days ago, I would have called out to Tobin, "Come and look." But I am solo now. All the things I sense—trees, wind, rain, ah yes, the rain—will not be shared with anyone, except my children. A rift, newborn in me, is deepening.

Elen thrusts her usual intensity into my face. Her hands are black from digging in the dirt.

"I must have a pet. I'm about to make do with a worm."

She drops it on the floor.

The worm wriggles on the linoleum, blind and deaf.

Like me, it feels vibrations.

3 Rumblings

Have I finally, verifiably, made a grave mistake?

4 Impulse

I guess this is where I should open a vein—in case I need to get an IV started later—and spill some facts about how it all began.

The minute Tobin and I meet in the gallery, we know we will be married. The thought circles in our heads like a crazed dog chasing its tail, as we speak the tentative getting-to-know-you words.

"What's that?" he asks about the blue beaded necklace wound around my ankle three times.

"I made it."

"Can I have some for my foot?"

"Sure," I say, not thinking he's serious.

But he is.

Attraction is electric: ions so deliciously charged, they reach for each other. Until the polarities reverse.

5 Orientation

Looking back, especially at the good, is more painful than I had imagined.

One minute I feel bloodless; the next burning inside as if I were hot to the touch. If I could stab deep into the meat of us, skewer every first detail of Tobin and me—even the tilt of the earth—maybe I could find some sign that we would end badly. Something I had failed to notice before. Like a flock of crows. Or snakes crawling along the sidewalk.

Remembering has its own logic, its own mythic nature, neither true nor false.

6 Tiger

He was the first man I saw that night as I paced the gallery.

It's an opening for an exhibit of drawings by a group of sculptors including Tiger Manning, whose ex-wife Delia is a friend of my boss at the arts journal where I work by day. By night, I'm in a semi-punk band called the Shaved Legs. I had pushed to no avail for it to be called Mammary and the Glands.

Once, at the arts journal, Delia took me aside for a fashion consultation. "You are such an attractive young woman. I really wonder why you wear anklet socks."

" 'Cause I love 'em," I say, deliberately speaking babyish.

It's ten years before mini-socks will feature on the waify ankles of runway models.

She looks pained. "But they ruin your outfits."

"I know. That's why I wear them."

Her deep breath shows exasperation. "I could take you to Marshall Field's, and we could get you some nice hose."

"Thanks, Delia," I say. "I appreciate your concern, but I buy these in the children's section of Woolworth's."

"Indeed," she says. "They look like the Communion socks of a West Side Mexican girl."

"Precisely," I say.

"And the blue beads around your socks?"

"Let's not go there," I say.

She has invited me this evening to the gallery opening featuring her famous ex-husband. As a concession to her, I am wearing light blue stockings. But as a tribute to Tiger, and to wickedly insist on my right to pursue eccentricity, I have applied startling tigrene makeup.

I'm with my strawberry blond sister Chloë, who has come from work at the Chicago Symphony. She is happy to look like a grown-up in her dark blue dress and pearls, to mill around, and to load up and get loaded on wine and cheese before going home.

I look around the packed room for Delia or anyone I know. Most of the crowd are Addams Family look-alikes. Pallid, gangly young men in black pants and women with long layered hair murmur without looking at each other or the drawings on the walls. Both sexes sway slightly as they sip wine, inhaling cigarette smoke deeply to accentuate waists cinched tight with thin colorful belts. The scents of Ralph Lauren cologne and cheap chilled wine ferment in the air. All around me is an ambience of practiced ennui from the posturing youth and professional cordiality from the older, graying men and women—most of them architects or textile artists.

But I have already seen him. As chic as a '20s movie star, ash blond—like fair Chinese hair, fine but thick—with bangs swinging into his eyes, high cheekbones, face angular, tanned, smooth, his uptilted head catches the light while scanning the room, as if searching for allies. Among all the darkly clad people, he gleams so brightly in that first moment, he could be the sun outside a train window. Everyone and everything else are just scenery whizzing by.

I have painted half my face and neck like a tiger, and although he must notice, he doesn't look twice. Being so much taller than I, he doesn't see my teeth.

The moment I see him, I purr to my sister Chloë, "That's my future husband."

"He's so perfect, he probably won't age well," she says. Arm in arm, we take a wide turn to look at him more closely while avoiding collision. We're both so small compared to him—occupying the area of most domestic animals—he can't see us.

A grandiose version of the Little Prince, he wears a scarf in summer, twisted around a slate-gray shirt under a creamy linen suit, perfectly tailored.

"All other men seem like a species of dog compared to him," says Chloë.

(Stay away, flame-hair!)

A week later, he'll tell me without a hint of vanity, "My looks are a combination of Peter Fonda, David Bowie, and Dr. Kildare." But his name is Tobin Kleinherz.

The secret name I give him is Wears-Scarves-in-Summer.

He is accompanied by a very short well-dressed young man. They wander the room talking together and actually looking at the work on the walls. Tobin's smile is tentative and vulnerable at first, then complicit as he leans down, listening to his friend. He straightens up, vigilant, seeming alert to atmospheric shifts in the room. His ambiguous focus settles on me. But there are so many conquests to consider.

Aware that he has the attention of every female in the room, he asks anyone within earshot to go dancing. Not wanting to be part of a pack, I start to leave.

As I walk by, he suddenly sees me and is riveted by my ankles.

7 Petrified Ice Cream

Until I saw Tobin, I believed in the 31 Flavors type of existence. I wanted to live in many countries and have many children with a different, delicious man each time.

I was petrified of marriage.

8 Bronco

It's late when I get home after the gallery opening, and I go straight to bed. But the thought of Wears-Scarves et cetera renders me semi-wild with worry, doubt, panic about how, and anticipation, excitement, imaginings about when I will see him again. My bed is a bucking bronco all night long and I never fall off to sleep.

9 Phone Accent

The next day the phone rings and I pick it up. A man with a German accent asks for me. How Wears— How Tobin got my number I never do find out.

Tobin tells me he is studying here in Chicago on a fellowship and that he is an artist. I can relate. I've been trying to establish myself as a writer, actress, and musician—any job that is nonlucrative and without a pension plan, any opportunity where the pay is sporadic and the odds are against me.

Basically he is phoning to invite himself and a German friend over for dinner tonight at my place.

10 Leather and Silk

When Tobin enters my apartment for the first time, he's wearing sleek black leather pants. I don't notice much about his friend—he's just a guy.

It's hard to focus on anything above Tobin's waist, but when I am able to concentrate on his words, I realize Tobin is animated, interesting, and pretty funny for a German person. Not bad qualities for a future husband. But I am still most impressed by the pants.

I seat myself at the piano. Both men stop talking and sit down to listen. Not your typical American response. I begin to play a piece. Tobin recognizes his countryman Beethoven.

"It's a rondo," I tell him.

After we eat the dinner I prepared, Tobin says to his friend, "See, not all Americans are uncultured." Then he adds to me, "Play your Beethoven rondo again." What American male would remember my repertoire? I think to myself. And command it, I neglect to think.

As I sit on the piano bench and play, I feel Tobin's eyes boring into my silk pants. He must really love Beethoven.

Obviously, we have much in common.

CLUE NUMBER ONE

No clue.

11 Silent Nights/*Stille Nachts*

A couple of silent nights go by. Then one more. Other men come to my doorstep, but I don't buzz them in.

I wonder where Tobin is. Hadn't he felt the same thing I felt the moment we met?

12 Sonnets

Tobin wasn't my first love. And I have to ask myself, is it love if it doesn't last?

Frantic with memory, I unravel. Spinning to start over again. And again. Re-remember.

I started loving ultra-early. In rhyming couplets from the first grade.

I loved two boys in my class at Saint Constantine's, my Catholic grade school. Peter had dark hair and Trent, red. Peter was great at spelling and Trent was acrobatic: he could catch a football one-footed. Peter gave me a Valentine with a flower pasted on it, and Trent gave me chocolates. I couldn't make up my mind.

We memorized our love letters so the nuns couldn't catch us. Nights in bed, I set the words in my mind, ready for school in the morning. Trent dashed them off before the first bell. Sometimes they rhymed, these young sonnets:

Dear pretty girl, are you lying
or were you really crying?

Peter was lovingly poetic in describing how much he wanted to kiss me.

More than the best Christmas present.
More than I want to kiss my dog.

Trent was jealous, but practical.

If Peter steals you from me, I'll find you. I don't care how far away you are.
Unless I can't buy enough gasoline to get there.

In third grade, my sister Chloë helped me compose late into the night. We thought up rhymes for love: *glove, above, dove*. She recited our creations to Trent until she stole him away.

She reasoned the bad news in rhyme. *"Dear still very pretty one,"* she began, having memorized Trent's words, *"I hear your words so true, but the messenger is lovelier than you, her hair of red, our love is dead, good-bye, don't cry."*

In fourth grade, Trent moved next door and we loved each other again. But the love was a wounded one, diminished and more desperate. Sometimes he called three times a day, not just out of puppy love, but to get the homework. Other times, he fled for days.

His inconstancy made me jittery, made me care too much about his reactions—his smirk when I wore pink, his smile when I wore stockings. If I hadn't been so loyal, I would have refused him when he came back to me.

While Trent's fickleness was disturbing and distracting, I had never stopped loving Peter. In fifth grade. Still in sixth. In class, our crazy one-liners made each other laugh and sometimes the class joined in. The teacher had a soft spot for both of us, but she tried to put a stop to our disruptions.

When I arrived on the playground in the morning, Peter's eyes brightened. Because he didn't play hard to get, as Trent did, and he was easier to please, maybe I took him for granted.

We polished our poems in night air and sent them during the day. I loved the words, pure and immutable, as much as I loved the boys. With only the promise of a kiss, our love was chivalric. We longed, we pined, we wrote, we recited, we languished.

I changed to a public school in seventh grade. Although I saw Trent occasionally, it was thirty years before I saw Peter again. It was at a bookstore. I opened a book and the dedication page read: TO PETER HIGGINS. As I walked out, I noticed that the author would be speaking there that evening. I returned later, and sitting in the front row were Peter and Trent. "Oh my God," I said, and they kissed me one after the other.

It seemed that Trent and I had a blank page between us.

But Peter said, "I can't believe you're here."

At the book signing, his wife said, "I've heard a lot about you. Peter talks about you all the time."

Amazed and flattered that he remembered me so well, I looked into his eyes. There I sensed an empathy for me that was miraculously intact.

I still think of him as the one who never betrayed me, even though he's married to a writer and has four children now.

In everyone's life there must be people and places that remain untainted. They are our refuge in the spasms of pain we call memories.

I overheard a man in a café talking to his friends. "I moved to Santa Fe because nothing bad ever happened to me there," he said.

13 Shift

Close to midnight, nine days from our first meeting in the gallery, a ferocious cosmic force—or was it meek coincidence?—brought Tobin and me once again to the same place, on Earth, in Chicago, at the same moment. I was to have left on an all-night train for the East Coast to work as a pianist, but I didn't; he was supposed to be traveling to the West Coast with his sullen friend, but he wasn't.

Maybe coastal faults shifted, jostling us to the same street in what used to be a field of wildflowers, making us feel we will be tumbleweed if we are not together for the rest of our lives.

Wears-Scarves-in-Summer is crossing the street with a tiny, pretty blonde when he notices me. Embarrassment shows quickly on his face, and I hope it's because he's with her and not me. Instead of introducing me to his elf-partner, he says to her, "I'll see you later at the club." She tucks her minuscule head into her doll's coat and walks off into the neon.

An awkward moment, then a gust of night air makes me shiver and invite him back to my apartment, only a block away. First we look at the lake, which we both know is our future, and walk most of the night along it. At about four in the morning, we arrive at my place. Without a word, we fully undress and get into bed, pretty much the same as we will do for the next nine years.

14 Chopin

The following morning we go for breakfast and the sun singes my shoulders in an outdoor café.

Afterward, we walk up to my apartment's air-conditioning and I practice the piano while he rests on the couch.

"You are the most mature person I have ever met," he says after hearing me play a Chopin waltz.

I am nineteen months older.

I am practically certain his next sentence will be a proposal of marriage.

Instead he says, "I am on the verge of falling deeply in love with you."

Oh, come on, I think. Just fall. But I lower my eyes and take a risk. "I knew the minute we met that we'd be . . ."

"So did I," he says.

Exhilaration followed by deep exhalation.

"Then why did you . . . ?"

"It is hard to describe," he says. "I knew, but I still wanted to live my old life."

"You mean you were staving us off?" I ask.

"What is 'staving off'?" he asks. "I don't know this expression."

15 Two Castles

Later that evening, after a long dinner, he says, "This is odd for a German."

Pulling me onto his lap, he looks into my eyes. A flicker of worry passes over his face. Oh no, I think, he's going to tell me about . . .

"I've been with the same girl for seven years," he says. "I was supposed to marry her until I met you. She is studying to be a veterinarian. Her family owns two castles."

Two castles! Maybe he should give this some thought. . . .

"I told her I'd be back, but I won't." He sounds like Arnold Schwarzenegger.

Much later that night in bed, when he is starting to roll on top of me, he says, "Am I too heavy?"

Thinking he has said, “Am I to have you?” I reply, “I think it’s a little early for that.”

He says, “What did you think I said?” and when I tell him, he says, “Don’t you think it’s a little early for that?”

Even with the language barrier, we are in sync. Strangers, made on different sides of an ocean, entangled, as the quantum theory goes, know each other instantly.

16 Stone Pier, Turquoise Lake

The next few weeks race by as if in a film montage: Tobin braiding my hair, Tobin taking me to his apartment the first time and making me a dinner of stuffed clamshells, Tobin throwing rose petals on the floor to make a pathway from his chair to mine, Tobin picking me up and carrying me into a steaming bath, Tobin buying me a lavender dress and red shoes, Tobin telling me he wants to know everything about me, and Tobin in the dark—how he feels.

On the twenty-eighth day, he wakes me in the middle of the night. He has been drinking a whole bottle of wine by himself and reading my journals. And that’s all right with me.

I don’t know that in a month’s time he’ll be flying back to Germany with a journal I would have preferred to be verboten in his suitcase. After he’s read it, he’ll phone me and say in a worried voice, “Are you sure you want to marry me?”

“Why?”

“Because you’ve had such an amazing life, with so many . . . amazing men. I don’t know if I’m good enough.”

But I’m pretty sure he is.

But tonight he sits on top of my lower back, the journal’s spine against mine, his mouth in my ear, and says in his basso voice, “A great spirit wrote these words. *Meine Liebe,* let’s get engaged.”

Of course I say yes. But the demented romantic in me is troubled. It took him a whole four weeks to ask.

We celebrate at dawn by the end of a stone pier on a turquoise lake, whisper to each other the things we will need to know.

17 Clean

Watching the sunrise with my beloved is a hard act to follow, but the next night with me as an initially unwilling human candelabra is even more magnificent.

I wake up alone. The cloying scent of smoke from snuffed-out candles is still in the bedroom.

I feel rearranged, in a good way, from the intensity of our love-making and do not want to rise.

Tobin is already in the kitchen. "Have you ever cleaned out this refrigerator?" he calls in his thick accent.

"I don't know," I answer.

His laugh gives me a sexual jolt. I get out of bed, without clothes or a sheet (this is not a film), and walk into the kitchen. Tobin is tawny, bent over and peering into my crummy refrigerator. I look inside. Tall containers are in line with tall containers, small jars stacked on top of each other. The white interior sparkles as I imagine his soul does.

To augment his satisfaction, I assure him, "I have never cleaned it," and I hug him, my hero, my man. He is almost a stranger. I call Tobin "my love" over and over. He presents me with six wineglasses bought while I was sleeping. We drink from them and burgundy spills on my breast. The small candle burns on the back of my thigh are painful, but I am too happy to pay them any attention and I don't show him where they are.

18 Ships or Love

Their bodies—fragile boats—are afloat.
Water seeps into the carved-out part
of his chest, her belly, their thighs.
How they rise and fall together—
their skin, illumined from above
and from each other.

They stretch limbs like masts,
bed linens taut to catch the wind,
to carry them from certain shore.

They push off each other, setting ravens free.

Love and water for days and nights.

A dove returns with a twig in its beak.
A sign that land, though unwelcome,
is almost in sight.

19 Eyelash Music

I blink and Tobi has already returned to Germany to finish his degree in painting. We write letters until I visit and again until he returns to Chicago for the wedding. His parents tell him, "You can't marry while you're a student." But on our wedding day he won't have finished his degree yet. He's definitely my Indian brave.

While Tobi is buried in books about art in Germany, I'm creating art in the new wave scene in Chicago. I've become involved in a music production called *Eyelash* that records then magnifies the sound of eyelashes with and without mascara. Okay, go ahead and laugh, but the musicians I work with are the strangest and most brilliant people I have ever met. Lawrence or Lon, a juggler as well as a keyboardist, talks about "the omniscience of tone and the focus of chordal resolution." "I like to talk to you," he says to me, "because you understand." But I'm not sure I do.

I am in charge of some graphic work. Occasionally, I help out with melodic lines inspired by the music of eyes and eye hair, magnified.

I am so in love with Tobi, I try to withstand the attention of other males. But I enjoy it too much. Sensing that I am unavailable, they crank up their ardor a notch. Bill, a lawyer, is quixotic, shifting between admiration for me and my art and tormented by what it stirs up in him. He seems wholly undeterred by my engagement. He cooks Chinese for me—fried tofu and bamboo shoots—catering to my vegetarianism.

"I am formally engaged," I say.

He winces. "How quaint," he says, caressing my bottom.

As we eat, I am so attracted to him, my head aches from trying to winch thoughts of Tobin from my heart to my forebrain. After vanilla almond Häagen-Dazs, I leave Bill, with difficulty, return home, hoping to have a letter from a foreign man who will be my husband, and I do.

In cartridge pen, he writes: "Dear Eyelash, I love it when you bat them at me. Your eyes are my home. Love, your Sunglasses."

20 Flaschenpost

Letters must be sealed with a lick. Think of that. Human saliva, traveling distances, near and far. This is the fundamental difference between mail and e-mail. Spittle. The intimacy of the mouth, its words lining the roof, slipping off the tongue. The warmth of speech. When Tobin courted me, e-mail had not yet been invented. Would he have captured me online, the flickering monitor, cold—sending words without envelopes or contemplation? Messages in bottles, bobbing on cyberwaves?

21 My Name Is Pearl

There have been many famous Pearls: Pearl Bailey, Pearl S. Buck, Minnie Pearl. Had I kept the name, I might have been a lot more successful.

Claire, although beautiful, is a name for lovers, and artists, with all their accompanying suffering. My full-moon name is Pearl Claire McLeod. Some people hear the last name (pronounced McCloud) and ask, "Is it Native American?" I wish.

I actually took my first breath on the full moon on a night when the planets were unusually clustered on the left side of the sky—which ensures that I will be remarkably independent my whole life. (Think: divorced, single mom.)

My mother strolled me about in Hyde Park, Illinois, a former buffalo-stampeding prairie, near the University of Chicago, where intellectual roaming, extinct in other areas, is enthusiastically cultivated.

We soon moved, and I grew taller and more freckled in Evanston, Illinois, a home on the range for Northwestern University and its preppy student body. The general community is economically, racially, and philosophically diverse, with some surprisingly hip family units.

Some of my early classmates called me Pearly-Girly. Even then I would have preferred something like "Miss Karenina." After attending Saint Constantine's grade school and developing a taste for the fervent theatrics of the Catholic religion, I new-kid-slunk into Nichols Junior High public school. Now I had to wean myself of weekly Mass.

Turning my back on sultry smoke from musky incense in the Sacristy proved more of a sacrifice than I had imagined. Festive rows of red votive candles burning prayers toward heaven, the can't-help-noticing practically naked Christ whittled down for our sins (so that we might live . . . in sin), and exotic Latin words that could just as easily have been profane as sacred, were a feast for me. Leaving that table created a void that would have to be filled later.

My second taste of schism began when I changed high schools midway through my sophomore year. Going from Evanston Township High to Lake Forest Academy was as jarring as one minute saying swear words with my new friends and the next saying the stations of the cross with my old friends. I blushed to think of one group finding out what I was doing with the other.

The two high schools were archrivals. Switching was like changing sides during battle.

During sophomore year, I wept every day walking home from school because I missed my old friends. They may have been wealthy, but it wasn't noticeable. Maybe all the kids from large families wearing hand-me-downs served as camouflage.

At my new school, everyone's father seemed to be the CEO of Coca-Cola. They mentioned Mercedes and Jaguars and designer labels in the same breath as swim meets and football games. Not knowing, I asked, "What's a label?" This was incomprehensible to the girls, but quickly endeared me to the boys. Yes, I looked the part of the almost anorexic, sleek-haired Lake Forest girl, but I didn't ever feel it. Maybe that's typical.

My name, like the labels the other girls revered, pigeonholed me. "Pearl" was as preppy to them as the pearls strung around their necks in a shiny display of what it meant to be cultured. But I thought of a pearl as a castoff, solitary, unable to be categorized—a stunning dollop of irritation from the sea.

his name is clive

The months toward the end of high school, when Clive coursed through my veins, are the most vivid in my memory.

I meet him senior year during my period of greatest fascination with, as we called them then, American Indians. Our great Lake Michigan, seen as a blessing of inestimable value by the indigenous people, inspired me to read every book about them.

As I'm biking along the lake on Sheridan Road before school, an eerie sense of déjà vu wafts by. In a past life, as an Indian princess, I may have galloped this road bareback every day.

When I make it to homeroom, Clive whispers to me, "I like your spookiness and dilated pupils." I didn't know my pupils were dilated, and I don't know who he is.

Tall and so skinny his muscles are not visible even to the female eye, Clive has serious dark eyes behind thick black glasses. It doesn't hurt that he looks like an All-American Native American boy. He even wears his shiny blue-black hair to the shoulders.

The bell rings and he walks me to my first class. In those few steps down the hallway, I learn he is Clive Tucker, the editor of the school paper. A poet, he throws pottery, and he's reading *Black Elk Speaks,* which he lends me.

Whatever the words were I couldn't find in myself to speak at that time, Black Elk supplied, to the point that I date my diary entries with the names of months such as *Moon of the Snow-Blind*, *Moon When the Cherries*

Are Ripe, or April, my birthday month, *Moon When the Ponies Receive Wrapped Gifts*.

There are days I want to feel American Indian in a stingingly WASP high school. Clive, full of admiration and anachronisms, notices everything about me: ass-tight blue suede midi-skirt, lace-up soft leather bodice—bought for three dollars at the Winnetka Community House annual thrift sale—feet slopping along in too-big men's Frye boots, long hair in braids with a headband.

I smear dark foundation on my face. I'm all dressed up with no powwow to go.

A week after our first meeting, Clive takes me to the movies. On the way back, it's raining. He pulls up our driveway.

"How come you live only with your mom?" I ask.

"My dad divorced my mom when I was three," he says.

This sounds exotic to me, not realizing my parents are heading down the same road. "Do you like your dad?" I ask.

"Sure," he says. "He's a formal sort. He's great. Very thick in the wallet."

The rain gives me an excuse to stay in the car with him.

He takes my hand and puts it against his cheek.

We sit listening to the rain. Although he's usually making me laugh, he's silent.

"Thanks for the movie," I say.

"My pleasure," he says.

"I love you," bursts out of me, as if I had Tourette's. The slant of the rain makes me say it. Tree branches bending over his car make me. Gusting wind rocking us.

My hand feels tears under his glasses. "I know," he says. "I think I love you too."

To leave him in peace, and preserve the rainy mood, I slip out of the car and walk the slick driveway to my house.

We don't mention this evening again, but we continue our adventures together. At night, Clive and I strip and wander the Skokie Lagoons like Indians. During the day, he photographs me in junkyards, my naked skin against the rust. To amuse me, and keep me posing, he delivers a monologue accompanied by the click of his Nikon. "Johnny, I told you to get down from there! Look at your filthy hands, I'm gonna smack you silly. That's disgusting, Billy, take your spoon out of Sarah's ear. Sarah, quit eating your hair or I'll drop-kick you to kingdom come. What did I tell you about juggling your food? Go to your room, all of you!"

Changing the roll of film (and ignoring our imaginary children), his long fingers, expressive as a potter's, pose me again.

"Pearl, Pearl Claire," he says, "your breast is a rosebud against the metal. Ooooh, that's perfect, white hips on the oily motor. This must be *The Moon When Your Butt Looks Super-Cute*! Let me carry you over the bed of rusty nails, my sweet, and place you on the barbed wire."

I laugh and squirm in resistance as his gangly frame scoops me up and puts me down near a coil of barbed wire.

"The hairs on your thighs are golden. Tilt toward me, honey. I'll catch the last moments of light, and then we'll go."

Out of, what seemed to me, the blue, he asks, "Do you think we should have intercourse when school's out?"

"Maybe, Clive. Let's think about it," I say with an ease I'm far from feeling. And think, *intercourse*—enticing word choice.

He smiles his dark, sensitive smile. "Okay, we can plan it so it'll be right."

Years later, although I'd never suspected it, Clive tells me he's gay. "I always knew," he says. "Although I didn't have a name for it. But I knew I loved you too."

For now, though, we are each other's muses, creating our lives as if they are pieces of art. When the big day arrives, the first intercourse, we sit cross-legged on the motel bed facing each other as if to smoke a peace pipe. When the hands of his watch pass over the appointed hour, we start to take off our clothes until we are bare. He bends at the waist to fold his clothes, then mine. As an afterthought he jumbles them together and throws them on the floor. It's a bit like a performance piece. As agreed, he opens a window to let in some moonbeams, and I regard his inflated member with some concern. He's as generously equipped as a porn star.

"Don't worry, it'll wilt when I get near you."

Which it won't, we both know, so we laugh.

He opens *Black Elk Speaks*, places his limp cock between two pages, and says, "The perfect bookmark."

"Oh God," I say. "Such blasphemy."

Then he shifts to the edge of the bed, begins by kissing one of my feet.

Afterwards, I can't help but begin to notice that while everything else is profound between us, sex turns out to be little more than schtick for his everyday stand-up. "He and she are no longer encumbered by their virgin status," he says. "Calories burned: four gazillion." Tossing his shiny black hair, he takes a deep breath and says, "I'm starving. Let's go dine at the vending machine, my dear."

His flippancy is contagious. "As you know, I don't eat anything that's come out of a package," I say. "Nothing with even a hint of sugar, and nothing sparkling."

"I don't know how you can live without at least three sodas a day," he says. Starting to walk down the hallway to the machines, he yells, "Well, I want a Coke to celebrate your deflowering!"

And I have to yell back, "Funny, I don't feel defleured."

When he comes back, he's got three Cokes. "Is sex your only bad habit?" he asks, ever curious, because he reports about me daily to his mother.

"I make it a habit to eschew habits of any kind."

I don't want to be hindered by needing anything. Not food, not sex. As I imagine nomadic folk might do, I cultivate freedom, to be ready to flee at any time.

Clive has habits: coffee, pulling his forearm hair out by the roots ("To go beyond the pain," he quipped when I caught him), bird-watching, and, most notably, smoking. Before college, when we set off on bicycles across the state of Wisconsin, Clive has to stop and hunt for cigarettes. (I've never even tried a cigarette; the blue vapor is too dreamlike for my day.)

Now he's slurping from all three cans and making me laugh.

"I don't even feel thirst," I go so far to say.

"But thirst is not a habit," Clive says. "It's a need."

"I don't need needs."

More things to tell his mom later.

I don't want to be tied down by the body's real desires, intangible as they are at that age anyway. But most important, I don't want to be anyone's prey. If I have no habits, the hunter can't find me.

After my divorce, I'll be at a party where I meet a former high school acquaintance, a so-called jock. "God, I envied you and Clive," he'll say.

"You had the most magical relationship. Everyone thought so. We all lusted after you and couldn't figure out how that skinny, weird guy got you."

Before senior graduation, my parents announce their divorce. Around the same time, I am chosen to solo for the high school Spring Festival of music. Their split puts me into a zombie-daze, and I practice piano six hours a day.

From third grade on, I had been under the spell of my Hungarian teacher, Mimi, herself a pupil of Béla Bartók. Her devotion to her students, especially to me, makes us cry during lessons when we make mistakes. Or maybe it was something to do with her knack for barbed sarcasm when listening to less-than-perfect Czernys. She tolerates nothing less than complete dedication, even for finger exercises.

On the day before my performance for the festival, I bike recklessly through the streets of Lake Forest, ignoring stop signs, trying to get hit by a car so I won't have to play Bach Concerto in D Minor with chamber orchestra, for a full audience in the school's gymnasium.

Clive tracks me down with his bicycle and brings me home. "Let me carry you back to the piano where you belong," he says. The next night I play Bach flawlessly with my eyes closed in full spotlight. Like the blind, I can see music.

Shortly afterwards, I audition for Northwestern University Music School playing Liszt's Rhapsody no. 11. My performance is apparently unaffected by my trance and they award me a four-year music scholarship. I don't use it. Never even tell my parents. They are too busy breaking up our family to notice. My reaction to their troubles is to see them down tunnels. Mom lingered in a long straight corridor while Dad stood in a shorter one. Peripheral vision seemed to form protective walls around them.

Clive is the only person I can see normally. My mom, now living alone, allows him to spend the night with me whenever his mother can be misled. When I am especially fragile and tell him I need to be "a barnacle" on him, he stays the whole weekend and tells his mother, "I'm going camping." We sit on the sofa in the living room, drawing each other. Sometimes I ask him if my voice is coming from my mouth, because I'm not sure it is.

david and lisa

Scarier still, the second of my younger sisters is invisible to me. When she walks in the room talking, there is just empty space. Clive had taken me to see the movie *David and Lisa,* where, if memory serves, Lisa sees the world blanketed in snow during summer. Although Lisa taught me the power of neurosis, I didn't believe my eyes could perform such tricks. Just a few weeks later, I was swearing I could see with my eyes closed, through my eyelids. But not even this kind of vision could help my parents as they split apart. And it didn't help me trying to write college applications.

sacre coeur

By default, I end up going to Manhattanville College outside of New York City, a Sacred Heart school, where my brilliant mother with her photographic memory and my aunts had attended on full scholarships. Living at college allows me to reacquaint myself with the contrast and comfort of religious rigor in a secular world. But the best thing about Manhattanville is that it gives me a scholarship to study a year abroad at Oxford. There I'll return to my roots and board in a convent.

Although music had been my religion, I drop it during college and, like a convert, fervently embrace the written word. I discover my true love: reading the ideas of decomposing men. It takes studying Schopenhauer's dismissal of women in a philosophy course for me to revolt and discover female writers.

my name is claire

One reason I let my piano repertoire rot, at least for a while, is my discovery of the freshness of language, the renewal a name can bring.

The first day of college orientation, I turn over my name card and change Pearl McLeod to Claire McCloud, the name I have been using ever since. A name that makes me fittingly oxymoronic, if one thinks of *cloud* as amorphous and *Claire* as clear.

For my family, the switch is difficult, especially for my parents, who have a nagging suspicion I am divorcing them. I staunchly ignore them if they use Pearl, pretending not to be that former girl they knew. This leads them to think they are calling all their children the wrong names. I don't want to cause disruption, but I always seem to.

For Clive, the transition is easier. He says, "Claire suits you," and writes me from his college, the University of Minnesota, using my new name on an envelope that contains his poems about me.

Later when I marry my German man, we both take each other's last name. Having already changed my name, I need the stability of a double-barrel. So I went by Claire McCloud-Kleinherz. And he became Tobin McCloud-Kleinherz, despite his parents threatening to disown him for it. Love made him brave as an Indian then. My children are both McCloud-Kleinherz, but I tell them, when they marry, they can do what they want; they can take their spouse's name, even if it's Smith.

inner clock, anaïs nin, cheryl tiegs, johnny carson, and naughty nancy

The years before my senior meltdown were also fairly strange and left their mark of strangeness on me. I think that's one of the reasons Clive found me irresistible.

Sophomore year of high school, I have a fixation on Time. With mononucleosis and attendant liver complications, I miss an entire semester, but I pass. To show that I am the inner clock of death, I smudge dark circles under my eyes with eyeliner, emphasize the hollow of my cheeks with tan makeup, and powder my face shock-white. I wear a rusted watch with paralyzed hands on my wrist.

My mom is laissez-faire.

"Okay," she says, frantically mashing a mound of peeled potatoes for dinner. "Why don't you write about it?"

I waft away, trying to find my sister Chloë, who shares a room with me. She knows the drill—shielding her eyes as I approach, burying her strawberry blond head into *Anna Karenina* before she pulls on pajamas for bed.

The next morning, when I come darkly and dismally into the kitchen, Chloë scrutinizes her cinnamon toast. For weeks, the only person really looking at me is the one staring back in the mirror.

After I'm less jaundiced and weigh enough not to be blown off the sidewalk walking to school in the fabled Chicago windiness, I am allowed to return to high school.

I wear regular makeup now. Chloë sniffles with relief. Kohl lines my eyes to emulate Anaïs Nin, whose novels and journals I have nibbled at and then devoured. I try bangs as an homage to her and my burgeoning yet ultra-shy sexuality. I add an attractive brush stroke of peach blush à la Cheryl Tiegs.

Imagining myself on Johnny Carson, I play Liszt's Rhapsodie Hongroise no. 11, a piece I am mastering. My practicing intensifies to five hours a day, and I capture first place in a few competitions, but the regular beats of the metronome have little relationship to my chaotic emotional life.

Junior year, I have a complementary-color phase. My body can tolerate only purple and yellow clothing. I'm sure the Indians, as we're called at sports events, asked the question, Why did Claire McCloud need to be so visible? I had landed the ingenue lead in the play *Little Mary Sunshine.* I relished my part, Naughty Nancy, a spying minx who trades her charms for secret information. That's what high school seemed to be about: playing the person you are *not* while trying to stay true to the secret self you *are.*

After the play, I abandon the purple–yellow kick and adopt jeans and a jean-shirt, scissors-cut by me above the waist. Exposing my belly button before it was fashionable, I walked the halls, imagining eyes riveted to nothing but the flesh, pale and impermanent as my family.

22 Family

Growing up surrounded by Catholic families of eleven, twelve, and fifteen children, I was embarrassed to admit that my slacker parents had "only six."

I have three sisters and two brothers, with names beginning with *C:* Clint, Catherine, me (Pearl/Claire), Chloë, Charles (incomprehensibly called Brian), and Carey.

Because my parents practiced Catholicism, they were able to practice the fine art of benign neglect. I thank God and them for that. The intact structures of their religion and our neighborhood made raising children seem almost effortless.

Sipping scotch and water on front porches, our parents and their friends knew how to laugh and relax—a mythical beast in our generation.

We roamed in packs throughout the neighborhood while our parents drank, laughed, danced, and argued politics. We fell off bicycles riding double on the handlebars, broke legs leaping from rooftops and trees, and split our heads on concrete playgrounds. We wouldn't have dreamed of interrupting the partying parents unless our arteries had been severed. And maybe not even then.

23 Frozen Rain

When Clive and I entered windy days and nights, did he wish to change?

We lifted our clothes off our bodies like floral kites and ran through islands, rushed nude into water knee-deep.

He unclasped the silver choker on my neck, and our cries were white-throated: a singing girl and raven boy.

His photographs preserved my breasts, naked in a junkyard, rust against white skin, but couldn't catch his changes of mood, or the secret life he would follow.

Everything in him wanted to break free, like clouds releasing rain, the night's splash against our car on the first night we meet and my words to him, "I love you," prophetic because I will.

Caged behind steaming windows, I can't understand why he cries while we wait and do not kiss.

If I found the bicycles we rode across hills, the trees we sketched out of charcoal, the tall grasses where we slept, the freezing rain in the morning, could we start again?

24 Learn to Lose

Oxford brings me closer to our culture's geniuses but takes me farther from Clive. Still, just as I visited him in his freezing college dorm in Minnesota, he visits me in my convent digs in England. He is already backpacking in Europe and actually meets my train in Oxford, without my asking, and helps install me there. While I immerse myself in the study of metaphysical poetry, he travels.

For the long Christmas break, we meet in Paris, travel back home, and take a quick trip to New Orleans, where we, unexpectedly for me, end our romance. It's Clive who leaves me. Even though his mother would insist, years later, that me breaking up with him had "driven him gay."

I return for the next term at Oxford knowing we will never be together again. All I know is that Clive made me laugh and I still love him. He may have been elusive at times, but he seemed perfect to me.

The cream-colored convent wall, pinned with our drawings of each other, was what I woke up crying to every morning. I never attributed his rejection to anything other than my faults, which I assessed during bouts of hand wringing.

Like cells programmed to die, there is something inherently rotten about love. No one explained this to me. Just as no one can explain childbirth. My American friends told me to "practice Lamaze," but my old-school German doctor gave more seasoned advice: "Practice your screams."

The loss of Clive made me practice suffering, hour upon hour, like I practiced scales and Chopin and Scriabin. I learned then how to lose, to long, to be tormented. He pained the way for Tobin.

25 Frozen Rain II

In Oxford, we kiss on a platform where he meets my train.

"How did you find me?" I ask, me and my nine pieces of luggage I couldn't lift alone.
"I know you that well," he says, "with all my heart."

My desire fades inside a hotel in Paris.
He doesn't know that I have been sleeping with the Brazilian attaché's son, who slips his Portuguese tongue into secret places learned from forbidden French porno.

In our orange hotel in New Orleans, he sleeps alone, his jealousy burning me into him like a brand, his tears searing with what he doesn't say.

I am left with a memory of a January night.
In his St. Paul dorm room, I wait in bed for his return, looking at wall-sized posters of men kissing men, the hours accumulating like snowfall.

Down the hallway with another man, he reins in longing, whispers to himself, "But I love her," all night long. From separate beds, we both take in moonlight. And the cold snap sharpens.

I can't cry, can't believe that endless winter, empty hallways, and dark rooms could silence our sound love.

26 Pinocchio

Is there any better time than the beginning?

The first seconds of a movie, the first few sentences of a book, even the first words of a love affair are exhilarating, full of excruciating promise. If the tale is good and the teller even better, there's no turning back.

Tobin, I never wanted to turn back. Never, until now when I begin every day with our ending and try to develop, like a scared child, from that lethal point.

We began at the beginning, but I can't anymore.

"Midway on life's journey, I came to a dark woods. . . ."

And it was fitting that I became lost.

"Once upon a time, there was a tailor named Geppetto. . . ."

And it was fitting that he loved his puppet son into a real boy.

The words *once upon a time* bring me into a world where sadness is magical.

Once upon a time, we were lovers, like all lovers, alike in our adoration as we peered into each other's core and came lip to lip with . . . faults. These never went away, but the adoration did. It seems to be an inexorable process to break us all down—women and men alike—and we, who have loved and failed will find a piece of our spirit gone. Gone.

If we could have lied after it was all over, only our noses would have grown. I never loved him anyway! I never loved her! But no, there are letters and lingerie and tears to prove it was love. Dried roses and champagne corks at the bottom of the drawer.

Strings that were attached are now tangled and broken. Unbearable as it may seem, nothing, neither our children nor we ourselves, will ever move the same way again. We will put ourselves back together, not as we were—sliding belly-pure into the world—but like handmade puppets with limbs slightly skewed and seams showing where the parts have been crudely mended. The stiffness we feel is love denied, ossified, collecting in the joints, turned to wood.

27 The Face You Never See

But I did love him.

Early on, Tobin finds one of my discarded drawings and uncrumples it from the wastebasket. The next day, I find it framed on the wall.

Although he is the real artist, he says, "You're the artist. The natural. Everything you do . . . It comes out of you like other people sweat."

The drawing is melodramatically called *The Face You Never See*. It's a sketch I tossed off of a face with a penis-nose, breasts for eyes, butt cheeks for the face, and a vagina-chin. He tells our friends about it: "She thinks of these crazy ideas nonstop."

I don't know if I'll ever find anyone who appreciates my garbage as much as Tobi did.

28 Pizza Art

"I'll only be away for a day, *meine Liebe*," says Tobi, before taking a bike trip with his friend Klaus. "But I made you something to remind you of me."

He has a sweet smile as he leads me to my pristine refrigerator. On a plate is a cold replica of his penis made out of pizza dough.

One day stretches to three, so I have to put it in the freezer.

29 Master

I break the news to Mimi, my piano teacher, that I am engaged to a German.

She says (after a long monologue about not *all* Germans being bad, that Beethoven, Bach, Handel were *good* Germans), "Claire, you may not have money, but an American passport is worth more than any money," and then she gives me her famous hawkeyed yet sidelong glance, accentuated by a long drag on her cigarette. "And Claire, Claire, dahlink, your charm"—puff puff—"is your master key."

Though she is a master of scales and compositions, her teachings on love are even more absolute.

30 Making Waves

When you meet someone, it is a beginning.

Life is a flood: Beginnings and endings flow into each other like waves—churning, intermingling, and finally indistinguishable as they wash over the shore and then head back into dark, open waters.

When you meet someone, it is the end.

31 Flood

Tobin hangs up the phone and silently cries.

"What's wrong, my love?" I ask.

"Just my parents," Tobin says, sitting in his sunny, small studio in Heidelberg, West Germany, where I am visiting him while he finishes his degree. "They're telling me they are hesitant to pay for the silk suit I picked out for our wedding," he erupts.

It's his last year of graduate school.

"They are getting showers down their back because I swore to them that I would never marry while I'm a student."

He crouches down on his bed, which is barely thicker than a rug on the floor, and covered with his drawings.

"You mean *shivers,* darling," I offer.

We had been writing letters for three months when our passion and his grammatical errors reached a pitch that propelled me across the ocean.

"All I mean is, I'll marry you when I please. I love you. They can't tell me what to do," he says, throwing a sketch into the air.

I watch as it wafts to the wood floor.

"I think we should start by buying a secondhand washing machine, so your mother doesn't still have to do your wash," I say.

"How comes?" he asks. Making *come* plural is just one of the many things he says that I find enchanting.

"Well, it might be good for you, sweetheart," I say. "In America we start doing our laundry at age—"

"We're not in America," he says, "but yes, I'll buy a clothes washer."

I wonder if it is only a cultural difference, his resistance. His mother's touch on our sheets gives me the willies. But he might miss it.

Apparently, dryers have not yet been invented in Germany. At least no one we know uses them. Even in winter, wet laundry hangs outside or is strewn about the house like stiff sculptures, twisted and grotesque. All the running cycles of equipment in Germany take three times longer than anywhere else in the world. To them, duration must equal efficiency. Perhaps buying a dryer is open rebellion against a generation of women proud of their impeccable laundry skills. German women fold clothes with such precision, they don't need ironing. But they iron them anyway.

He comes back the next day with an old-fashioned washing machine with two devices: one for only washing, not spinning the clothes, thereby necessitating the other for wringing them out. I think aloud, "Double the work. How excellent."

Luckily Tobin doesn't understand or encourage my brand of humor. He is so excited about the new machines that he kisses me on my eyelids before we fall asleep to the churning of device Number One.

In the middle of the night, I wake. The moonlight is exceptionally bright on the parquet. My hand dangles off the bed and feels five inches of water where the floor should be. The futon is almost floating.

I hear a sputtering click. Squinting in the dark, I notice the electric outlet of our night lamp half-submerged and swollen. I sprinkle some floor water on Tobin to wake him.

"We're flooded," I say. Not yet with memories.

He jumps up onto the floor with a splash, heads for the bathroom, where the washing machine's hose is disconnected and flailing about, spewing rinse water.

After working all night to mop up the water, we put the heat on full blast to dry the parquet, even though it's the middle of one of Europe's hottest summers. We sleep all morning, and then he fixes lunch for us outside in one of the seven gardens that stretch out in front of his apartment.

"Thanks," I say, eating the dark bread with tomatoes and creamy herring. "This is delicious."

"Thanks for working so hard all night with me," he says.

When we come back in, I hear it.

"What's that popping?"

"What? You mean popcorn?" he asks.

"No," I say, putting my finger to my lips.

Then we see. The floor is buckling and forming wood tents that cave in, pop, and crash inside themselves, breaking up the parquet pieces like dominoes falling, not in sequence, but in chaos.

We watch. A huge buckle billows in the middle like a model volcano, then explodes, throwing pieces almost shoulder level.

I move to the wall, as if dodging bullets.

"I can glue it all back," Tobin says.

God bless him. It's our only chance.

His is a small apartment, but like everything in Germany, it is high quality, especially the wood floors. Of course, it will cost a fortune to repair.

Tobin buys fans to run all day to dry the floor evenly, "like a gourd," he says; otherwise, it will mold.

In a matter of days, the entire floor is decimated, the stench of rotting wood and molding glue, overwhelming.

"I know I can clean it and glue it all back again," he says.

I don't want to break it to him, but the warped floor chips won't even make good firewood.

I admire the way he refuses to give up. Denial is by far the most effective defense against reality.

He's on the floor for hours a day, placing and gluing the good pieces as if it were a puzzle.

"That looks pretty good!" he exclaims when it works. But it looks like an old quilt, uneven and skewed, with gaping holes even he admits can't be fixed. His parents lend him money for the floor repair, but they still won't commit to his wedding suit.

You can smooth over rough surfaces, but the foundation may still remain shaky.

32 Deer Brain

"You don't eat butter!" Tobin's mother, Brunhildegard, exclaims.

"Well," I say, "um, sometimes . . ."

Tobin intercedes. "She'll eat butter, Mama, but it's just not a big deal."

"During the war," she says, cutting a slice of her homemade linzer torte, "we didn't have any butter. Or meat."

The next day at the midday meal, Brunhildegard passes a platter of meat, swimming in a thick gravy. I take a fork-tine full.

"Please," she says, "help yourself."

"That's enough, for me," I say, "but it looks delicious."

With internationally recognized alarm in her eyes, she says pleadingly to Tobin, *"Aber, es ist doch Hirn!"*

"What did she say?" I ask Tobi under my breath.

"She says it's brain."

"Oh, in that case . . ." I feel quite sick.

"Just take a little more," he says quietly, "and I'll keep her talking."

He gives himself a huge helping, and she nods approvingly. *"Guten Appetit,"* he says loudly.

Handing the platter back to me, she says desperately, *"Reh Hirn."*

Tobi smiles and tells me, "She says it's wild deer brain."

"Now I'll definitely take seconds," I say, almost giddy.

To stave off my stomach's upheaval as I chew the meat, I think of foreign cultures and their allure. But really, deer brain in any language—I don't care which, German or Old Frisian or Navaho—is still *brain*. If my future mother-in-law were Native American, she might have offered me eagle-talon soup or buffalo-eyeball stew. And I would have had to eat it with relish. Or without. Or with ketchup.

33 Macaroni in the Ears

We have to climb a small mountain to get to the family doctor's office. I already have vertigo without going uphill, but the stomach pains are definitely exacerbated.

After running some tests, the corpulent German Dr. Kemper sits me and Tobin down in his office. "*Herr Kleinherz und Fräulein McCloud,*" he begins. . . .

After a few sentences Tobin blanches.

"What did he say?" I ask.

"He says your bilirubin is very high and . . ."

"What?"

". . . that you might not, that you will only live for another twenty years."

That seems like a long time to me.

"Are you sure?" I ask, taking his hand.

Tobin speaks to the doctor for a few minutes.

Turning to me, and holding both my hands in his, he says, "Twenty years maximum."

"Sounds like a prison sentence," I say under my breath.

"Vielen Dank," says Tobin, shaking the Herr Doctor's hand.

Once out of the office, I start laughing.

Tobin looks surprised, and we set off down the mini-mount. "I thought you'd be feeling sad," he says, stepping over rocks to walk closer to me.

"That doctor is crazy," I say. "I'm going to live a long time. With you."

When we arrive back at his parents' house, the table has been set for *Abendbrot* (evening bread): mounds of dark bread thinly sliced, salami spread like petals of a flower on china plates with ripe tomato slices in the middle, chunks of raclette cheese near a basket of *Brötchen* (rolls), and a couple of *Bretzel* (soft pretzels), and a pale gold bar of fresh butter. If I were not nauseated, it would be lovely.

At dinner, I can't eat. Tobin distracts his parents by telling them about our visit to the doctor. They listen impassively, more concerned about my uneaten portion of food.

"He was putting macaroni in your ears," says Tobi's father, Karl-Jürgen, referring to my dire fate.

The mother explains: "My husband means the doctor was not telling the truth. When Karl-Jürgen was a prisoner of war in Russia, that was the Ukrainian expression for lying."

"But why," I ask, "would a doctor—?"

"Ah," she says, handing me a roll and the ubiquitous butter, "I think he believes what he says, but that doesn't make it true."

Actually, I am convinced it's all the heavy German food that is making me ill. Of course, I can't say anything. She'd think I was putting pasta in her ears.

34 Vertigo

I'm landing in Chicago after my visit to Germany, and on the tarmac, I see a wheelchair being rolled up to my side of the aircraft. I have a horrifying thought that my mother has arranged this.

After seeing the German doctor who diagnosed a death sentence two decades away, my dizziness did not abate.

My parents insisted I come back to see an American doctor.

As I feared, the stewardess finds me and tells me my wheelchair has come.

"I really don't need it," I say.

As if warned by my mother, she ignores me and helps me out of the seat.

Once in the wheelchair, back in my own land, I feel I can fly. A song races through my head—a piano instrumental.

The first thing I do, after greeting my mother and threatening her person if she ever orders me another wheelchair, is to run to the piano—the vertigo has vanished—and play my new composition. I call it "Waldi" after the region of Germany—Schwarzwald—where my fiancé was born. This would be the equivalent of him calling me Cook Countess, for Cook County, my Chicago birthplace county. Being back home makes me feel liberated in a way I don't really understand, but I don't want to be free of him.

35 Twelve Times

Our wedding is in a church on a hill in Lake Forest, Illinois. A misty June with my three sisters in antique white cotton dresses, rented for fifty dollars each. Pale pink silk sashes circle their waists. My dress is a lily in an Italian summer breeze with a cream silk sash. French lace is in my hair, white baby roses in my hand.

Tobin has joined me in the States after three months of airmail lettering. What we don't realize is that our knowledge of what marriage means is like my German at the time: practically nonexistent.

The men are in black tuxes, except Tobin, who, sleek as a shark, wears a silver silk suit, paid for in humiliation and with an advance from his parents on his inheritance.

My sister Chloë's voice lavishes "Ave Maria" with such meaning that Tobin cries.

I am uncharacteristically dry-eyed.

His parents, who were telephoned twelve times by my dad to secure their attendance, are crying for other reasons.

36 The Gamble

A ragged child plays in the sand, her scarlet dress dipped in elongated waves. Tobin and I won a little money at the casino last night. This is good because we barely had any money to begin with. But what is bad is that most of our money fell out of my pocket as we made midnight love on the deserted beach. That's why we are here with this orphaned girl, searching a beach in St. Croix during our honeymoon. Digging in the sand for what is already gone. Tobin is taking it well.

"Do you think we were here, or more over there?" he asks.

Wearing a green bathing suit with a zipper down the front, a light pink towel over my hips, I say, "I'm not really sure, my darling. I do remember something sticking in my back at one point. Maybe the edge of that fence over there."

"Oh my God. There's a twenty-dollar bill. None of our fifty-dollar bills, though, my love."

"So sorry," I say.

"That's all right; it's not your fault," he says, but I wonder if he is regretting the loss of crisp green bills. I know I am.

"I love you, Tobin."

His strong golden arms squeeze my wet shoulders, smooth my long damp hair.

"I love you, too. My wife—it's amazing."

"Isn't it!"

It is hard to recognize myself in this fabulous, married way. At the time, it doesn't feel like a gamble. We are blinded to any risk.

People say, "You are the most beautiful couple we have ever seen," and we believe them! Trying to live up to their appraisal, we spend hours in front of the mirror, dressing to go out to meet our public.

CLUE NUMBER TWO

You are already losing.

37 Vertigo II

Marriage is a high-flying risk. Dizzying and invigorating as diving through clouds or throttling a car at full speed. You are socially, legally, economically, sexually, totally joined to one person. A person you choose in sickness and in health, but the priest didn't say in misery, did he?

38 Pincushion

I wake with a joy-filled heart. Sue me. I remember good times with Tobin. So sue me. (He did.) But details are elusive unless I pin them down.

Memory is a pincushion, with painful ones marked by silver in blood. Sharp and deep, the pin's tip probes where the pain is most vivid: *Ah yes, that's us in Paris kissing near the Louvre; that was him near the orange tablecloth raising his hand; ah, there's his mother in her brown wool stockings; oh, that's me in a full bath, candles on the porcelain rim, crying into the water, submerging myself so the children won't hear. . . .* The needle pricks suffering and joy—each stitch a word that hurts, or a knot that binds—sticking the best to the worst until happiness is a dull ache. I didn't expect that kind of ache. But here it is.

The ache of how it was to be held by him, the skin on his arms. I can't think of this anymore. Now the good moments bring more anguish than the bad.

Odd questions about us have a way of pricking me. When we woke in the morning, had my smile already formed? Or was it because I was next to him? And when the children came, was my sleeplessness only because of them?

Yes, memory is a pincushion. It doesn't predict misfortune, but it'll allow you to revisit the aftermath. And although the heart recycles emotions, it pumps an anemic message all the way to your brain: *Are you sure it was that bad? Or that good?*

39 **Peter Pan**

"There is an expression, *meine Liebe*, in German, that says, *ich bin über meine Schatten gesprungen*. That's what my parents did by coming to our wedding," Tobin says at our umbrella-shaded table on our honeymoon. "They jumped over their own shadows," Tobin says to me.

"Bully for them," I say, knowing he won't get it.

I rephrase. "Well, it took a few long-distance calls, but I'm glad they came."

Not.

His mother had taken my hands in hers during our first meeting in Germany. Speaking in a British accent acquired in Berlin after the war when she worked for an English company, she had said, "Oh, Tobin, she is so beautiful, and look at her delicate hands."

Later he had told me what she said after having taken him aside for a motherly consultation.

"*Du sollst sie in Seidenpapier wickeln. Du kommst nicht weit mit so einer Frau, mein lieber Sohn,*" she had said. Meaning: "You should wrap her in silk paper. You won't go very far with such a wife, my dear son."

At *Abendbrot*, she asks me, "What subject did you major in?"

"I couldn't make up my mind," I confide in her. "I studied theater, art, French, then majored in literature after attending three universities, one in a little place called Oxford, England."

"Dein zartes Mädchen hat nie etwas Richtiges gelernt," she says in a stage whisper to Tobi.

In bed with me, after much hemming and hawing, he translates: "Your frail girl has never really learned anything."

"Because of World War Two and her family's social level, my mother didn't graduate from high school," he says, squeezing me close. "She's jealous of you," he adds.

The sun umbrella tilts precariously with a sudden burst of island wind.

"So they're pretty agile," I say, thinking how much older and more rigid his parents are than mine. "They hopped over their shadows. I like that expression, Tobi, it's picturesque."

"Shall I teach you more German, *meine Liebe*?" he asks, sipping on the iced pineapple juice we're sharing at the hotel restaurant.

"No, I'm too tired to declinate."

He leads me back to our bed, and we fall asleep in each other's arms; it's been a long day searching for money in the sand.

Late that night, I hear Tobin ransacking the drawers of the hotel dressers.

"I can't find them," he mutters. "My favorite sunglasses are missing."

In my drowsy haze, I think he's looking for his parents' shadows, the ones they leapt over.

40 Shadows

Toward the end of our five-day honeymoon, Tobin says, "We have no more money. Maybe enough to get to the airport."

Remembering the chunk of money his parents gave us as a wedding gift and that my parents paid for Tobin's bachelor party and for our honeymoon because it was too awkward to explain to his foreign parents, I say, "I was hoping we could go to at least one nice restaurant before we leave. We could use our wedding money from your parents."

Tobin shifts his weight. "Under no circumstances is that money to be used for anything other than a car. When we get to Germany, we'll need one."

In long gray bathing trunks, he looks like a boy, his blue eyes eager for my compliance.

I shake my hair, make a turban with the hotel towel. "Yes, I understand."

I survive on huge coconut ice cream cones. We buy pineapple juice to drink all day at the beach, and at night we split conch fish at a cheap restaurant. I'm intensely hungry, and he teases me about being fat, shaking my skin as if it were Jell-O.

"Do you . . . think I'm fat?" I ask.

"Are you kidding? You're tiny, like a ballerina. You're my *Spatz*."

"What does that mean?" I ask, hoping it isn't something like our English *spaz*.

"It's a small brown bird. I don't know how you call it."

"Well, I'm not a tiny bird," I say, "even though I'm starving."

Why can't he see me, I think, feeling like a shadow in a cave.

One afternoon, we splurge and rent a moped, ride up and down the coast overflowing with tourists in cafés eating and drinking. Torture.

The night we leave St. Croix, we take a rickety Jeep that speeds us to the airport in the middle of a tropical storm. As we get out, I whisper to Tobin, "Don't give the man anything, because he almost killed us." I sling my purse over my shoulder, notice my husband slip the driver a wad of money so thick that the man blesses him.

41 Burn

I try not to scream as I rush to the shower and turn on the cold water. The pain seems to turn my skin an alarming purple. Tobi runs in from his art project.

"Get me the vitamin E tablets," I manage to say.

Lying on our bed, I poke open the pills and squeeze the oil on my burns.

"I'll go to the all-night *Apotheke* and get you some pain pills," he says, stroking my damp hair. "I'm so sorry."

"That's okay," I say. "You know what a freak I am if I take drugs. Just stay here and finish your work."

I had been making pasta in a huge wedding-present pot. The water was boiling when the lid of our tiny stove smashed down, spilling the pot on my thighs and legs.

It's our first night back in Germany after our honeymoon, or *Flitterwoche,* as Tobin says in German, sounding, for once, more ethereal than in English.

"Try to sleep, *meine Liebe,*" he says.

"Don't leave me," I say, drifting off.

In the morning Tobi rolls over toward me, careful not to touch my legs. "You moaned all night in your sleep," he says. But the pain of the burn, like all horrible things, subsided.

By midafternoon, the vitamin E elixir had almost erased the purple and, after a few months, the scars completely disappeared.

42 The Daily Newspaper

"It's the same thing, *Liebchen,* if a man hits a woman as a woman hitting a man."

We are still newlyweds, living in Tübingen, and this is a recurring argument.

"All I can say, Tobi, is that you're a lot bigger than I am. It's easier for you to scare me."

"*Blödsinn*" ("nonsense") "my sister scares the hell out of me."

During the "discussion," he had roughly squeezed my arms, which attach to my piano hands.

"Look, darling, I don't know why we have to talk about this."

"I just want you to understand that if you grab my newspaper, it's the same as me grabbing your arm."

"Like this!" I say, crumpling his *Die Zeit* newspaper.

"Or like this!" he says, tapping my arm.

"Tobi, hitting a thing is different from hitting a person! *Die Zeit* doesn't hurt, but my arm could. . . . You could have hurt me."

"But did I?" he asks.

"No," I sniffle. "This is a strange conversation."

"I'm sorry, *Liebchen,* I'll do anything to make you happy."

And in this recycled movie line, I'm left wondering what anything might include.

While he reads, I clean the bathroom a few times, knowing he will reclean it anyway. "You call that a clean bathroom!" he'll exclaim.

I go for a walk because five o'clock is my favorite time of day—when the sun is slanted on everything it touches. I'll watch as the Strassenbahn train gleams to a halt—a few Germans in work clothes step off—and then glides by to the next stop.

43 **Blue Notes**

As the world is darkening, I walk around our neighborhood smelling the last vestiges of fresh *Bretzel* from the bakery on the corner, deflect a few women who say, *"Guten Abend, Frau Müller,"* because they think I am the wife of the baker—who does look remarkably like Tobin.

Before it's truly dark, I turn for home and my Tobi. He looks up from his newspaper and indicates his lap with a pat of his hand. I curl up onto him and then we go to bed.

In the morning, I look out the window of our small apartment onto busy Kimmelstrasse.

A red car stops at the corner, and a bald man gets out with his gold trumpet, blows a few notes, and climbs back in. His tune is blue, and the car bulbous, like those in comic strips. I've seen this before, but I can't fathom what it means. This scene is expected yet mysterious, and I return to my husband, a little alarmed.

44 **Hills**

We talk about when we first met and I am shocked to hear his take on the momentous events.

The night I was playing the Beethoven rondo, he said he had wondered what it would be like to "fuck an innocent virgin" like me. Of course, at the time, I was unaware of his fantasy and I was decidedly not a virgin.

"I thought for the first four days that there was something clinically wrong with you," he says. "You were more electric than other people."

Even now I am a live wire, shocking him back. "You should have asked me to marry you sooner," I say.

"Twenty-eight days was crazy enough," he says, kissing me on the head.

"It's because you come from a quiet mountain village," I say.

"No, there are just hills."

I am only slightly dashed.

45 He Cried over Unfolded Sheets

Tobin, like many European men, is a tad more domestic than our home-on-the-range American breed. He is concerned about our household, dusting off books, checking dates on milk cartons.

We're not aware that most German–American marriages are the other way around—the man is American and the wife is the doting hausfrau.

Tobin looks in the linen closet and, shockingly, he is actually tearful. He sees that I, American woman and slob, have stuffed sheets in the shelves without folding them. He brings this loudly to my attention.

"At least I don't use baloney as a bookmark," I say, because I know some Americans who might.

"When they're all wrinkled, it feels bad on the skin."

"Is that why your *Schwanz* feels bad unless I touch it?"

He laughs a little, but then he sheds another tear as well.

Later, I shed my old skin and begin, like a good hausfrau, to iron the sheets flat—then flatter yet.

46 Vinyl

Mid-'80s, synth-pop era.

While Tobi finishes his degree, I decide to answer an ad I read in the paper searching for a singer in a German band. After auditioning, they call to tell me I've been chosen to make an album. It's called *Die Liebe wie ein Webergrill (Love as a Weber Grill)* with two German guys called Kriegston. The Strassenbahn takes me to a World War II bunker, where we rehearse. Even in summer, the thick concrete walls make it refrigerator-cold and the noise level is atomic. Call me weird, but I'd like to retain my hearing, so I ask the guitarist, Günter, to turn the levels down. Because I'm American, anything I say or do is cool.

After a few months of practice, we're in a recording studio, where I meet Dieter, who asks me to sing on his upcoming album with his group Vino Blanco.

"Kinda like Oingo Boingo," I say because Dieter, unlike the members of my group, speaks English.

"Yeah," Dieter says, "we'll be the German Oingo Boingo. Okay?"

"Bingo," I say, and disappear into the sound booth to finish my song.

While recording with Kriegston, we tour Germany. During a performance on an outdoor stage in the Black Forest, with my sleek red one-shoulder dress, no one would guess that I'm pregnant.

Vera K. performs after us, and we stay to watch her, even though I'm exhausted. She rocks more than most. Tobias thinks the *Neue Deutsche Welle* (New Wave) should change to the *Neue Deutsche Gefühl* (literal translation: "New German Feeling," but we call it, to ourselves, *The New Emotionalists.)*

"Avant-garde rock will be filled with opera lieder," he says. "Just wait until the end of the eighties and you'll hear it."

Tobin's cousin is in the rock group Kunstwerk, and although Tobin likes the group, the music is too bland and electric cold for him.

On the tour bus back, Günter, the guitarist, is toking up a storm. Thinking of the little boarder in my belly, I say to him, *"Bitte nicht."* But he continues. I slam my hand against the window of the bus. The bus driver asks me to stop, but I continue. Günter extinguishes his joint and the bus rolls on.

A few days later, we're back in the bunker to rehearse the last few songs on the album. Günter turns the bass up and there's a low vibrating thump that almost deafens us all.

"I think you just killed my baby," I say.

We drive to the studio for a final session and it's a disaster. Tobi and I wait and wait all day, then into the night. The bassist takes nine hours to get a "cool sound." The sound engineer is also no slice of cake. *Kein stück Kuchen.* He is slow and fumbling and fails to record take after take. He has the nerve to say we did it "just for fun." If one of us had a gun, there'd be a bullet with his name on it.

I'm asleep under the table when they call me in to sing. The last song "Funk" is not even finished when we leave at dawn, but everyone is just too damned tired. I don't even care if there is a nuclear bomb, I'll be happy to sleep.

I've composed an End-of-the-World Waltz in case everything goes *kaputt.*

47 Munich, 1983

It must be the tight turquoise plastic pants that are giving me such a horrible stomachache. We're in Munich at a music industry party.

I see Tobin, smoking a cigar to fit in with the moguls, warming from the purebred German beer into full inebriation.

I find the bathroom. I hear laughter and Tobi saying, "We're gonna have a baby in a few months."

"Super," someone says.

The pain is bad, and I see blood. I grab a towel in case I get sick and walk into the foyer. I catch Tobi's eye and he rushes to me. "I'm really sick," I say, leaning into him, "I think I need a hospital."

"Where's the hospital?" he yells.

I'm doubling over as he searches for someone who isn't soused or high to show us the way. No luck. It's as if he's asking for another bottle of champagne. Everyone is flying as high as he is.

"Don't worry, darling," he says as we both stumble to the car. "We'll get you there."

Lying down in the backseat, I hear his key missing the ignition a few times before the pneumatic rising of our Deux Chevaux car. As we set out, rain and thunder accompany our silence. Every turn is painful, and after an hour, Tobi stops at a restaurant to ask directions again.

Even though I know we'll get there, the way is not clear.

48 Semidarkness

We're back in our bed in Tübingen, after the ultrasound told us our baby is dead.

Somewhere in the city, a light goes out, and I am just awake enough to sense the change from semi to more complete darkness. I sit up, anxious that the bomb will really hit. To a sleeping Tobin, I say, "Darling, a light just went out."

Like in our small, striving lives. "I'm afraid we're all going to die," I say, pressing against his body.

"Why don't you play the End-of-the-World Waltz," he murmurs.

I imagine heat whirling, colors, beautiful and deadly, incinerating us all. I feel a twinge inside my empty womb. I want to go on living. I remember last week when the child inside me had kicked, as if to say, "I'm alive too, Mom."

49 Sideline

I'm worried I can't have kids, because my side has been hurting since the miscarriage. The only advantage I can see to not being pregnant is that I'll be able to drink again.

50 Living Things

The exhibit is filled with cages and resembles a zoo more than a graduate show.

One wrought-iron cage is empty except for the word LUFT hanging from a string.

Surrounded by a small audience, Tobi stands by his professor, who is discussing my husband's graduate work exhibit. "Mr. Kleinherz's work is post postrealism with installation art emphasizing the futility of halting technology. . . ." He points to a large piece, a birdcage with a hand-drawn thermometer. What appears to be a live sugar glider is moving around cut-out parakeets and one real starling. He says, "*Drei Grad Celsius Unter Moderner Kunst,*" which is the title of the piece as well as Tobin's show. "Three Degrees Below Modern Art."

A female student starts rampaging about caged animals and other trendy subjects. She touches on vegetarianism and although I agree with her, I am annoyed with her strident tone. The professor laughs at her. He seems glib, having less of a firm ethical or intellectual stance than disdain for her type. Turning toward the young woman, he says she should "*ask the bird* if it would rather be in an art show cage or in a cage in the real world."

Slinging her rucksack over her shoulder, she and her group of friends leave the gallery. When they get to the door, they yell something, probably a German obscenity, at the professor. And maybe at Tobi too.

The professor asks Tobin to say a word.

For the first time this evening, Tobi looks over at me and says, "Thanks, everyone, for coming to my show. Your comments and reactions will help determine my grade. So don't leave. If you look in the other 'environments,' you'll notice that none of the other animals are moving. Obviously, they are merely painted or constructed. But I do worry that art in the future will be nothing more than taking living things and caging them for others to observe."

51 Party Animals

Carnival celebration in Paris. Christmas break from Oxford. Years ago. Clive and I have been invited by a stranger to a party. She is Lea, a Hawaiian with an almond body—practically nude—dancing with us in a club. It seems impossible to refuse her, so we meet the next evening outside the courtyard of a house large enough to be an embassy.

We enter the front door. Caged dancers gyrate to Brazilian music. Clive and Lea grab me and we walk the stairs toward a skylight and onto the sun roof. Clive says, "Ah, my two wives," as Lea walks to the roof's ledge, her shiny long black hair flicking her buttocks.

We've had a few Ricards—a strong anise-flavored liqueur—between us, so I tell her not to fall. Clive hugs me, then nudges me toward Lea. He watches as my cashew body stands near her—a sculpture of light and dark—and says, "You two are more beautiful than a star."

"Or the moon," I say.

"But not the sun," Lea adds. She takes off her top and says, "I'm ready for the pool."

We follow her down two flights of stairs into hallways where couples, presumably strangers, are pressed against each other.

At the edge of a lighted pool, a few women are dressed as slaves. Although I can't use them, I don't want them to go away. A rosy fountain in the middle of the blue water glows like plutonium in a sci-fi movie.

Young men with gold leaves in their hair fornicate in the pool. Wildly, with a steady wild rhythm. Violent, but muffled in water, turquoise bubbles rioting to the surface.

Wearing a forest green bikini, I stand between Clive and Lea. My hair is sandy blond to my shoulders. We jump in the water together. Some men follow my green like twittering birds. It's here that I meet a young Italian—a cousin of Lea's who will, for a few evenings, become my lover.

An older man grabs Clive's hand and urges him onto the fountain's slab. He waves weakly at us. There's a dancer's cage next to him and he walks in, starts dancing with a black man in plumage.

We are clapping and splashing and laughing. Lea unties my bikini top. Clive dives back into the water to us and kisses me. He's just silly enough to whisper furiously in my ear, "Claire, don't let anyone put you in a cage. Not even if you're a bird. Not even if it's unlocked. Claire, when you're inside, all you think about is freedom." Then he tries to say it all again in French, slurring the word *liberté* so it sounds like *library*.

We pull ourselves out of the pool, wriggling on the tiles from the exertion. A dark man carrying two trays of food steps over us, saying, "Pardon," as if we were all in formal wear and not half-naked on the ground like gasping fish. Clive extends an arm to try to snatch a passing meal. No luck.

Not having eaten, we leave Lea to go find a café, walk from the bursting gold-lit house, feeling free like paupers, hungry as the sky goes blind.

I think then that I will never be caged. Will never even do the wild thing of getting married.

52 Purse Option

Tobin searches for it for months because, as he says, "It'll be near you more than I will." It's wine-colored leather, supple and versatile. It closes with a strap at the top, cinching to become small and secure; or, if I need to carry my music, expanding.

On our first wedding anniversary, he wraps it in gauze with a pink silk ribbon tied around it and a single white rose. Those who say a handbag is but a carrying thing have never seen this purse.

53 Birth Announcement

"*Das wird toll sein!*" ("That would be great!") I say to my friend and fellow new mother, Birgit.

I've had a few months to recover after giving birth to Elender Marie, nine pounds thirteen ounces, twenty-three and a half inches and perfect!

"*Na ja,*" she says, looking at both of us, me and tiny Elender. Our other friend, Christa, about to give birth, sits across from us in a large chair with a cushion under her belly. "*Wir könnten fahren bis Berlin, da gibt's die Reperbahn, gell?*" ("We could drive until we get to Berlin, where there's the Reperbahn, you know?")

"What's the Reperbahn?" I ask, speaking in German. Then I remember that Tobin told me he was there once, shortly after our wedding, and was offered a *Fick Frühstück* (a "Fuck Breakfast"), which he declined in favor of coffee and a croissant and intact marital vows.

"A street where all the prostitutes are," says Christa with a yawn.

And it would be perfect, of course. All three of us gorgeous girls, there, on the strip. Christa, post-delivery, with her shiny short black bob, me with the shoulder-length hennaed hair, and Birgit, with golden waves falling down to the small of her back.

It's not that we want to flaunt our hot mommy bodies; we just want to be outrageous. While breastfeeding and diapers have their appeal, we need to spin a fantasy for ourselves.

"I think we should each have a different length of skirt. To be subtle," Birgit says.

"Subtlety is not what they're looking for!" says Christa.

We all laugh.

I stand up to find my coat before I bundle up tiny Elender. "We're too beautiful to be prostitutes," I say.

"Danke," says Christa.

"Although Tobi says they *are* stunning on the Reperbahn," I add, remembering when he had said that to me, his new bride. I had cried and he was surprised. We were on a bus at the time, and he comforted me the whole way home.

54 Collarbone

When I gave birth to my daughter, my husband thought I had gone mad with the pain. I had. Screaming in German, I almost foamed at the mouth.

"Scheisse! Verdammt noch Mal! Schiess mich in den Kopf!" ("Shit! Damn it again! Shoot me in the head!")

My eyes glazed over for thirty hours before my daughter Elender Marie was eased out.

I didn't swear during Marcus Sean's birth; I just reminded myself silently, "Don't have any more children." After forty hours of back labor, they finally pulled him out, all eleven pounds, with forceps, breaking his collarbone. The German doctor assured me, "It didn't matter," *(macht nichts)* because his bones were soft, but I would have preferred his collarbone to have started out intact.

55 Full of Grace

Both Elender and Marcus were born on Sundays.

Most deliveries do not occur on this day of rest, but I was in a homeopathic hospital in Germany, and the doctors told me, "The child will come on the day it decides."

56 Infancy

Although the practice is unheard of in the United States, except in the newspaper after the parents have been arrested, Tobin and I leave our two infants—Marcus is born thirteen months after little Elender—every night to go dancing in Tübingen nightclubs. Sometimes the song *"Liebetron,"* from my Kriegston album, comes on and we go wild, twirling together in the middle of the dance floor.

Every night at seven o'clock exactly, we zipper nine-month-old Marcus and twenty-two-month-old Elender into sleep sacks and put them side by side into their cribs. Then we leave for the evening.

The neighbors across the hall, a lively Yugoslavian family who entertain friends in their small apartment from morning until late at night, watch out for our children.

The mother, who is a cleaning lady, says, in broken German, "Go, have fun. We hear if baby cry. No worry."

My parents in the United States are horrified, naturally, by this arrangement; but in Germany, it is the norm. I feel a bit apprehensive at first, but after months of dancing till dawn and nothing happening, I am fully accustomed to it.

One evening we return late and our babies are not in their cribs. We rush to the neighbors' apartment. They laugh and invite us in. The husband, who has lost his job due to a back injury, says, "Your babies are smoking and drinking. Don't worry."

We peer into the smoke-filled living room. The TV is on full blast, the radio is blaring, people are dancing and drinking.

Yugoslavian preteen children, with dark circles under their eyes, are pouring coffee for their parents and offering us sweets.

We search the crowded room for our children.

In the corner, Elender and Marcus, still in sleep sacks, are being held and bounced by a dark elderly couple. As we approach, it seems Elender has a cigarette holder in her hands. Marcus looks distinctly as if he is chewing on a wrapped cigar.

The woman hands Elender to me, smiling toothlessly, speaking a few words in her language.

"Danke, danke," I say, hugging Elen close to me. Taking one of her hands in mine, I notice she has acquired bright red nail polish. As I examine them, a young girl says in perfect German, "I painted her nails. I want to be a beautician."

"Danke vielmals," I say.

Tobin takes the cigar out of Marcus's mouth and lifts him from the old man's lap.

The old man rubs Marcus's head and tries to say "good boy" in German.

"Ja, ja," says Tobin, the proud if somewhat tipsy father.

As we make our way through the smoke, we are offered every type of hard liquor, which we refuse.

"Nein danke," we say to our babysitters as we exit their apartment like dutiful parents and bring our little ones safely back to bed.

57 **Rot**

Even though Tobin and I are a well-known item, young women start disrobing when they dance with my husband. Maybe they think the blaring "*99 Luftballons*" and whirling lights in our favorite club, ROT, meaning "red," will distract me so I won't notice.

An endearing thing about Tobin is that he really is unaware. "I thought she was having a bad bra day," he says when I explain to him how one was reaching inside her blouse to finger her bra. Usually it's the tall women with uni-brows who are the most obvious. I feel like a yelping little dog, "Hey! Hallo! I'm his wife!"

Luckily, I have rarely experienced jealousy, especially with Tobin. To his credit, he is attentive only to me.

Because we live in the center of Tübingen, near the club scene, we often invite people back to our place.

"I can't believe you have children. Your apartment is so cool," a young tattoo artist says.

She makes me show her our sleeping babies in the dark.

What she doesn't know is that every day before Tobin gets home, I meticulously rid the house of any baby evidence. Pacifiers are scooped off pillows, toys are hidden in the bookshelves, high chairs are carried into the porch. If I don't, Tobi says he gets in a *schlechte Laune*. Which means a "bad mood."

Another evening we watched television to better my German. It was a show about terrorists, including the Baader-Meinhof people. Tobin turned to me and said, jokingly, "Children are terrorists."

Thinking of his mother and father, and, to be totally honest, most parents, I said, "So are parents."

I know he loves his kids when he sees them, but it crosses my mind: Maybe he doesn't like to be reminded they're here to stay.

58 West Berlin, 1981

Two years before Elender comes to planet Earth, shortly before we're married, we're celebrating a new year.

We all drive together from Heidelberg to West Berlin—Tobin's best friend Klaus and his wife, Birgit, and me and Tobin.

We're in our second bar on a young evening of an old year. And what a place. Hard-core alcoholic dive, dark old wood, old people—hags, crazies, conservatively dressed women and men—all out for their routine night of serious drinking. Wine is cheap, cheap, and cheap, poured into ribbed glasses or onto each other. Bottles are everywhere as décor, lining the walls like books on shelves making the bar very living room–homey. *Gemütlichkeit* rules.

Tobi is excessively wasted and puts on a show with another performer, who is a door-to-door toy salesman. He opens his trunk for us to buy some of his wares. Tobin buys me a small toy car that is a cross between a hippopotamus and a bug. Adorable. It drives slowly across our table, crashing into glasses. Tobi talks to it as if it were his pet, making it drink out of a bottle cap.

The salesman is surrealistic, saying whatever comes to his mind, mostly obscenities, in German, of course. When he enters the bar, his monologue begins with, "Hello, you cunts and creeps; good evening, you lousy motherfuckers." His style is as picturesque as it is vulgar, at least for me, who can barely understand anything other than the ease of his delivery.

A man with a red wizard hat sits at the table next to us. Lecherous bastard, he leans into my personal imbibing space, tries to put an arm around me, in full view of his deranged, if not mentally retarded, wife, who wears clothes that don't fit but somehow cover her body. At the solid mahogany bar, two ancient men, virtually in rags, sing *"Auf die Nordsee Küste . . ."*

But the loudest, drunkest maniacs are none other than me and my fiancé, Tobin, who is making a point of talking to every single person in the bar before we leave. "I think I've greeted everyone in the room," he says to me, laughing. Then I'm up on his shoulders, juggling matchboxes. I jump down and do a few handstands to raucous applause. We win a bottle of champagne, and I bring a glass over to a little Jesus-like man sitting alone. He says, *"Vielen Dank."* The bartender says he has never spoken before.

We run to our car and Tobi proclaims to anyone who will hear, "I can drive better drunk than anyone sober."

And, in truth, he is a great driver even on the autobahn, where there are no speed limits, especially for us, tonight, flying into our new year.

59 If

If you were still my husband, I would say to you:

Take hold of who we are. It may not last.
We look through wet, iced windows at lighted streets. Could be our life; may go on, may end. I am round and thin, peach cobbler with blue eyes. You are tall and lean, taking youth from a wineglass, tired, wary eyes with shadows of guilt behind every smile.

Maybe I scared you. We were married only a few months
when I did something that took you a long time to be able to speak of. It terrified you so. I didn't mean it that way.

But now that you are no longer mine, I must tell you:

I can't bear to say I love you but can't have you,
that there are reasons for loving you, that you merit love, as we all do, and yet at the same time, you destroy my love intentionally, use our family to create ash for your new growth. . . .
That I don't know you after all these years
empties me, making my body see-through. I am so sad.

Too much has changed. But what has changed for the good is admitting I love people who have disappointed me.

And abandoned me.

60 Day Trip to Stuttgart, 1982

There is a runaway ache in my palms.
I must grab the world and give something back.
A magician in the street says, "Can I have a volunteer?"
A crowd has gathered to watch the show.
The magic man chooses me, and I go to the center to assist him.

He is dark, Italian, chiseled from another era.
He asks, "Can you hold these four orange balls in the palm of your hands?"
I do.
He says, "Squeeze the balls with closed fists as hard as you can."
I do.
He tells me,"Open your hands; stretch them out for the audience to see."
I do.
The balls are gone.
Miraculous.
On that day, I have no thought
of common parlor tricks.
Just the orange disappearing into thin air,
and how seeing eye to eye is impossible,
mystical, raw.
Wonderment wrinkles my senses,
passion squeezes my body.
Tobin, my new husband, does not know that
I can also disappear.
He has gone ahead to buy Egyptian cigarettes in the Stuttgart train station.
I run wildly
to catch up with him
down a street where cars are prohibited.
I spot him
weaving in and out of a crowd
in his greatcoat.
I follow his tall figure in secret,
noting his every move.
I need something, anything,
to let my man know
that magic lives in South German air.
That we may hold as tightly as we can,
but everything will escape us.
He enters the station, climbs wide stone steps,
goes to the multicolored kiosk. He pulls
his wallet from his back pocket, asks for cigarettes.

I'm right behind him, a faithful American shadow,
feeling now like a sorceress.

Under a moon-sized clock, travelers stray by
like lost stars. The vault of the station ceiling
is dark as night. Orientation is up for grabs,
four orange balls still hovering in my mind.

I begin by taking off my coat.
My hands are not mine,
but they obey my command.
My sweater is unbuttoned,
falls to the cold station floor.
My shirt is next, then undershirt,
then bra. Pants, socks, shoes, and
underwear are in slow motion.
Silence is forming a golden ring
around me. So are many Arab men.
Others are gathering in a crowd.
Everything is in black and white,
but I am invisible orange.
I stare at nothing but the winter air of this German *Hauptbahnhof*.
I am creating a dream, and so it is as if I am dreaming.

My husband turns around, lighting a cigarette,
the end of it glows orange, flickers,
as he wonders what the crowd is watching.
He walks toward me and my silent devotees.
He looks in the center of the spiral
to find me, his small wife, naked to the universe,
except for my gold waist chain, a gift from him,
that glints in his eyes.

Seconds move like planets, imperceptibly spinning.
Sovereign in their own orbit.
I merely look up at him.
His face turns red, then purple, then gray, then a hideous white.
He manages the words,"What . . . are . . . you . . . doing?"

Slowly. Distinctly. Between his teeth.
I am unafraid and calm as cold bacon.
I could try to explain: My hands held
and lost.

He stoops to pick up my bundle of clothes.
Opening his coat, he includes me in it.
I am close to his body, yet far away,
wrapped in a world that remarkably fits us both
as we descend the stone steps.

Here's what's visible to the ear: his bold boots
on those stairs and my soundless bare feet.
After a block, he gives me my shoes and socks.
I put them on slowly, still hidden in his coat.
Darkness closes in from Schwäbische forests,
fills the city.
We are silent.

A moment can be invisible.
He never refers to this evening until two years later.
At a beer garden, he tells a group of our friends.
The details are crisp and no one, especially Tobin,
looks beyond them.
Everyone is laughing, including me.
I try to picture that walk in the cold night,
his coat protecting my nakedness, the color of the street, the shades of the air. I try to recall; were we heading into darkness even then?

61 — Naked

Taking for granted the effect lack of clothing has on another person is not wise. Mimi, my piano teacher, says, "You cannot truly know someone until you see them naked."

I wanted Tobin to truly know me. I had exposed myself to him a thousand times, but this time, I exposed him. He used to smile his bright, warm smile when I flouted convention and call me his "little anarcho." But after that night, his mouth tightened when I said anything wild or unexpected.

I thought my stripping-down was a way of living up to his expectation of me as untamable. Instead, I planted an unwanted seed of doubt: Is she more than I can handle?

Perhaps I was testing him to see if he would love me no matter what I did. Foolish game. But I didn't want us to be a normal couple—the love we felt was too magical for that.

Huddled under his coat, I couldn't help thinking: Wouldn't it be tragic if love could vanish as mysteriously as it had appeared? As unfathomably as those little orange balls? Maybe not completely, all at once, but a different sort of disappearing trick—a slow disintegration.

62 Pairing

The mental institution of marriage builds a grand house on the shaky foundation of physical attraction.

63 Paring

I'd prefer my marriage to have the structure of a beehive, or the form of an apple.

64 Scar Crossing

I tell time by my children. When Elender is two and a half and Marcus one and a half, they each hold one of my hands while I shoulder a backpack, push with my feet three rolling carry-on bags, and try to follow Tobin, who struggles with a trunk. We are going to cross the ocean to move to my homeland. We settle into our seats, and after a few minutes, incredible, we're all in the air!

Half-drowsing during the flight, as much as possible with two toddlers, I think about how we have stored our lives. The movers converted a lion cage into a container for the Bösendorfer grand piano. We shipped the rest of our things, whittled down substantially by Tobin's system. He said, "We can keep what we need, love, or use."

"What about things we hate, but are addicted to?" I forgot to ask.

Exhausted by it all, we are looking forward to the nine-hour ride even though our flight has a stopover in Reykjavík.

In midflight, Tobin asks the stewardess, "Can I have a scissors?" To open Elender's soy milk. Before going to the bathroom, I think about warning Tobin not to use the scissors with Marcus on his lap, but I resist. I don't know if I'm imagining it, but he seems easily angered by any directive from me ever since the children were born.

I walk down the aisle to the door marked VACANCY.

A baby screams as if being branded. Marcus, I'm certain. I run back to our seats. His index finger is almost severed. Tobin is holding our baby's hand in the air, trying to make the blood run in the opposite direction. The stewardess gives us a first aid kit. Then another. Marcus's blood soaks through the gauze of seven kits.

"I could have cut off his finger," Tobin says, tears splattering his face.

"He'll be all right," I say. "It's not your fault."

Yes, it is.

I keep pressing the red gauze, afraid of the blood and how it came about. Every time we bandage him, he tears it off, and we start over, this time pinning his hands down. The stewardess says, "It's hard to clot in this altitude." And hurries to the cockpit.

When she comes back, Marcus is a ball of bleeding and screaming.

"The pilot," she says, "has radioed for a doctor at the airport in Reykjavík. He'll stitch him and decide if you can get back on the plane."

We are landing in twenty minutes.

Elen is white-faced and still.

I am flushed with hot blood even as Marcus's is draining.

Tobin has cut through all of us.

The passengers near us give up trying to sleep and pace the aisles.

As we land, I look out the window and see a medical van pulling up. The stewardess takes us off first to meet the doctor. He leads us into a van.

"Okay. Lucky boy, your plane comes down here," he says in halting English, stitching quickly. "Blood will stop, maybe now. We will see."

An hour later, as the doctor seals the last stitch, he says, "I have bandaged whole arm, young man, so no danger you pull off again." He allows us back on the plane. Marcus's finger will heal nicely except for a scar, its smooth thickness reminding us of our crossing over into night.

PART TWO

Love is the dog we let into our bed, even when it bites.

TUNNEL VISION

I wake the child I was, the girl who sees her mother down a tunnel.
The tunnel is Truth and water.
The girl is fearless of fear.

There is one sister, of her three, she can't see.
And the others fill like shells with ocean's noise.

I am in the middle, half in, half out of the waves.

Night dreams. The child me is sleeping.
She sits upright in bed, her long honey hair
falling in rivers down her back, awake until dawn,
and all the snakes on the roof slide away.

Her back warmed by the sun,
a bright lozenge that rolls
into place at the window corner.
The air is dry as light.

The walls are salmon-colored, wallpaper dirty and peeling.
(She never noticed until this remembered moment.)
The ceilings curved and high give the room a tunnel-cold.

Her mind fills flaws with perfect book surroundings:
the plain jumper is a party dress,
socks on her hands, an ermine muff.

Not much has been taken from her.

She is not yet me.

65 The Key

As soon as we are settled in the States, I have a faint sense something is out of tune.

After Tobin falls asleep, I play the keys quietly for hours, writing music, songs and instrumentals: "Waldi," "I Met Him in a Gallery," "The End of the World Waltz," "Peru," "Hold Me," "Hot Night Hotels," "The Last Day of Trust . . ." For his Christmas present, I learn a Bach partita and Chopin's Ballade no. 1.

He can hear me through Chopin or Bach, but I am mute and invisible everywhere else. On the street he'll pass me by, and I'll run after him pleading, "Don't you see me?!" When the children and I spot him getting off his train, he looks right through us.

On the other hand, when he wakes from a nap, he pulls me close to him. "Oh, it's you!" he says, as if recognizing me for the first time. "I'm so happy it's you."

After a late-night piano gig, I run from my car to the apartment. We don't live in the best neighborhood—in fact, it's downright dangerous—so I try to compose my nerves. But when I get to the door, I realize I've lost my keys. I ring our doorbell. No answer. I ring and ring, looking behind me into the dark bushes. No sign of life. I drive to a Pancake House and call home. More ringing. No answering. I drive miles to my mother to pick up an extra set of keys.

In the morning, I tell Tobin what happened.

"Yes, I heard it ringing," he says, greatly irritated, "but the phone is not next to our bed."

I don't think there's a chord progression to resolve his words.

My mind dodges back to a train ride, my junior year abroad, from Dublin to Killarney with Rick, my British boyfriend (who would have protected me from the wild Picts, if necessary) on a five-day vacation after his champagne-drenched graduation from Oxford.

We are eating homemade sandwiches from his mum, in our compartment, when a thin middle-aged man sits down in the seat near us. That something is not quite right with him seems immediately clear.

Like a gerbil, he rummages through piles of papers taken from a large overstuffed leather satchel. Pulling his pockets inside out, he looks to be on the verge of tears, his lined face sagging, his eyes darting wildly from the rushing pastoral scenes outside the train window to the papers, and then back to his inverted pockets.

After much searching, he looks up to us and says with his thick Irish accent, "I've lost two, smahl keys!" His intense eyes seem to hold a much larger tragedy in view, but we put our half-eaten sandwiches down and set about trying to help him.

Now I'm trying to unlock the door between Tobin and me, and he goes on sleeping.

66 Biters in the U.S.A.

Prostitutes try to befriend me as I roll along the sidewalk with my double stroller. It takes a lunatic running after me in the middle of the afternoon, the stroller overturning and our sleeping toddlers landing on their heads, miraculously unscratched, for Tobin to realize we have to move out of our large but affordable apartment to a better area.

While Elender and Marcus are still small enough to require bowls of hot oatmeal—three helpings each—we move to a two-flat house in my childhood hometown Evanston.

Elen has a bizarre propensity to go berserko if the oatmeal is overcooked. Even the slightest bit of mushiness makes her scream, "There are no biters! Where are the biters! I want biters!"

"They eat like four men," I tell Tobin in case he starts in again about our food bills. I prepare litanies in my head against his criticisms: *Why do I buy raspberry jam from the Greek grocery store, even though it's four cents cheaper at Jewel? Because it's closer and the owner knows me and the kids.*

I recall Tobin's mother canning the berries from their summer-home trees to make marmalade, one of Elender's first German words. A rich purple with seeds, like biters, we spread it thick on dark full-grain bread.

But we have no berry trees of our own here. Just a small maple in the front. I can't climb very high on the small budget Tobin allows us from his work as a graphic designer, supplemented by occasional gigs painting murals in buildings. Our standards definitely exceed our bank account. But we are, I think, safe.

67 Orphans

Elender keeps climbing on the railing on our front steps. I'm annoyed, but she's only four and a half years old. When I yell at her, again, to get off, she disarms me, "Have no fear, my lovely friend," she says, "I won't fall."

She and Marcus wander through the house playing Orphans, which involves carting bags and suitcases, wearing layers of clothing, hats, and sleeping on floors with blankets. As I prepare breakfast for the "orphans," Marc walks by and says to Elen, "That lady is nice; she's gonna give us something to eat." It's just seven o'clock in the morning.

I know I'm exhibiting burnout symptoms, but by the end of today it'll be third degree. First of all, there is the summer humidity that does not abate, even at sunset. Elen and Marc have been laughing, then fighting, then crying. All day long. Although usually great chums, they are tired, sweaty, and irritable with each other and need a bath.

Like the wicked witch in "Hänsel and Gretel," I grab a skinny arm from each of them, drag them into the bathroom, strip off their dirty clothes—they are whimpering by now—and throw them in the dry bathtub. They are crying full force now, and I don't care; I flip the faucet with enough presence of mind to turn cold on first—they are both screaming from the shock of icy water on their summer-hot skin—but I really don't care. I could be a Nazi saying, "Into the showers, women and children first."

As the water level rises, I am sobbing.

Yes, the day has been hard, but just the usual mom-with-young-kids kinda day. There's no excuse for my wickedness.

I'm trying to forget last night with Tobin. He doesn't seem to have a clue about what I do during the day. I told him Elender needed new shoes and he said, "What's wrong with the old ones?"

"They're two sizes too small. And besides that, she needs ballet shoes."

"For what?" he asked.

"Why are you quizzing me?" I asked. "Don't you think *I* know when the children need things?"

"They have food and a roof over their heads," he said, and stomped out of our bedroom.

Now Tobin is about to come home to us.

The children settle down as the water surrounds them.

I splash with them and they begin to play.

CLUE NUMBER THREE
The children are losing.

68 Postures

To help make ends meet while taking care of the children, I teach six piano students each week at home. I also have a gig every Thursday night in a private restaurant, singing and playing the piano. I'm also the event planner for a trendy art gallery. I demo food most Saturdays, some Sundays, at a sadly now-defunct, fondly remembered health food store called Oak Leaf Produce. I model for artists in their homes. Being an artist myself, I want to make unusual poses. Twisting myself into twenty-minute postures—all of them painful—my blood tries to circuitously reroute to reinfuse my numb limbs. My modeling career culminates with a show called Claire with forty artistic renderings—all fully clothed, thank you very much—of *moi* in a gallery. Talk about an ego trip.

Fortunately, my own artistic development costs us not a naked dime. I win a scholarship to an acting school in the city and to an arts center in the suburbs, where I study printmaking.

I work part-time in yet another gallery—Native American—called Six Deer Pronging. Navajo and Hopi artists from Santa Fe personally deliver the jewelry we order from them. Their sense of time allows for lingering, as if each moment were a five-course meal. Nothing like our Midwestern no-nonsense, meat-and-potato variety. I am often unaware a Navajo artist has entered the gallery. He might be standing in the corner for several minutes before I walk by and notice him with his large shoulder display bag. After a quick shocked breath, I say, "Oh, hi. I didn't know you were there."

Still standing still, he smiles. "Howdy." He's stocky, wearing jeans with a silver-and-turquoise bear belt buckle.

"I'm Claire."

"I'm Big Clay."

"Good to meet you . . . Big Clay. Neat name."

He sets his display bag on the floor and opens it.

After looking it over, I say, "These are really beautiful. But . . . did you make the Kokopelli necklaces we ordered? The boss says they sell really well. Or the hanging deer pendants with the turquoise moon?"

We both change from a squat to standing. He is silent for several minutes.

"I made the silver coyote," he says finally, "with bone moons. I hope you like it."

"I do," I say, going back to sit at my desk. It's no use. The Indians create what they feel like creating. As usual, I'll write out the check my boss signed and have to explain to her again. I'll hand it to Big Clay, who will thank me and stand silently over me while I work, until he thinks it's time to go.

Even though I'm selling art and I'm a mom, in my heart, I travel with Big Clay and his folk. I, too, do what I feel like. Maybe that's why Tobin tells everyone, our friends, his family, his colleagues, "She doesn't work."

His words freeze me. To him I'm a statue sitting for everyone at all angles: an artist posing as a mother, a mother posing as a wife.

69 Shoes, Paper, Scissors

Even though I "don't work," I seem to be events-planning at another gallery in downtown Chicago that specializes in European paper-based sculpture. My boss there is omnisexual and wears black clothing that fits her skin as if it were dripped on like wax. Over this, she drapes pearls—not around her neck, but encircling her whole body in a tantalizing sweep.

I have been accused of being flamboyant, but next to her I am a Mormon matron or at the most extreme, a vixen librarian. She offered her body to everyone, including me, on several occasions.

Her name is Simone Leckerbaum. (Another Kraut!)

She doesn't show enthusiasm for anything except carnal relations, most notably, but not exclusively, with her co–gallery owner and current boyfriend Julian. They are as inseparable as the pope and his infallibility.

Blasé and sultry at the same time, Simone can't be made of flesh and blood—her body and face are perfect enough to have been fashioned by a mad scientist's knife and know-how. The jagged angles of her asymmetric platinum blond hair make her look like an anime character.

She seems to follow her own personal homing-beam to the cool, yet effortlessly adheres to a style of hipness that has no guidelines and does not tolerate any infraction from friends, lovers, or employees.

Speaking with the ease of one unencumbered by emotions and the quotidian, Simone comes, evidently, from wealth, and it stains her very teeth a bright white, despite the incessant smoking and coffee drinking in which she indulges. As far as I can tell, she doesn't eat.

Today she is uncharacteristically agitated, as only a lesser mortal (like me!) would be. "He left a few pair. But my clothes are cut up into shreds!"

Apparently, her boyfriend Julian found her in bed with their tax accountant—another impeccably stunning female being, only much younger than her, and of Japanese descent—and went all Edward Scissorhands on her shoes and clothes.

"After he found us, I changed the lock, but he climbed up the tree and broke in a window," she says, adjusting the pearls nestled under her breast. "At least fifty pairs of shoes, slashed! Some with holes in the toe, some with the strap snapped in two, others just hacked at. And he knows how much I live for my shoes. Oh, and my boots! Thigh-highs from my parents they brought back from Germany, snipped in half. Goddamn the son of a bitch."

I shake my head in sympathy as I clear away food trays on tables near pulp-paper sculptures.

"He says he's going to come over and shoot me today. And he's got guns," she says, laughing. "Anyone want to stick around and see if he comes?"

I'm thinking of the airplane and the scissors, of my small Elender and Marcus at home with Tobin.

I can't help imagining the blood-splattered pearls and her lifeless body impaled on a monstrous paper phallus in the corner of her gallery space. It's not an image I wholly dislike.

"Simone," I say, "I think we should all call it a day. It's late and I wouldn't put it past him. Have you called the police?"

"Of course," she says, yawning at my alarm. "My parents are basically the chief's best friends."

Emanating a slight odor of cowardice, I slink out the door as soon as she gets on the phone.

70 Tiger Breasts

"I must come over and see them."

"You mean . . . my breasts?"

Luckily, this phone conversation is not being taped.

"Yes. It's very important. Sometimes after childbirth, the breasts—well, they are not exactly perfect. You know what I mean."

"Yes."

"I'll be there at three tomorrow."

"Make it two, while the children are still in school."

"Okay, see you then."

"See you."

I'm talking to none other than Juaro, my hairdresser, a long-hair specialist from Brazil. It would be an understatement to call him a control-maniac, borderline nutball. But he is truly gifted when it comes to long hair like mine. I have turned all my Evanston neighbors onto him. Even Tobin and a few other husbands put up with him. Tobin says, "He takes three times longer than anyone else, but he's three times as cheap."

"After he gave me a trim," a neighbor with ultra-long locks tells me, "he tried to convince me to let him come to my house and get in the shower with me, so he could make sure I was washing my hair correctly!"

On your first hair consultation, Juaro actually gets out a microscope. He plucks a hair from your head and makes you—there's no choice involved here—look at it under the lens while he holds forth like an Oxford don. Stressing the importance of a freezing cold-water rinse to stimulate the hair follicles, he plunges your hand in a bowl of ice water. "Cold!" he says, as if your wincing wasn't a sign that you were sentient. "Nada! Your hair loves it."

He cuts the rubber band from his waist-length ponytail. "Always cut, to minimize hair damage," he screams in your ear. "Never pull, never un-twist."

He shakes his lustrous hair like a model in the old Clairol ads. "See how strong my hairs are? They love cold water!" He interrogates you. "Do you use a proper pH hair conditioner?" Never mind answering. Anything will be wrong. He divulges the proportions of apple cider vinegar to filtered water in a whisper so intense, it could be prayer. He louds up for a second. "Don't ever forget a drop of olive oil."

I have to admit, my hair looks fantabulous, but last week his haircut and lecture lasted three and a half hours. At the end, he stared me down with his deep brown eyes and said, "You may not believe me, but I care more about your hair than you do."

"Trust me, Juaro," I said, "I believe you."

Along with this hair-gift thing, Juaro is world-famous for body-painting.

He wants to make me into a tiger (déjà vu of an animal kind) for a client's photo shoot. Naturally, I'll be naked, à la *Goldfinger,* only the paint is water-soluble so it won't kill me. His one concern is that, having suckled my young, the nipples may not be perky enough. I know they are, but he's a fanatic artiste and must decide for himself.

The doorbell rings at two o'clock on the nipple, and I take off my shirt.

"Good," he says to my firm chest, "but not exactly what I'm looking for."

"Okay," I growl. "Thanks for coming."

If I were a tiger, I'd mess him up.

Instead I button up my shirt and see him out the front door.

I pounce back into the quotidian; Lois Lane by day, Tiger Balm by night. No one, not even me, knows who I really am.

71 Little Red Wagon

The children are barely four and five. *See,* I remark to my puzzled mind, *how early it all started.* The artists I draw with and model for have arranged an entire exhibition of Claire portraits in a local gallery. It's opening night, so I'm bringing some quiches I made and wine. I also have several large prints I'll be selling.

I've told Tobin for weeks about it and he knows I'll need the car. I specifically requested it. Why did I need to?—as best I recall, he never "requested" anything—I ask myself now.

To my utter delight (in an alternative universe where husbands are lauded for being monsters), Tobin comes into the kitchen dressed in tennis whites and says, "I need the car to go play tennis."

"What? It's the opening. We have to bring all this stuff."

"I'll come later."

"Tobin? Are you kidding?"

Monster grabs keys and racquet and heads out the back door to the garage.

"You have to take the kids," I scream at his back, my heart pounding through my blouse.

"I will," he yells back.

Elender and Marcus are in the backyard and I hear him say, "Kiddos, Daddy has to go play tennis." So I assume they are going with him.

In the front yard, I load up the red wagon parked under the maple tree, carefully arranging my shrink-wrapped artwork so it won't fall or get creased.

I'm about to head out like a refugee on the suburban sidewalk when I hear crying from the kitchen. It sounds like my children. I run up the stairs and find Marc and Elen tear-streaked.

"Why did you leave us?" sobs Marcus.

"Where did you go?" asks Elen with a whimper.

"I thought Daddy was taking you," I say. "He told me he was."

"He's playing tennis," says Marcus, looking at me accusingly as if I were the bad guy.

In our universe, the mother gets blamed for anything in a little red wagon.

72 Rude Awakening

After walking a mile with the children, I arrive at the gallery. My brother Brian meets me at the door. "Where's Tobin?" he asks in brotherly outrage. I burst into tears and he helps me bring the kids and the wagon inside.

When Tobin arrives, he has a strange, arrogant swagger as he walks the room filled with all the images of his wife. I don't think I've ever noticed that swagger before.

Brian grabs me and whispers, "What? Is he jealous?"

I can't imagine how he could be. He's the successful artist. He's the professional.

"He's having a hard time," I say quietly.

"When wasn't he?" Brian says, almost as an aside.

"I don't know, Brian," I say. "He's between projects and . . ."

"Aren't we all," he says.

"Maybe he's depressed," I say.

"Maybe he's a narcissist," he says. Then he whispers in my ear, "Or maybe, let's just forget labels and go back to the good old-fashioned he's an asshole."

It hurts to hear, but he's making sense.

73 Height

"Let's all be silent for ten minutes," says Tobin.

We're walking in the mountains—the Schwäbische Alb—on vacation in Germany, singing à la the von Trapp family, and Marcus and Elender are, admittedly, becoming quite boisterous. But surely the hills are alive and absorbent enough for two small children's echoing voices.

Tobin looks at his watch before stepping over a boulder. "Ready, set, silence."

We climb down now at a steady clip. Watching Elen and Marc, who are only six and seven, negotiate some pretty steep terrain, I am dizzy with panic.

I trip over a little jagged rock and it cuts my ankle. "Ow!" I howl.

"Quiet!" admonishes Tobin.

We reach a lichen-covered plateau, the same one, in fact, where Tobi had taken me before we were married and insisted I walk topless in the sunshine.

Now Elen and Marc are running in circles, quietly, through the grass and edelweiss.

In a daze, I walk to the edge of the field toward a sheer drop. *They would all be better off without me,* I'm thinking. *A second, and I'm over the edge. They'd think it was an accident.* These thoughts are fleeting—induced by height and the proclamation of Tobin.

Suddenly Marcus is by my side. "Mommy, the ten minutes are over."

Oppression over.

"That's great!" I say.

"Mommy?"

"What, sweetie?"

"Did you ever think about killing yourself?"

Silence.

"No. I'd never do anything like that. I love living, you know. Especially since you two guys came along."

"And who'd take care of us?"

"Exactly."

Although both of my children have tested "gifted," Marcus's gift for reading my mind is even more impressive.

I'm not clairvoyant, though, so I'll know only later that this was our last trip before Tobin and I both jumped.

74 Obscured View

It's astonishing how the trees have lost their leaves overnight. Yesterday when the children and I drove along the lake, we were straining to look through leaves to see the churning silver blue water. Today, there are only branches obscuring the view.

The maple stands naked in our front yard.

75 Score

"Don't take my jumper!" screams Elender as if that were the object of the game. She's playing with Marcus, who, having been entranced at age four by the beauty of chess moves, takes the game seriously. Marcus winces because he knows she'll refuse to continue if her "jumper," as she calls her knight, is taken. But if she quits in a huff, he is happy to sit like a little Buddha, playing against himself hour after hour. It's hard not to marvel as the little boy (mine!) with blond shoulder-length hair quietly concentrates on the patterns before him.

After we return from our family trip to Germany, I bring home music scores from the Northwestern Music Library. I want Marcus and Elen to become aquainted with abstract feelings evoked by great music. My plan for them to listen and follow along comes true at night. They climb into bed, flipping through scores of their favorites: Beethoven symphonies and Rzewski's variations on *The People United Shall Never Be Defeated!*

Years later, Elen says, "I was following along to impress you. Only Marcus really understood."

Marcus, being younger, is always in Elender's shadow, so it's good to realize that he might be a shade more of a genius in something! For me, conducting is akin to being a god: lift the hands and beautiful sounds begin. I always tell Marcus, "You can be whatever you want, Markie, but Mommy wants you to be a famous conductor of a symphony."

If life is a game of chess, it's hard to resist helping your children make their first moves.

76 Zhivago White

New Year's Day, what seems like a long time ago.

Tobin and I, Elender and Marcus set out in the snow to go to the park. Our footsteps make the first marks in *Doctor Zhivago* white.

Rick, my British boyfriend during my year abroad in Oxford, had said, "When we have our first daughter, we'll call her Lara, for Julie Christie's part in the film." I should have married him; he was mostly nice to me.

Now, years later, my husband and two children reach the park grounds. Tobin puts his arm around my wool jacket.

Marcus, too small to make a proper snowball, throws snow in the air like sugar. Packed like a snowman himself, he can barely bend at the waist to scoop up more of it.

"Mommy, look," he laughs, falling into the billowy ground.

Elender, in a lilac coat, runs in zigzags across the park, like a fairy. She is the most graceful child anyone, even the blind, has ever seen. Says her mother.

There's a layer of slush far beneath, and I slip, roll in the snow. Elender runs back to jump on me. Tobin stands above us. "I'm hungry. Can we go back now?" he says.

"But, Daddy, we just got here," says Elender, slithering cold and wet on top of me.

Tobin slaps the snow off his thighs. "I'm in a bad mood. I hate these Sunday walks. . . . Everyone out with their family. Let's go."

It's a new year, and as we slip home with Elen and Marc crying, I make the resolution that anyone who melts my children's happiness will have to roast in hell.

77 Cornerstone

Romantic loving comes easily to those steeped in its tradition. My mother frothed in a tragic wave of unquenchable desire for most of my life.

She woke me in the middle of the night to call France. In Europe. At fourteen, I spoke better French than my mother did, and she needed me to ask for him. She didn't want his wife to know she was calling. *"Est-ce que Rémy est là?"* I asked.

Feeling important but groggy, I listen into the receiver for his French wife's reply: *"Oui, oui, il est là. . . . Qui est à l'appareil?"*

Not knowing quite what to say, I come up with, *"Une amie."* I hear static and her long breath echoing over the wires—she knows I am the daughter of her husband's lover—then silence.

It started in 1962, when my mother already had five of her eventual six children. She's thirty-two years old and I am seven. Down the street, a twenty-four-year-old French exchange student—tall, male, and handsome—rooms with our neighbors, the Brinkers. Mrs. Brinker is suffering from postpartum depression and needs more space for her breakdown.

"His name is Rémy and he needs a place to stay," says my dad to my mom, who doesn't think it's a good idea. "All I need is another kid," she says.

"The children can learn French," my dad counters.

Obviously, he was right.

"I'll be home at midnight," my father tells my mother on the phone. But he isn't home at midnight. And not at one or two. Or three. Or even four. Out with the lawyer boys, he can't keep track of why he isn't home. My mom roams the house, sits near the phone.

Rémy wakens, looks out his window, watches her in her long nightgown, running out into the street. After standing on the porch, watching her white against dark gray streets, he goes to her. She is a small brunette and could fit comfortably under his chin.

"If I were your husband, I would not do this to you."

She straightens herself, turns away from him.

"How dare you talk to me about my husband," she says, and walks up the porch steps to go inside.

But does she get inside? Maybe my dad comes home right then. At that exact moment. Maybe he doesn't. Timing, in any language, is all.

One night they dance at a neighbor's party and he leans his French face close to my mother's ear. "If I were your husband, I would not make you so many babies!"

She stops in the middle of the song and leaves the dance floor.

My dad notices Rémy pacing the sidewalk in front of our house, never going anywhere. His close-cropped dark hair looks exotic on his imposing head as he turns right, then left. The whole neighborhood, except my dad, knows he loves *ma mère.*

After three months, he suggests Rémy might be "too dependent" on my mother, and "should consider dating."

A month later, when Rémy has gone on only two dates, my dad tells him, "You'd better leave."

My mom says, "I am going to a prayer retreat. I need it." Apparently! What I don't know until later is that she checks in with a nun at the retreat, but leaves immediately to meet Rémy at a motel.

"But Mrs. McLeod, we are starting prayers in the chapel!" I imagine a bewildered Mother Superior saying.

Rémy drives down from Canada, where he is visiting friends. The motel air-conditioning is as loud as the airplane he will fly in a matter of days to Paris. They leave, weeping, to find another motel.

My mother calls home.

"All five of the kids have come down with the chicken pox, and the Brinkers had a kitchen fire," my dad tells her.

"I'll pray for the Brinkers," she says.

"And our kids," my dad says.

Dad makes spaghetti for us and the Brinker children.

A few spaghettis later, Mom comes back to us.

Years later, she confides in me, "After Rémy went home to Paris, I sent myself a dozen roses every week because he couldn't." I remember the neighborhood commotion those vibrant deliveries caused.

"After he moved back to Paris," she says, "we wrote each other two times a day for seven years."

Priests on both sides of the ocean intervene, tell them, "Stop writing, stop loving, just stop." A Jesuit friend of my mother's goes to the extreme of traveling to the Schwarzwald, where Rémy is stationed in the army. Even as a teenager, I tried to script their impossible love into the movie I would one day direct:

DAYLIGHT. OUTDOORS. SCHWARZWALD TREES DARK AGAINST SNOW. A CLEARING WITH YOUNG FRENCH SOLDIERS.

FATHER THADDEUS (Gregory Peck), saying Mass, raises the chalice. RÉMY'S face (Gary Cooper) reflected in the gold. After Communion, the priest takes RÉMY on a walk.

FATHER THADDEUS She's beautiful . . . an amazing woman, but she belongs to her husband and her family.

RÉMY (Nods)

FATHER THADDEUS She sent me to tell you to renounce her. I have a letter. It's thick. I have it in my pocket. Will you promise here before God that you will give her up?

RÉMY (Nods)

FATHER THADDEUS Good. Then I can give you this. (FATHER THADDEUS gives the letter and leaves.)

DAYLIGHT OUTDOORS. GUNSHOTS. THE SOLDIERS ARE AT RIFLE PRACTICE.

RÉMY (Aiming at the target) (Bang) I will never (Bang) give (Bang) her up. (Bang) Never (Bang) never (Bang) never.

The last shot's a bull's-eye. But in real life there is no shredded target. He asks her, but my mom says, "I can't leave five small children." We are cuter than buttons or snaps. He knows she can't leave. He took me to ballet in Winnetka; he taught me *un, deux, trois, quatre, cinq*. He understands the power of numbers in any language: They are two, now we are five. Soon to be six, and six is a mystical number.

"You must get married. I'll never be free," she tells him.

He does, then invites my mom to stay with them, the newlyweds, in Paris.

His wife thinks my mom, a mother of five, will be an American matron. Naturally, when she sees her extreme beauty, she slams down *le beurre* on the table. And my mom has to book a hotel.

"Don't be cruel to your wife," my mom tells Rémy before she agrees to help him find a job in the States.

He tries to be gentle when he tells his French wife, "I'm leaving you. I am going to live in Chicago."

She knows the French tradition of men having affairs. And as a teacher of history, she understands the power of tenacity. "She's just a mistress, *mon chéri,*" she says. "I'll make dinner now."

He follows her to the kitchen, looks straight at her. "I loved her before I met you. I didn't want to marry you. You asked me, remember?"

Tears roll down her schoolteacher face, but her classroom calm kicks in. "This might be the proper time to tell you I am pregnant."

My mother doesn't ask him to, and even if she did, he couldn't leave his pregnant wife.

Still, their affair continues. When he's too weakened by guilt, my mother is strong: She becomes a travel agent, flying back and forth to France thirty times in five years.

She chooses herself. Not just a wife and mother of now six children, but a lover in an alternative reality.

What this taught me, when my mother's faraway gaze took her from me, was that she was a woman. A woman first and then a mother, in that order. She taught me well in each role.

But this was not the only received knowledge from her. "Always wear lipstick," she said. "People treat you better." Too true. And, "The answer to the universe is in Dvořák's Symphony no. 8 in G Major." Also true. And, "If it's worth doing at all, it's worth doing badly." Fair enough.

Poetry, the moon, and the infinite moods of Lake Michigan were favorite subjects, but love and its elusive quality were her life thesis.

She kept herself for herself, for Rémy, her woman's need sovereign. She was gorgeous porcelain in those days, a rim of dark hair framing light green eyes. She was mystery, to us and to the men who loved her—and she still is.

When Rémy lived in our house those first three months, I knew nothing of my mother and her forbidden love.

Nothing of her journal. Only later, before I meet Tobin, do I read: "I take his still-wet sweater from the wash and drape it around my neck, as if it were a hug." This gesture lodged in my heart, something so sweet and private, I hoped I'd do the same when I found my true love.

Seven years after they first met, Rémy meets my mother at a French train station. "You look . . . sadder," he says.

"Only because of missing you," she says.

"I beg you to stay," he says in Paris hotels and more hotels. But she always comes home to us.

"I die a little each year I am not with you," he writes.

His wife has given birth to a boy after the first girl, his blue ink on airmail announces. Then another boy. He faxes, he phones, later he e-mails. His is the divorce that never happens.

As I grow up, my mother and Rémy talk into the night. For them hope is a telephone. Even the name—Ma Bell—is romantic. They talk during my mom divorcing my dad. Talk about us, all six of us, and about his three.

They fit together the puzzle of two worlds separated by an ocean, floating on a timeline that rises and falls with names, faces, and dates. A ribbon of absence and ink. But *their* lives, after forty years of bending and squeezing, remain the missing pieces, the edges, worn and misshapen, are unable to meld.

"Twenty years ago, I decided to let him go," she says. "I piled his letters on the sandy beach and set them on fire. I regret it now. But I saved one scrap."

I imagine their letters—thousands of them—(many I read sitting next to my mother) turning into confetti over the ocean, settling like snow on the waves. She shows me a bit of paper, charred but still legible. It says, JE T'AIME.

I didn't judge her then. And I barely do now. Only later will I understand that true lovers like Rémy and my mother didn't need to live together—they never did—to belong to each other. And if they had?

Thirty-five years later, my mom and Rémy are still beautiful-rooming it—facilitated by the handy airplane—then allowing the ocean to separate their lives.

At age fourteen, I am sleepy as my mother nudges me from dreams to play a part in her *Anna Karenina* world. (Minus the train ending, I hope.) My young life is pallid in comparison to their ocean-crossed love. When she wakes me, *my* story flees, and her elaborate one takes over.

78 Blind Spot

I married a German, one of my sisters married an Australian, another an Italian, and the other married an American. Anyone can see that's an impressive three out of four carrying on our mother's tradition. I shouldn't speak for them, but I will. In our minds, a foreign man could sweep you away in the blink of an eye. That blink seems like true love, our vision of it as clear or clouded as Rémy's long-distance voice when he asked, "Is your mother home?"

Two out of four of us are now divorced. That's me and one who married an American. It proves that nothing can be proved about love.

Marriage is the blind part of the eye, behind the optic nerve where everything converges, and you just cannot see.

79 Dogma

In comparison to my mother's, my domestic life is fairly uncomplicated. The McCloud-Kleinherz family all live under one roof and we follow some basic rules:

1. *Love each other.*
2. *Kiss and hug.*
3. *Listen to each other.*
4. *Care if someone is hurt (body or feeling).*
5. *Think of the bigger picture: GODS, NATURE, MUSIC, ART, LIFE, COLORS, LOVE.*
6. *Do not poke into each other's wounds.*
7. *Big hug and kiss after school.*
8. *Don't feel sad when another person has a good thing, because you might get a chance to do it.*

9. *Rejoice in another's good fortune.*

By the McCloud-Kleinherz family: Claire, wife/mom; hubby Tobin; Marcus and Elender

Signed in black ink by each of us. Marcus's signature takes up most of the bottom of the page. Either he was emphatic or just learning how to write.

80 For Argument's Sake

Tobin and I tried in an intimate moment to agree on some guidelines for us as a couple.

1. Don't argue about money.
2. Don't argue in front of the children.
3. Go to bed earlier.
4. Don't argue in bed.

Funny how we never followed them.

81 Name-calling

It feels like a year since my husband called my name for any other reason than to remind me to pick up his dry cleaning.

"Look, Elender, there's an art store," I say. "I bet Daddy would love some of those paints."

Or "Marcus, see that mural, your daddy painted one a little like it in Germany on a castle wall."

I think if Tobin knew how often I talk about him to the children, he would call my name again.

82 Sunglasses

I watch women driving their sport-utility vehicles. They usually have salon-perfect swinging hair and they wear ultra-chicifying sunglasses.

I don't want their SUVs. I have nice hair, thanks to genetics and Juaro. But all I've ever wanted, for the past several years of marriage, is prescription sunglasses.

83 Proof That We Can't Stay Together

Deep winter is approaching and we belt ourselves in for an exhausting ride. The children are another year older, another year more adorable.

Blinding light reflects on a thin dusting of snow. The children and I take a walk and fall on the sidewalk, not breaking anything. I have the unsteadying thought that if Tobin had been there, he wouldn't have caught our fall.

Morbid thoughts creep into my brain as I set about the steady drip of daily life. Thoughts like if I don't wear a seat belt in the car and I'm in an accident, will I be instantly killed or just permanently crippled?

Later, when we're divorcing, I won't wear a seat belt anymore.

84 More Proof

"The kids don't need school photos. It's not in the budget."

Tobin says this with his back turned on me, a body position that is becoming more and more familiar. He walks out of the room.

"But, it's only seven dollars and thirty-five cents. . . . I'll get another piano student. . . ."

My voice trails as his form recedes, then vanishes. I phone my favorite neighbor and she runs over with an envelope containing fourteen dollars and seventy cents for both children's photos.

I'm a beggar with a red dress on.

I'm further and further back in the photo, until I'm at the edge, blurry and *lost.*

What we want to see requires careful cropping.

85 More Proof Still

I've been up four nights in a row with Marcus, who is running a fever. The thermometer's last pronouncement: 104 degrees. Although alarming, this is not unusual for him when he gets sick.

During the day, I keep Elen busy with projects, since we usually go out every day but can't now. It's our dinner time, and Tobin has just arrived. Elender jumps into Daddy's arms for a smooch. He kisses her, then reaches for me and delivers a long one on my lips.

"I'm exhausted," he says, and sits down with Elen in his lap. "How's your brother, big girl?"

"He's better," she says, then adds, "but still really sick."

I serve the dinner, tuck Elen into her bed, check on Marcus, whose thermometer has dipped to 101. If the course of his illness goes as expected, he's over the worst.

Tobin is in bed when I walk into our bedroom. I tell him the temperature reading, and we go to sleep.

At 4:00 A.M. Marcus wakes screaming. I comfort him, slip the thermometer in his mouth. His temperature is still low, but he'll be up for a while. And I'll need to sponge him off if it rises again. I hug him, pick him up. In my ninety-six-hour haze, Marcus blurs as I stand over him. I manage to carry him into our bed. As always when either child is sick, I let him sleep on my chest. In that position, it feels as if nothing bad can happen to them. But tonight I'm so exhausted, I feel sick myself. I sense Tobin waking up.

"Darling I . . . I've been up for four nights in a row, and I can't do it again," I say.

"Oh, come on, he's not that sick," says Tobin.

I thrust myself from the bed to the closet, grab any bag, and start throwing clothes into it. I don't know if Tobin is watching. Maybe Marcus has already fallen to sleep. Pulling on a coat, I walk out of the house. I don't know where to go—am too ashamed to explain this to my parents. I can barely walk but I do, for hours in the dark, getting nowhere. I end up in front of an older friend's house. She's an artist, a mentor of mine, not totally friend, or family.

She takes me in.

"We moved from our large house to this small bungalow so our kids wouldn't be able to move back in when they fight with their spouses."

"Very practical," I say. "Should I leave?"

"No," she says. "You can spend the night, but I'll call your husband; he'll be worried."

It's about 6:00 A.M. as she dials my home. Tobin doesn't answer. It just rings and rings. She says under her breath, "A man who doesn't care where his wife has gone. This is a bad sign." As if I were unsure about that.

The next day, I ask a neighbor to go over and check on my family.

"They all seem fine," she reports back. "Marcus is up and about. Tobin cleaned everything, did laundry, and baked two pies."

Marvelous. If I didn't have the sneaking suspicion he had done it all to show me how much better he is than I am at domesticity.

Tobin performs well when we have guests, or when I work, or, as he'd put it, when I "don't work." Or when his parents are there to watch.

"Did he ask about me?"

"No," she says. "He was busy washing windows."

We look through wet, iced windows at lighted streets.

Dimming into dawn.

86 Their Faces

Elender's high, round forehead catches the sunlight first as she crouches under the slide's handhold bar to whiz down the metal sheet.

Marcus is behind her. "Mommy, watch me!" His light hair almost matches the silver of the slide as he falls smoothly down. And I catch him. His face has round cheeks that bunch up like peaches when he smiles. Which he is doing now. He is sunny—they both are—and it will be hard to see their faces, a few years from now, changing to accommodate their parents' distress.

Elender runs back around and climbs up again. "Mommy, it's fun! You try."

The urge we all have to share is awake in her.

"Yeah, you too!" says Marcus.

The deal is that we'll share the bad too.

I climb up, feeling the rungs small and bonelike under my sandals. Remembering now how their upturned eyes with a hint of apprehension marveled as their grown-up—me—follows them through the silver rabbit hole.

When I climb back, pulling them through backwards up the slide, their faces are older and too capable of my kind of tears.

87 More Proof (As If I Need It)

When the children are six and seven, Tobin's parents visit from Germany. I prepare *Frühstück* every morning at 6:00 A.M. I'm early because I want to be finished before the children are up. The usual lovely table set for breakfast. Right!

I'm making an übereffort.

Fresh roses are on the table—a must for Europeans—toast is buttered, strawberry jam in a green ceramic bowl, assorted flavors of yogurt in single-serving containers, hard-boiled eggs in egg cups (one soft-boiled for Tobin), ready to crack with little silver spoons. Salami slices fan a white china platter with tomato wedges for color; fresh-squeezed orange juice is in a clear glass pitcher. I don't drink coffee, but I've made a pot. Hot chocolate for me. (Tip: When entertaining Germans, always cook twice as much as usual.)

Tobin's parents come down for breakfast, fresh as linen, fully dressed, looking as if they've been up for hours—reading, writing, listening to Beethoven symphonies, balancing checkbooks. They lack the vulnerability other people show in the early morning.

Tobin's mother, Brunhildegard, sniffs the coffee. *"Der Kaffee riecht gut!"* she says. ("The coffee smells good!")

"Gibt es Tee?" ("Is there any tea?") asks Tobin's father, Karl-Jürgen.

I say I would be glad to make him some.

He can't hear me, even though I'm shrieking in perfect German. He has hearing loss in both ears from the bombing when he was a World War II soldier, although he had never joined the Nazi party. She assists him, talking loudly in his ear. The only problem is that she misamplifies the things *I* say.

"Claire says she can't make tea!" she yells in his ear.

"No, I would be glad to," I protest.

He dismisses me, saying, *"Macht nichts. Forgiss es."* ("It doesn't matter, forget it.")

There is absolutely nothing I can say to right the situation.

Later that night, Tobi tells me his mother got him alone.

"Du kommst nicht weit mit so einer Frau. Du solltest dich scheiden lassen," she said. ("You will not go very far with a wife like her. You should divorce.")

"My parents should be happy to have such a daughter-in-law," Tobin says, kissing me. "You gave them two beautiful grandchildren, learned German fluently, and cook breakfast for them every morning."

Toward the end of my in-laws' visit, I am teaching piano as I do every afternoon. I have three students in a row, and with each student's arrival, Tobin and his parents are speaking louder and louder.

They are in the kitchen, the usual setting for an argument. Water is running. The sound of chopping could mean the Germans are slicing salami or lopping limbs.

Between lessons, I go to the kitchen and ask, "Could you possibly keep it down?" They stare at me, their eyes like searchlights from a guard tower.

Tobin grabs me. At six feet four inches and 185 pounds to my five feet four inches and 108 pounds, he's not a violent man, but he's not unimpressive either. He slams me into the kitchen wall. I am so shocked, I don't know what he is saying. Is it just me being shaken or do I see a satisfied look on his mother's face appearing along with the bruises on my upper arms?

After dinner, I pack clothes for me and the children.

Instead of putting them to bed, we stand in the hall, all three of us, with backpacks.

Elen is so tired, she asks to go to bed. Marcus whines.

It feels worse than giving up, but I'm so tired, I need someone to tuck me in too. I put away our gear and tuck my children in for the night. In a minute all the lights are out.

Mommy can't run away today.

CLUE NUMBER FOUR

You don't want to go home, but you have nowhere else to go.

88 TV as Weapon of Choice (Final Proof)

Shortly after the in-laws visit, Tobin is watching a public television series on World War II, a subject on which he is borderline (as in, run for the border) obsessed. He is watching and watching and watching and watching and I come into the room.

"Tobin? I have to talk to you."

No answer.

"The children's day care has to be paid by tomorrow."

Background rumbling of World War II weapons of destruction.

"We are three months late."

No answer and more artillery sounds from electric box in front of German husband.

"Tobin . . ."

He turns up the box. The children run into the room to see what the noise is. I turn it down as if I am a god silencing thunder.

Tobin grabs the nearest lamp and hurls it to the ground. More loud noise and shattering of glass. The children stare. He picks up the television and stands over me as I cower—not the most dignified of positions, especially in front of the children. Television is about to turn my brain into rot. In an odd and electrified moment, we both know he is going to kill me in front of our two children.

But the killing stays where it is, in the box, before it wars with our special family needs.

89 Suitcase

"I'll leave. I'm sorry."

Silence.

"I'll get some help. I know you can't stand to look at me right now. I'll leave."

More silence.

His suitcase is in the hall, and I'm not stopping him. He picks it up with a hitch that seems almost jaunty.

The silence blocks out even the word *divorce.*

I am calm because right beside the urgent misery is our love in a down/stay position. I give the release command, and it wags its tail and licks my face as Tobin walks out the door. And then it howls all night.

90 Purring

I am sewing—making myself a jangly bracelet out of black elastic and old, broken earrings—when Tobin walks in the front door. Even though I have been crying most of the ten days he's been away, I feel great now. That's because his gaze is on me. The gaze that makes me feel beautiful. My eyes lowered, the needle whirring in and out—a somewhat submissive purring.

I can't look back at him.

"I know I love you," he says, and threads me in his arms.

91 The Trap

The trap is nature at its most persuasive.

A young beautiful man and woman, descended from Adam and Eve and their unquenched desire for nakedness. Take away the ocean between them and bring forth the fruit of their quickening hormones and they shall know the sweetness of children. Close the trapdoor and wait.

92 Flooding

Frantic knocking on our door in the middle of the night. It's our landlord from the second floor of our two-flat. "The basement is flooding on your side."

Back in our bedroom, the alarm clock's phosphorescence shows Tobin's face, snoring slightly. A sleeping prince. "Tobin, we need to wake up." (*I* already am, mister.) "The basement is flooding. We need to get our stuff up off the ground."

He rolls over. "I'm sleeping," he says.

"I can't lift the stuff all by myself."

No response.

Pulling on rubber boots, I trudge down into the knee-deep cesspool. Tobin was going to elevate our boxes and stored furniture, but domestic inertia set in.

By the time I've salvaged the most important boxes, brought the ruined things to the garbage outside, and laid papers and blankets out to dry, I can hear the birds beginning their chirpy announcement of another day.

I slip back into bed with Tobin.

Tobin wakes for work. He's painting a mural on a building in Lincoln Park today.

"There's still water," I say.

"Oh."

"I couldn't lift the heavy stuff."

"Maybe the kids can help you," he says. "I have to go to work."

After breakfast, Elender and Marcus get on their rubber boots and we brave the depths. They think it's pretty fun to swirl around in the dark pool.

Our landlord comes down. "Where's Tobin?" he asks.

"He had to go to work," I say.

"But he lifted the things out of the way last night?" he says.

"No," I say. "He didn't get up."

"Didn't get up?"

"We're trying to do it now," I say.

"I think it's dangerous," he says. "There could be a live current down here. I'll call someone to drain it and then *I'll* help you tomorrow."

A few days after the cleanup, I am nauseated all day long. It takes a few months of stomach agony before I go to the doctor for tests. Apparently I have giardia. "Most people," she says, "get this in Tibet."

The sewage water in our basement, I think. While Tobin was sleeping, parasites seeped in, invaded our house.

93 Mad and Nomad

Moving is sheer madness. But I have a personal goal of owning a house before I am forty, and Tobin and I, despite everything, have pulled it off. We have bought a town house, still in Evanston, but in a little shadier (not from more trees) area. We are leaving the basement that floods to go to our starter house. A new start for us all.

94 Ring of Cows

"Princess, princess, this is terrible. Everybody should stay together in peace. Why all the trouble? I don't understand this culture. Nobody is happy. My wife and I were married in a ring of cows. Now that was a sacred ceremony."

I'm eating lunch with my Indian friends, Dev Sharma, a retired businessman from New Delhi, and his wife, Kalpana. He and his wife cannot fathom all the divorcing that goes on in the United States.

They and the light-filled rooms in their house are sanctuary from the flood and Tobi's inert form in bed. I haven't said the word *divorce*, because it is a noxious gas I don't want to breathe, but my dilated pupils tell them things are not right.

"Princess, princess," Dev says, "you look so sad." Calling me *princess* squared is, in itself, enough to make me weep. Or follow him like a guru.

I could lie and tell him I'm exhausted and sad because of our recent move. But I can't lie to a man like him. And anyway, he and his wife seem clairvoyant.

Close to eighty years old, Dev has only the faintest traces of gray around his temples, smooth café au lait skin, and clear, cow-brown eyes that make him look fifty. Instead of a hidden painting, I attribute his eternal youth to the meditation he practices three hours every day, from 5 A.M. to 8 A.M.

"Did you ever stop?" I ask.

"No, not even after triple bypass surgery. I awoke at dawn. Throughout my life, meditation has been a nonstop flight."

95 Portent

Kalpana was once one of the most successful film actresses in India. She is aging, although much younger than he. Her eager face and happy eyes hint at her earlier screen appeal.

"Can you show me a picture of you in one of your films?" I ask.

"Oh, that was such a long, long time ago."

But she brings in a photo of herself at nineteen. With her hair down to her waist, *she* was as beautiful as any fantasy princess. Now her beauty has shifted inward, making her angelic in everyday life.

She nods gently to her husband. "Now please, you will read princess's palm."

Surrounded by enlarged photos on the wall of himself with Mother Teresa, with Kalpana and Lady Diana, with Gandhi, Dev-ji (the honorific form of Dev) reads my palm. His otherwise imperturbable face shows alarm, as if he sees my death written on the skin. Tracing the connections and conflicts of the life line with the head and the heart line, he says, "I am sooooo sorry for you, princess, princess. This is terrible, terrible. You will always struggle, but everyone will help you. They can't stop themselves, because you have divine intervention written all over. When they help you, they are helping God."

96 Indian Wife

"Don't be frightened," Kalpana says, taking me aside in the kitchen, where golub jamun dessert is being prepared. I'm quaking, that's all.

"He's a man," she says confidentially, and a little apologetically, as if her dog had lifted its leg on my float in the parade. A man? Where? Is he single?

Of course she knows that my utter respect and love for her husband makes his reading even more disturbing.

"What I would say from your palm is that you have a challenging life," she says, looking at me with the tender Zen of a famously beautiful woman.

Hey, I am life-challenged!

"Don't worry," she says. "Your life is exciting. Much happening. Not the usual for woman. Be happy. Stay with the right boy. Too bad you are already married. Mr. Sharma and I could have helped you. You would have made such a good Indian wife."

Oddly enough, I'm thinking of hot water waking me and the songs I made up in the shower while Tobin listened under the sheets.

"My Indian wife is singing," he always said when I returned to him in my robe, still steaming.

But now Kalpana is still holding my hand, and I fear the palm's prophecy, the message cut like faults in my flesh.

PART THREE

A maiden at twenty may be unmade by forty.

TEN HOUSES OR ONCE WILD IN GERMANY

She is the murderer, the celebrant, the convict-priest giving blessing. Convinced of his soul, she scratches his calm, holding his hand like a crab on parole.

Wait. She is weeping; they are running. Mollusk-colored streets are sliding before them. They have only ten houses to go; he is holding a gun, hers has fallen, making a sound babies make with their spoon on an empty plate.

He is the murderer, the celebrant, the executioner in sudden tears. Even our chairs knelt before her innocence. He turns their furniture upside down; no way to sleep, to rock, to eat. She is almost put to death by fatigue, and still they run.

Look. Tiers of terror are rising like gun-turrets. The tenth house is a familiar place with frosted windows. But there are no doors.

97 **Boot**

> We're out of money, it's time to think.
>
> —Lord Rutherford

Our marriage and family have made Tobi and me into strict budgeters with no margin for error. Yet errors occur. I've told Tobi about the parking tickets.

"We don't have money for police stuff; it's not in the budget," he says.

And a teensy Heil Hitler to you!

"Last night," he says, "I dreamed I was looking at our '68 Mercedes. I was thinking it was a symbol for our marriage, beautiful to look at, but falling apart."

And they tell ya dreams don't come true.

It's Tobi's turn to pick up our kids. But I'm in the habit of double-checking because he's often late or doesn't show up. I jump in the car. It's been booted. I run a mile in the snow, make it very late, but spot the kids looking for their dad. Another mom drives us home. Tobin arrives in time for dinner. I ask him, "Where were you?" He grabs his drink and walks into another room. "I'm here now," his words trail. Instructions: Place hands on throat and squeeze.

"The car's been booted," I say, following him.

Without a word, he turns on the TV to watch another public television history special. After all, he doesn't need the car; he takes the train to work.

The next day, instead of spending money on food, I take all my money, borrow more from a neighbor, sell some clothes at a thrift shop, and walk to the village hall to pay for the boot and the tickets.

Tobin doesn't ask how we got the car back, but he does say, "I have possible collectors coming over. Why isn't there any food?"

98 Loot

As the cliché predicts, the real trouble begins when we enter our seventh year of marriage.

"I can't live like this any longer," I say.

"Like what?" Tobin asks.

"You'd treat a dog better than you treat me," I say.

He looks at me, snarling, as if I have stolen his bone.

There doesn't seem to be one moment I could flag and wave, signaling *Yes, this is when it all started.* There were no semaphores warning of danger.

But I'm nauseated by the spoiled way he grabs me when other men admire me, yet ignores me when we're alone, withholding affection for weeks, yet beaming at me in front of his clients.

"Oh, here's my wife," he says to a famous artist standing near his work. I may not be arm candy, but I can be devoured.

On our eighth anniversary, he hands me a large envelope in which I am astonished to find tickets to New Orleans. Before I can properly thank him, he races out with the kids to buy me chocolates and a dozen roses.

Leaving the children with my sister Catherine, we head off to the French Quarter for five days. I'm apprehensive for many reasons, not the least of which has to do with my first love, Clive. New Orleans was where he told me we should stop seeing each other.

The hotel is steamy, sweet, and a touch seedy. The mustard-colored bedspread—none-too-pristine by German standards—is a tasseled affair. Dusty voodoo dolls in a glass cabinet tell me we are not in Kansas or Chicago anymore.

After dressing for a few hours, we walk the streets and sit in cafés eating beignets.

"Wow, that couple over there is fat!" Tobin starts. "As if they really need those beignets. Watch them get up. . . . You're so beautiful. I want to grow old with you."

He touches my hair, and I want to reciprocate, but I can't.

"Just looking at you in those shorts," he continues, "makes me hard. You're my baby."

And you, Tobi, are Mr. Suave.

He drinks a beer. I have hot chocolate and half a beignet. I could easily eat twelve.

"Sweetheart, that girl over there chews her gum like a lizard snapping up a fly. Look. No, wait. That must be her dad. Typical, beer-drinking no-culture American slob . . ."

I sip at my hot chocolate. "Tobin," I say, "I can't take it if you're going to criticize everyone this whole trip."

Even though I'm a total Eurohag, I'm beginning to think, after all, these are my people.

The next day, paging through the tour guide, I mention, "I'd really like to do the boat trip and the zoo tour."

He says, and I quote, "I planned and paid for this trip. I have other ideas."

Why did you bring your wife along if it wasn't to give her orgasms? I fail to ask.

The sweat slides down my back like baby lizards. I lie down, and my heart growls for the days until we go back to Evanston. I feel emptied, unnourished by everything he wants to do.

The day of departure, Tobin wants to take two buses and a train to get to the airport.

"Tobin," I accuse, "we may be saving money, but we won't make it on time. Even the hotel manager says we have to take a cab."

But Tobi has an unarticulated motto: *Why do it the easy way when I can make everyone miserable doing it my way?*

"Give me some money," I say, "I want to take a cab."

"I'll go to a cash machine and get you some," he says.

Like families that no longer eat meals together, we have separate bank accounts.

"There's not much left in mine," I say.

His face shows a hint of reproach, but he doesn't dare say anything and walks off to the cash station.

A few minutes later, he returns. "I got some money, but I don't want us to take a cab."

"Give it to me," I say, gritting my teeth so I won't bite him.

"Be reasonable," he says.

Be rhyming.

After taking two buses and a train, we miss the plane. I hope everyone is staring at us as I melt down in the airport.

"I'll call your sister and tell her we're delayed," Tobin says, advancing to hug me.

I recoil from him, screaming. "You do this all the time—inconveniencing others—friends, babysitters, my family. I'm sick of apologizing for you. Catherine can't take care of our kids any longer. As a matter of fact, we can't be late. She was nice enough to do what she did. She has a life. We have to get home now!"

I'm coming across clearer than the loudspeaker announcements, and, to his credit, he says, "I'm truly sorry."

The minute we touch down, I use the one-two punch; I call a therapist and a mediator. "I have arranged an important meeting for us," I tell him.

Driving there, he doesn't ask questions; he doesn't resist. The emptiness has filled him too.

99 Dr. Jekyll & Mr. Hyde

Probably everyone has these two sides to them. I'd just have to live with them to find it out.

100 Lute

The most unexpected men can make you feel like a princess. In Oxford at age nineteen, I met a young man who—although ticcing nervously from just being near me, an actual female, after his years of public boarding school—played the lute for me.

His name was Robert and he peeled mangoes after finishing a fourteenth-century song about love and death and mangoes. As I recall, the word *mango* described female private parts.

At the close of Tobin's and my first therapy session, our therapist told him to "treat your wife like a princess for the week."

101 Straw That Broke

My Oxford boyfriend Rick and I were having an argument. The detatils are gone, but I remember the shoes and what Rick said a few years later.

I believe every couple replays their core argument over and over—the one assigned to them when they meet.

That night with Rick, we were on variation number 205. Rick, like most men do in these situations, retreated into silence. I erupted and threw shoes into the corner of the room. Something broke and I felt it inside me too.

A few years later, after we had split up for good, he said, "I know now that if I had comforted you that night and you hadn't thrown the shoes, we'd have stayed together."

Love is in the details.

102 Snow

Snowflakes are wet details.

Rain was our element.

Maybe the Midwest snow did us in.

103 First Last Straw

When marriage with its flammable emotions catches fire, there's no stopping it. Past, present, and future topple, meld, and smolder, becoming one and the same.

The first last straw is still bendable, slightly brittle, but the tip sparks and then brightens for the burn. Only a blizzard can put it out.

But not in our case.

Late at night, during the week I'm to be treated like a princess, I go outside to clear the walkway to our town house. The snow is wet and heavy and my back is throbbing as I lift the shovel.

Tobin's large form appears in the near white-out, walking toward me.

"I'm so glad you're here," I say, thinking he will help me, princess week or no princess week. But he goes inside and doesn't come out again.

I think of his long, strong artist hands in comparison with my tiny, delicate piano hands. Before tonight, I would have needed his hands, and he would have known it.

I continue shoveling—it will take a long time. I think I can hear Tobin's boots hitting our bedroom floor as he kicks them off to get ready to go to sleep.

I inhale the clean scent of midnight snow and it keeps me awake and numb at the same time.

104 Butterflies

Just hanging on to memories, my fingers gripping the pier: dark waves scallop the stone edge.

I'm recalling a summer in Chicago at the beach. We're all on the pier. Marc and Elen screech and run to us, chased by spray. Tobin hugs them, pulls my ponytail to bring me closer.

The wind is picking up, getting colder. Out of nowhere, thousands of butterflies surround us, circling our heads and the churning sky.

"Invasion of the winged ones," I say.

"It's a school of butterflies," says Marcus.

"More like a city," shouts Elen.

Sensing the coming storm, the many-colored ones gather under shoreline treetops, where they'll drop, en masse, to protect their fragile wings.

"How beautiful," says Tobin, watching Elen and Marc running madly about trying to catch them.

Just then a huge wave covers our children from head to toe. Screaming and laughing, they slip and slide toward us.

"I've got a blanket in the car," Tobin says, and runs down the pier toward the beach and the parking lot.

I walk slowly with them dripping and chattering from the cold. By the time we are under the trees, Tobin has returned and he wraps them together in a wool blanket.

"Like Robinson Crusoe," he says with a heavy accent that makes it sound even more exotic.

Looking out onto the lake, we seem to need each other still, the children cocooned between us and the last butterflies swarming, seeking refuge.

105 Lava

I imagine Tobin, the hero in our little film about Hell, saying, "Let's get outta here!"

Only, it is I who have been mortally wounded, by him. I'm such a pal, though, that I want him to live.

"Go, go on without me," I whisper.

Not to appear caddish, he mumbles some protest, all the while turning his back on me, ready to run.

"Hurry, sweetheart, before it's too late," I muster without air, as every predicted catastrophe descends upon us.

Writhing nobly on the scorched earth, I am grateful that at least one of us will survive.

If there were cheerleaders in Hell, they would be rooting for Tobin, juggling hot coals and forming letters with their smoldering bodies, screaming, "Gimmee an *f*, gimmee an *r*, gimmee an *e-e-d-o-m*!"

Like a unicorn trapped in a ring of fire, Tobin bolts.

I am alone, waiting for lava to liquefy my love. The pain of this ending is more degreed than any burn.

Explosions, hurricanes, floodwaters, volcanic eruptions, drought, pestilence.

Cut to a woman—me—who really should know better, crawling across the embers.

106 What We Have Here Is a Failure

Sitting with my husband in marriage—or in our case divorce—counseling, I had noticed our therapist's expensive neutral stockings, bought presumably with the help of our seventy-five dollars a session.

She had listened with professional respect to our stereo screaming, and had managed the phrase, "Have you two ever considered divorce?"

No, what does that mean? Di—?

Having wept during our last session, I tried to wring out my worst fear.

"I'm beginning to get a strong feeling that I'll be left alone to fend for myself and two small children."

Call me clairvoyant! (Or just call me Claire.)

"Don't be ridiculous; that would never happen," my husband and therapist said, laughing in unison.

107 Richter Scale in A Minor

Tobin, looking chagrined, like an errand boy who has delivered a package to the wrong address, sits me down at our dining room table and pronounces each word distinctly. "I think we should end our marriage."

Clearly, after two sessions, the marriage counseling's not working.

I'm not surprised, yet the shock is seismic.

I hold the edge of the table to steady the sliding in my chest, unable to measure the tremors inside me.

"Is she German?" I barely ask.

"No, there's no one else; that's why I'm so sure," he says.

Worse.

Perhaps coincidental, but this happens to be the same day an aquaintance of mine has commissioned Tobin's artwork, which will more than double his income, confirming my dad's long-held belief, voiced only to my mom, that "Tobin'll leave her and the kids as soon as he gets an extra dime."

I want to give up. But I can't.

108 Ships or Love II

Our bodies, fragile vessels,
break
spill
not into each other
but into dark waters.

109 Stillstand

I'm stealthy in the dulled afternoon. Sitting on the bare steps, I'm neither up nor down. If Tobin comes back late and I'm still here, he might trip over me. The children are in the basement playing. Now, there's a concept: *Honey, I want to play divorce.*

I haven't cried yet. Nothing has really happened.

I remember what my lawyer dad told me to do. I creak down the stairs, walk to my husband's desk in the den, open the drawers, rifle through files.

I'm doing well so far. It's been about two hours and fifteen minutes since my husband announced the death of us. We both could have been gurgling underwater. What was it he said, exactly? How did he phrase it? And what did I reply? Is there a reply to such a statement? I might clear my ears, remember everything later.

I sense the spy in my heart—her cool calm—the traitor who was frozen until now. I empty the contents of each file into a box. His records—bank accounts, credit card statements, insurance, Social Security number, children's German trust fund information—all this I will photocopy and return to their places. But the files with letters and drawings from me will simply disappear.

In the beginning, there was *no thing,* then a *pause,* followed by *something,* then a *thing,* then *every thing,* and finally *everything.* It is the pause that has intrigued me the most. In that pause is everything and nothing at the same time—the bridge that makes anything possible, the here to there. (I ask myself how did we get from our wedding to here?)

The moment I enter Tobin's desk, I am the pause before the striking of a match, the potential for fire but not the fire itself. I am the pause between lightning and thunder, the eye of the paper whirlwind, the barometric rising of my own front.

I am the storm he brewed to weather.

110 Chess

It is unclear to me if I am still his wife.

In my kitchen now. Alone, like a chess piece, I sit on the tiled floor. The black-and-white squares stretch into oblong, then change into puddles of dark and light. I slap my hands on the cold floor, and my breath spatters like dirty words.

Even pain tells me nothing now.

Standing one space away from checkmate, if I move the right way, I'll win; if not, he'll win. Either way, the game is over. And when it's over, there are no flags waving. No one is cheering.

The only mitigating factor is the children. No matter which side you're on, they are always on the side of love, their own infinite and unforgiving kind.

111 Bell Tolls

Did I hear it or did I think I heard it? Brushing my teeth early in the morning—the up-and-down movement on my teeth unutterably sad and pointless (Clean teeth, fresh breath? Why and for whom?)—the doorbell rings. I throw on a bathrobe (this could still be a movie) and run, like an eager mutt, to the door. Open it. No one. Oh. But there's a package on the ground. To Claire McCloud-Kleinherz. That's me, so I can open it. As if I'm still that mutt, I tear into the brown cardboard while dragging it like a carcass into the front hallway.

Inside is a large beautifully wrapped package—vellum paper with stencils of birds and trees and clouds in the style of Tobin's work—and I wonder if I should open it. Of course. It's close to my birthday, Moon When We All Get Greedy. Careful to preserve the paper, I unstick the tape and open the box. A supple green wool coat. With a hood, lined with patterned gold-green silk, like the French Lieutenant's Wife wears to tragically romantic effect as she looks out over the sea. The tag on the sleeve says what I already know. It's by one of our designer friends. Tobin must have ordered it recently—while he was deciding whether to end our marriage—when I had picked it out at a trunk show.

In one of the oversized pockets is a rare Hungarian book of easy duets by Leo Weiner in a German edition. Something I've been looking for since my childhood. How sweet of Tobin, I think. But then I remember. He is sleeping on the couch. And our time is dust collecting under him.

CLUE NUMBER FIVE

Birthdays make you wish you hadn't been born.

112 Just Living Together

In my twenties, many of my female friends lived with men, left them, or more frequently were left by them, and then lived with another. These pretty girls looked ravaged. By the time they lived with a third guy, they were desperate to get married. And usually, the third guy was desperately content to just live together.

I didn't want to get married and I certainly didn't want to live with anyone. I once drew a cartoon of a car with a man and a woman inside in front of a shabby apartment. The car is dragging tin cans and on the windshield written in shaving cream is JUST LIVING TOGETHER.

Living together, for me, seemed to have all the disadvantages of marriage and none of the advantages. At least for a woman.

All my boyfriends asked me to use their closet or keep a drawer in their room. "No, thanks," I'd say. "I leave no trace." I still wanted to be like an Indian who walks in the forest without cracking a twig.

113 No Ever After

Tobin puts a cot in his small office across the hall and moves out of our bedroom. The wallpaper there is light blue with clouds on it adding to the impression that he has been whisked away. At night, the light from his lamp shines under the door for six new moons. Then he evaporates.

On the night he vacates our bed, I draw a mural on the wall behind our headboard. Under the date is an elaborate castle with a princely man on one side and a princess on the other. I could have written: *Did not live happily ever after.* Instead I write: *Der arrogante Prinz blieb den letzten Abend zusammen mit seiner Prinzessin.* (The arrogant prince spent the last evening with his princess.)

Through my tears, it doesn't occur to me that he, just across the hall, might be crying too.

Darkness becomes its own wall between us.

He doesn't say a thing about it, but I leave a present on his cot every day. A blue stone, a feather, three almonds in a small bowl, a book by Alice Miller, a copy of a drawing I made that I know he loves.

His best friend, Klaus, calls from Germany. "You are really confusing Tobin, giving him gifts. He doesn't know what it means."

Neither do I, I think, reorganizing atoms with my slam of the phone.

I watch him sleeping, one night, and pray by his side as if he were dying.

114 — Specter

Returning every night at 4:00 A.M., Tobin switches on Mahler rock music loud. The children never wake up. As I squint down from the stairs to ask him to lower the volume, he looks up as if he no longer recognizes me.

I am the ghost I will become, and say nothing more.

115 — First Abandonment

Maybe I'm six years old. Our family is driving across the country in a station wagon to California. We stop off to see the Grand Canyon. Instead of staying in a motel, my dad parks near the edge of the canyon. We five kids and my parents sleep on foam mats in the flat, seats-folded-down back of the car.

At dawn, I wake to find no one. I open the car door and my bare feet hit the grassy stones, trying to feel a pathway. The air is cold and the fog makes me panic. Instead of getting anywhere, I find myself at the railing of the Grand Canyon, looking down into the shrouded abyss. Without wanting to, I start screaming. Suddenly my mother appears. "I'm so sorry, honey. We didn't want to wake you," she says, picking me up and taking me to the restaurant where my dad and brothers and sisters are ordering breakfast. I'm still crying when I ask for French toast.

"Nothing happened," says my dad. "You're fine."

But it did happen. I felt it.

The event itself and the metaphor are surprisingly fitting. Me, alone, in front of vast stillness, emptiness.

Unintentional harm hurts as much as intentional.

116 Remembering

Memory is in the body.

Tobin, I feel the Grand Canyon, its giant cliffs and rocks, its miles and miles of desert air.

My body is lost.

117 How to Poison

I am sure there are shelves and shelves of books that deal with how to inform children, gently, and with the least amount of harm, of their parents' impending split. Maybe Tobin or I should have read one. If asked, I would write a chapter:

Snake bites might be physically worse, but there is no antidote to the emotional sting your children will feel when you tell them. The effect may be protracted, possibly as long as they have a pulse. There is no minimizing it, so forget that and start practicing wringing your hands in front of a Greek chorus that watches your every move, chanting how bad you are doing, and never gives you any sympathy.

I guess I wisely underestimated just how wrenching even the thought of telling my children would be.

"Don't worry, your mom and I are getting divorced," Tobin yells at the door as I slam out of the house after one of our most venomous fights.

This is how our children, Elender Marie, age eight, and Marcus Sean, age seven, frozen on the landing of the stairs, are told.

I'm sobbing in the Mercedes, not knowing it will be my last trip in this vehicle; Tobi will repossess it the next day by parking it in an unknown neighborhood for the duration of his silent six-month stay across the hall.

When I return, the children tell me, "We know what's going on, Mom." Even I hadn't been clear on that until now.

Elender calls me into her room, where they are both huddled, still dressed, under her cover. "Daddy told us not to worry, that you are getting divorced!"

Marcus plugs his ears. "I don't want to talk about it!"

I wish I could cover my little dumplings with my skin, take away the smarting wound.

All I could think, rightly or wrongly, is that it was the usual Tobin brand of immaturity and selfish unconcern for others.

"Act like a father!" I yell internally to no one. Maybe an archetypal Father is listening.

It's irrelevant now, but I have to ask myself if I would have handled it any better.

This is true: An acquaintance told me, "I was in the Korean War and I went through what I thought was the worst, but it was nothing in comparison to telling my son that I was leaving."

Try as hard as you can to fool yourself, but you are not in divorce mode until the children know. And, once they do, everything that follows will leave bite marks.

118 Altar

The Bösendorfer grand piano houses it, my divorce altar. The pile is growing, and I arrange it daily. Love letters from Tobin, ticket stubs from our trips together. I even find the plastic couple from our wedding cake and put it on a jewelry box he gave me. It seems too apt, but the tiny bride and groom are broken apart, the glue from their stand having hardened and flaked away. Flowers brighten the pyre and candles burn.

Elender and Marcus and, most important, Tobin walk by it every day.

"Can't you take it down, Mom?" Marc asks.

I didn't know he noticed. That's how self-absorbed I've become. Bad Mom.

"Cool altar, Mom, but I think everyone knows already," says Elen.

But she doesn't know that I need the altar for myself. When she and Marcus and Tobin aren't home, I stand at the curve of the piano, survey the pile of artifacts and once-treasures, touch them softly as if they would crumble.

119 Crucible

After four weeks of rock-loud Mahler, I have mourning sickness.

Before leaving for his studio, Tobin hands me a letter.

The words that shred me are: *I am no longer in love with you.*

The world stops.

120 Life Investment

I still want more children, I tell myself.

A little girl named Ravel, with molasses hair who writes musical notation with a quill before she can speak. And a crinkly haired black boy called Tostan (never mind that my husband is German) who cooks the best pancakes the world has ever tasted.

Tobin hangs around the house, no longer speaking to me, even when the children are around. They say he tells them, "I will stay in the house, because it is one hundred percent mine, and you and your mommy will have to move out."

They're so small, they must have heard him wrong.

Little stricken faces turn to me, where I hide in bed biting the sheet.

"Is it true, Mommy?" Elender asks. "Is it true? Where will we go?"

Marcus reports in tears, "Daddy says it's his house. Is it?"

An explosion inside me goes nowhere. I want to send out comfort, but right now the children seem like an investment gone bad.

121 Grub

Only hunger can bring me back to the present.

It's been over a week since food has looked normal. Beets look like battered tomatoes, broccoli trees are green dendrites in the brain, beans look like the earthworm Elender will show me on D-day. Over a week since I cannot fix a meal for my children. Well over a week.

122 Padding

This morning, I go downstairs.

Notice the carpeting on the staircase is gone.

Tobin must have been up all night ripping it out.

The heels of my shoes echo as they grind each step.

All the padding on my life is disappearing.

Even my weight is dwindling.

And I need grounding.

It's early, the children are making Sunday breakfast with their dad, who turns his back to me when I sit down at the table.

There are not enough place settings.

Inadvertent?

Marcus looks to Tobin, then to me. "Daddy says you can't eat the food here," he says. "Because he buys it!" He sounds almost proud now that the horrible secret is out.

Elender spits out her food in a long, wailing sob.

Marcus continues. "Why are you so mean to Daddy, Mom? Mommy?"

I am spiked out of the kitchen.

I want them to eat the nice breakfast.

123 Gangrene

It's almost impossible to understand or believe what is happening. Most of the time, I feel like screaming and crying and begging Tobin, myself, us, to make it work again. Yet I know, yes I know, that our marriage is dying—as if the doctor had found gangrene—and there is nothing I can do to save it.

124 Raccoon Truce

Water lapping awakens us. Tobin and I end up at the same window, peering out into Indian summer air. Lit by a streetlight, a family of raccoons plays in our plastic pool. The mother dips her hand, while the father pushes in the side, letting water spill over. Two raccoon children, nudged one by one, drink and splash in the rivulets.

No words, no touch, we return to our solitary beds.

125 Lights Out

There is no light here. No songs here. I will never sing again:

The song of a complete family.
The song of him, that singular him.

126 Warning Through the Ages

Even though the children are whatever age they are, I revisit them younger and see who they were. Looking into their cribs, I say to them now something I would never have said then, "No matter what we do, we love you."

When they are older, they should yell at us, "What kind of love is that!"

127 I'm Injured Only Because I Never Did This Before

The snow crunches under the tires as I pedal ahead of my children, crossing an alley. We are biking to their piano lessons. Why? Because instead of parking the Mercedes in the usual spot behind our house, Tobin has left it elsewhere. I haven't been able to find it for a few days, even with the help of the kids.

The cabdriver, not expecting to see any bicycles in the middle of a snowstorm, is coming at me from the side.

I am in a daze, knowing Tobin is still living silently across the hall from my bedroom.

The headlights enliven me. Throwing myself over the handlebars like an acrobat, I land in the street and scream at my children to stay back. My bicycle, in the spot where I would have been, is completely crushed.

A dark stunned man gets out of his car.

"I saw you. I was going to stop," he says, shaking from head to toe.

I had felt dead, but my body thrust me back into life.

"Can I call someone for you? Your husband?"

If we were on speaking terms.

"Can you walk? Do you need a doctor?"

I tell the cabbie to call my friend Quentin, who lives close by.

Quentin literally scoops up me, the kids, and our bicycles into his Volvo and whisks us home.

That day, I call my first divorce lawyer.

128 Darkness and More Future

The day after my bike accident, I file for divorce. I let my first lawyer—there will be six—draw up the papers and have them delivered to my husband at his studio. I am emboldened by the pain of my injuries, even though I can barely walk. Tobin never asks why I'm hobbling around on crutches. He doesn't seem to notice my wounds now.

I cry as if it were my profession. I have cry-lines to prove it: They have never gone away. A woman at a party told me she cried so much when her daughter died that she almost went blind. She had two eye operations to save her vision. I should be careful.

Children.

Children like to make themselves the center of any universe. My children's father and I will have our forum in front of divorce lawyers, and they need theirs.

Whenever I return, numbed by the avalanche that has become our divorce, Elen and Marc want to talk to me. They are nervous and curious at the same time.

When they look this miserable, I want to curl inside a massive snowball and succumb to hypothermia. But I need to listen to them.

Marcus, age seven, asks what could, in another situation, be a rhetorical question. "Mom, can you die of sadness?"

129 Kitchen Aid

No matter how hard I try, I can't make meals, can't even go into the kitchen. It's the black hole. No longer a hearth.

Food, like life, seems rotten, and no amount of soaking, steeping, sautéing, broiling, baking, or cooking can change that.

As soon as Tobin leaves, the fire goes out. No one warned me about this. Not any of my self-inflicted divorced female friends. I wondered about them dropping weight. I thought it was stress that made them buff.

But why were their children heavier? Now I know. If you can't bring yourself to put together meals, guilt forces you to stuff your children with junk food. Of course, this is more expensive in the long run, while you starve to save the budget.

There are Meals on Wheels for the sick and elderly; I need one for a nuclear family, minus the nucleus.

I have grown accustomed to being in the kitchen with Tobin. He is a decent cook, if you love to dine on swine. A too-good cleaner-upper, he ziplocked and twist-tied carrot shavings or one bite of lasagna; rubber-banded and bagged our leftover rations.

After our meals as a family, he would graze through the cabinets and the refrigerator, chewing the last vestiges of supplies we had on stock for the next meal.

After a while, even the grazing didn't bother me.

Our first fight: In Heidelberg, I am throwing away a third-empty yogurt container. Although he is environmentally correct, and I have been raised to be a wasteful American, his utter contempt makes me proud of my heritage.

He retrieves the yogurt from the garbage. "You're not going to throw this away?" he semi-asks.

"No," I say. "I just store things in the trash to eat later."

No laugh.

"It's still full with yogurt," he says.

"What about this," I say, opening the refrigerator and taking out a jar of marmalade.

"And this." I scoop a violet glob of it and flick it onto the floor.

This is too much for the German sensibility, raised by parents of World War II, to fathom. Tobin shudders and slams out of the house.

And actually, years later, after having become more European myself, I will shudder in my children's American parochial lunchroom as I help scrape the mostly uneaten hot lunches into garbage bags for the Dumpster.

Now I stand in darkened hallways, unable to brave the kitchen alone.

I imagine accepting my own personal savior into my kitchen: an aproned matron filling the counters with fresh-baked pies and casseroles.

Marcus and Elender are used to home cooking. Their dad makes his own sourdough bread and pizza dough (X-rated at that!). I juiced carrots, celery, and beets for them after school; concocted their favorite *green drink* out of pineapple and coconut juice, oranges, apples, and kale with a dash of yogurt, homemade by slowly souring organic whole milk above the pilot light. So it comes as a surprise to my children that I now pick them up from school and, after they're buckled in for safety (does not protect against divorce), hand them each a Butterfinger and a Snickers. They look hesitant and then snatch the candy bars before I change my mind.

We used to sit around the table and eat and talk in the candlelight. Now at home, in our separate rooms, we are as solitary as three people encased in hermetically sealed bubbles, like the little boy I read about when I was growing up, who had to live like that because of a disease.

Starving, Elen and Marc grab bread and butter from the fridge. To assuage my own guilt and convince myself I can stay where I am, I yell from my bed, "You can nourish a child on bread and butter until college, with no ill effects."

130 Moving Target or We Can't Go Home

I can't stay home tonight; it's the first night Tobin is gone for good. My heart keeps overbeating toward the family room, where Tobin used to draw at his easel.

"We'll pretend we're Indians, and spend as much time outdoors as we possibly can, starting now," I say, after they finish their nutrition-pyramidly perfect bread-and-butter dinner. Elen's and Marc's eyes are huge.

"What about homework?" asks Elen.

"Do you have a lot?" I ask.

"Sort of," she says.

"I've got tons," Marcus pipes in.

"God will excuse you this once," I reassure them.

It helps to bring in God as an endorser, because they attend Catholic school—the only affordable school that educates gifted children. Tobin says he won't pay for it anymore. But I'll get them a scholarship and pay the rest myself. Going through our divorce *and* changing schools at the same time would be too much.

Elender, Marcus, and I leave the house and walk down the sidewalk. Mercifully, twilight makes it difficult to decipher the cryptic messages written earlier today in white.

It's not too terribly long before spring will be here, but for us, the only thing fresh is our life without a husband and father. On a warm evening like tonight, we don't need much gear. I have borrowed a car. Tobin still has the Mercedes. We drive close to the beach near Northwestern University and get out. It's almost dark. I teach them to run from tree to tree like Indians. We are moving targets that never get hit, immune to the slings and arrows. We're on the expanse of lawn in front of the Regenstein Library. Elen cartwheels perfectly while Marc tries. He gives up and complains to me. "How come I can't do it and she can?"

"Because you're a lefty. Let's take some of these home," I say, indicating the colored rocks landscaping the bushes.

"That's stealing, Mom," he says.

"You've got a point, but we need them to brighten our place."

"I'm not touching 'em," he says.

"Good for you, son," I say, as if *I* had taught him a life lesson.

"I'm hungry," says Marcus.

"Okay, how 'bout we go to Blind and Deaf for dinner and Hormone Café afterwards for some hot chocolate?"

"I want to!" says Elen, always the good girl, cartwheeling up to us. But I know she, like Marcus, just wants to go home.

As we stand there, the sky is suddenly darker than the trees.

131 Red Mustang

Elender, Marcus, and I walk into our favorite vegetarian restaurant in Evanston, Blind and Deaf. We'll be eating here frequently during the next couple of months, trying to order only the cheapest things on the menu: corn bread, twig tea, and garden salads with miso onion dressing.

Tonight Marc and Elen are sitting at the high counter, sharing a peanut butter/tofu milk shake while I order a tea. A very nice-looking man, slightly older than I, is standing behind me in line. "Is the food here any good?" he asks.

"Yeah," I say. "We've been coming for years."

"And you're still alive," he says with a smile.

As we wait for our orders, he abruptly says, "I bought a Mustang today."

"My husband moved out today," I reply.

"Trade ya," he says.

I laugh.

I know my son will be overjoyed to see the stranger's new car, so I call them over. "Kids, this man just bought a new car."

Marcus perks up and runs over.

"Do you want to go for a ride?" the man asks. "It's the red one parked right out in front."

"Sure," I say, seeing a closed convertible.

Elen looks up from her milk shake.

Remembering I'm the mom and should protect against rather than take risks, I say, "Can we put the top down?" That way he can't abduct us; we can jump out at any moment.

"Kinda chilly," he says.

"Just for fun," I say, as if fun and not escape is on my mind.

After we finish eating, we go outside with the Mustang Man—that's what we call him, since we never see him again after tonight. Maybe he moves away, or maybe it has to do with my yuck reaction to any middle-aged man who buys a red convertible. The Mustang Man and Marcus have an easy rapport. It turns out he and Marcus have the same March birthday.

The Mustang Man puts the top down and we all climb in.

"Don't ever try this without me," I whisper to Elender. She rolls her eyes.

Even though I'm paying lip service to safety issues, the only thing I fear is going home.

132 Benz

"When are we gonna get our car back?" asks Marcus as we walk back from school in the snow.

"I don't know. It's good to walk," I say.

"Yeah, but when will we get it back?" he asks again. "Daddy doesn't even need a car."

I know.

Tobin can walk to his studio, and I have two car pools, but he took the car. And the kitchen phone off the wall.

I liked the old Mercedes-Benz, but I'd take a rickshaw now.

133 Wood

In lieu of morphine, there's chocolate. I devour it, try not to. Getting out of bed is the equivalent of miles of brisk walking. I feel paralyzed. After a few weeks of no car, my nice dad saves me. But even the new-used Honda Prelude he bought and put, newly washed, in front of my house doesn't rouse me. And I feel slightly guilty because he is getting old and has disbursed most of his savings already on my siblings and me.

I remember the story my children's German au pair Petra told me. She had stayed with us after we moved from Germany to the United States so I could accept a scholarship to study acting at Second City.

"My grandmother who lived in Ravensburg woke one morning completely stiff. She was unable to move any part of her body except her neck—and that could only turn to the left. She was as rigid as a wooden puppet, and when they put her into a wheelchair, they inadvertently broke both of her legs, trying to bend them into a sitting position."

The leg part was hard to believe, but Petra swore it was true.

Her grandmother lived for thirty years in bed. She was the best friend Petra ever had. She could listen. That's all we need. Almost. But who wants to listen to someone whose marriage is disintegrating? Listen to them moan about their already precarious financial situation becoming disastrous during a divorce?

I need to see the humor.

I have no money, no car, no toilet paper.

I slog through snow like Julie Christie in *Doctor Zhivago,* but instead of getting to Omar, I reach a nearby restaurant and steal the extra roll of toilet paper.

134 Gott

> Nur ein Gott kann uns retten.
>
> —Heidegger

Only a god can save us.

135 Grief Backpack

I am unable
to drive that patch of road
near the lake
which turns toward home
without wailing
like a forest animal.

I abandon my car
with the backpack
of silver grief
I now carry with me
everywhere.

In the phone booth
I call anyone
to come pick me up.
It is so late;
no one answers.

136 Lost Connections

I call my best friend, Nina, who is also my husband's client. She hired Tobin, when she was still married, to do a painting for her loft. He created a new technique especially for her. He called it "lost connections" or, in German, *verlorene Verbindungen* because the dots, or blobs, don't connect to the lines. I remember him quietly ecstatic in his studio at night, under the hum of lights, as he squeezed a luminous substance onto the linear drawing so large, it looked like a sail.

Nina, although recently divorced herself, is stunned by the news of our breakup. Like all friends, she has to ask. "What happened, if you don't mind my asking?"

I do mind, and I wish I could give a definite answer.

137 Unprayer or Astral Escape

"Who do you want to stay in the house?" Tobin asks Elender, before he exeunts the marital property. "Mommy or Daddy?"

"I don't know," Elender says.

"Should I move out or what?"

"Well," she tries, "we're used to Mommy taking care of us."

"Okay," Tobin says, breaking down, "I will move out."

Poor little thing, she'll never forget this. She tells it to me over and over like a chant, "Daddy made me choose and I didn't want to, and then he cried."

When he scoops the children up on weekends, I sleep at friends' houses, unable to make a home in mine. At night, I leave my body, find it hard to get back in, awaken alone, moaning, as I squeeze myself into veins and arteries.

I often end up on Nina's couch. Sneezing. Then sleeping. She's a Russian architect, beautiful and living alone. If only I could find a way to be a little more like her, to not be allergic to her cats, who listen as she pours verbal honey over them. "*Natchinka, glosta nostchi lunka schpalenska;* they love it when I say that!"

Fixing me with go-green eyes, the cats wriggle on their backs as she rubs their bellies.

Nina's eyes are green too, and she looks like a cat with her close-fitting clothes revealing a lithe mocha body. She kisses me good night and walks to her bedroom.

It's difficult to sleep, knowing I'll have to be me again when I wake up.

Early next morning, Nina watches as our white Mercedes pulls up. Tobin's large elegant form steps out, bends a little to open the car door for his children. They lug heavy weekend bags all by themselves as he watches.

"Bye, kiddos," he says, ducking into the driver's seat.

Nina and I help rush the children into her kitchen, where she has set a breakfast coffee cake and a pot of hot chocolate on the table. They sit down to eat while Nina pulls me into the bedroom, her eyes wide with tears. "Eet is so beautiful, the car, the children, that man; I can't stand eet."

After breakfast, Nina and I start the day in her neighborhood's Catholic church. Elender and Marcus sit between us, kicking at the underside of the pew. Incense rises from dark wood to sun-struck colored glass. I am thankful for the silence, for my children, my family and friends. I am grateful the sickness of divorce might not be terminal, but I wonder if anyone can prescribe a prayer.

138 Love Eradication

We will be wiped from the face of the earth.
Come my love, let us forgive each other and begin again.

This prayer is what I mantra in the direction of Tobin every day.

139 Agnostic

I used to believe true love would solve anything. Now I don't know.

140 Clockwork

Before Nina was divorced, she lived in a huge tent with her husband and young son, Alexander. The tent was Nina's architectural dream, and so they bought a loft and constructed their tent inside. Splendid with winches, ropes, and pulleys, it made me think of clockwork, some part always in motion. Alex, afraid of nothing but restraint, would swing from rope to rope until bedtime.

I revisit that time—Alex dangling free—and wonder if it's primal, this urge to drop loose, without a safety net. To set one's own clock and push off on one's own.

141 Displaced Person

Walking back from the train after a downtown court appearance, I notice my Honda in front of our house. I almost say aloud, "Oh, I must be home."

142 Legalphile

My second lawyer says, "For a couple with no money, your file is starting to get very heavy."

This is what I have to look forward to in the next four years:

Numerous court appearances and being handcuffed for mistaking a court date and not showing up.

Going through six lawyers.

Tobin barging into my house—twice. First for a surprise inspection and then just to show he can.

The Department of Child and Family Services (DCFS) ringing my doorbell like the Welcome Wagon.

Tobin asks, "Can I have the kids for an extra week to take them camping?"

"Of course," I say. They are his children too.

To my great shock, after their camping trip, he takes me to court for trying to keep him away from his children. Because of this one action, the DCFS—more menacing than the IRS and the CIA put together—hounds me for years. The really scary thing is, Tobin seems to be enjoying this.

143 Advice for a Fresh New Hell

Note to self:

Develop a taste for patience.

Imagine Justice carted on rusted metal pallets and rolled up an interminable mountain with unoiled, square wheels.

Picture Sisyphus cross-legged on top of the pallet smirking at you as you try to push him up. A few times, he almost jumps off, dragging his heels in the dirt to slow things up a little bit more.

Visualize King Pyrrhus, fat and powerful, pushing boulders down to block the passage, just for fun, and Sisyphus chippping away at them with a cork bat.

Remember that for them, it's a game. For you, it's your very future.

Don't give up as you stop at the base of every hill, your feet smarting from bits of quartz, your lips parched and bleeding, and you taste iron.

144 Blood Sampler

"Mom, I'm bleeding a lot!" Marcus says excitedly, watching his blood drop on the yellow-flowered fabric he's practicing on. Usually Marcus is remarkably adept at not stabbing himself, but when he does, he enjoys it.

He and Elender requested samplers before they could write. I find them at secondhand stores, presumably from dead old ladies.

Now they are both working on a blanket patch for their dad's new apartment. No words like HOME SWEET HOME, just flowers.

After a few weeks, I ask Marc if he's finished.

"No," he says, "I took it all out."

"I did too," says Elen. "It didn't look right."

"Yeah, bummer," says Marc. "We have to start all over again."

145 Skyscraper Request

"I want to talk to someone—not you or Dad—I want to talk to someone else about what's going on," Marcus, just turned eight, says to me. This is how my children start seeing the black-haired, middle-aged, moderately obese therapist. She staccatos her pencil on her desk as she holds forth: "Your children are what we call *resilient children.* They are physically well-developed, extremely attractive, gifted, and they are able to process trauma and work through it. And, I want to congratulate you and your . . . their father because you have done something right. These children do not think the breakup is their fault. That is remarkable."

"What did you talk about with the lady?" I ask Elen and Marc.

"It's none of your business," they say.

But they give in and show me the scene they acted out for her. Marcus pretends there is a skyscraper and he and Elen are in the middle of it. They hop up and down.

Marcus says, "Even if you are on the top floor and Dad is in the basement . . ."

"We still don't want to be in the middle," finishes Elender, matter-of-factly. "That's how bad it is, we told her."

They crack me up. As if I weren't already toppled.

146 Feline Night

Made the screechingly horrible mistake of letting my children get a kitten. Even thought, in my bonkers state of needing to please them out of guilt, that I wouldn't be allergic.

I gave in because Elender and Marcus are like Saint Francis, Dr. Dolittle, and PETA rolled into two little people. They think they *are* animals. In fact, my sister Chloë says, "They look less like children than freckle-sprinkled fawns."

My first step into lunacy was going to the shelter, where they fall in blind, passionate, squealing love with a runty black kitty they name Night.

After taking her home and giving her a flea bath, they take turns gazing into Night's eyes until bedtime. That's when I notice the problem. If I could get a sharpened pencil and jam it down my ears, it wouldn't relieve the itching. I try to sleep but can't. A week of skin rashes goes by, and I don't dare say a word to the kids. I phone my asthmatic sister Catherine.

"You're allergic to the cat," she says.

"I don't think so," I say. "I'm not wheezing like you."

"Trust me," she says. "I get the itching too. Do you have the sharp-pencil-ear thing?"

"How did you know?"

"Trust me, it's *Night*."

I hate to be an Indian giver, but I have to be. Elender and Marcus think

I am the most gigantic demon-fucker in hell when I break the news to them. "I can't tell you how sorry I am, kids, but Night has to go."

Elender lets out a sharp scream, snatches Night from Marcus's arms, and runs upstairs to their bedroom. Marcus sprints after her.

A few days later, after Night is gone, the kids are teary-eyed on the couch, trying to do homework.

"Look," I say. "If you kids wanna hit me, you can."

They let me sit between them and we all cry.

A few weeks later, I pick them up from their shrink session. Marcus says, buckling his seat belt, "I told her we were sad about the kitten, but she kept asking if we were sad about Dad."

"Yeah," agrees Elen. "Of course we're sad about Daddy. Duh. But we're crying about Night."

"Her brain is not too good, Mom," says Marc.

Sometimes a kitten is just a kitten.

147 Contortionist

"Mom, I have to go to the bathroom!" whines Marcus, halfway up the stairs.

This is the first indication of something dire: My children's voices have changed. They echo, in hallways and rooms, through doors.

There is too much space now that Tobin is gone.

"Well, then go on up," I say.

"I can't. I need you to come up."

"What?"

"I need you to come up too."

"Marcus, you always go to the bathroom by yourself."

"I don't want to be upstairs alone."

Alarm.

I close the space between us, goad him with compliments. "You're a big boy, Marcus. You've never done this before."

But he draws me nearer with a yell, "Mom, hurry up!"

We run upstairs to the bathroom. He zooms in and I wait outside.

Downstairs seems far away until Elender calls up, "Mom, can you come down? I need some art supplies for my project."

"Honey, you know where they are."

"But they're in the basement!"

"So?"

"I don't want to go down there alone."

"Elen, what's wrong with you?"

"Nothing. Come down with me, Mom."

"Oh, all right."

I am caught between them, spanning two floors.

From inside the bathroom, Marcus wails, and I press my ear to the door, letting his words reach: "Wait for me, Mom, I'm not done!"

"All right, Marc! What's up with you guys?"

"Wait!"

"Mommy, I have a lot of work. Please!" Elender pleads, pulling me closer to downstairs.

Marcus hurries out, leading us to Elender.

In the basement, Elen says, "You can go because Markie's here."

The kids have more room now to contain more fears—the way my youngest sister Carey did during my own parents' divorce. Home from college, I notice Carey won't eat anything unless my mother takes the first bite. Like the King's official tester. When I ask my mother, she shrugs tolerantly.

"She thinks I'm trying to poison her."

"Oh, so that's cool?"

"She'll get over it."

"Why don't you refuse to test the food?"

"I don't want to make it a big deal."

My mother, like me, is aware of the physics of emotional time and space, how easily children can become spooked.

I feel like a contortionist, having to be upstairs and downstairs at the same time. If only we had another bathroom on the first floor. Elen and Marc won't enter their dark bedroom anymore. Unlike most children, they used to be unafraid of the dark.

Now they act as if every room is dark and I must go in first to turn on the light.

Marcus takes to wetting his bed frequently. The first few times, he cries bitterly. "I'm sorry, I won't do it again," he says over and over, half in his sleep, as if he were in the Deutsche Wehrmacht, where young soldiers were flogged for what Marcus is doing. His feeling of unwarranted shame is worrisome.

"Marcus, it's not a problem. All boys wet the bed once in a while. Here, let's make this cozy. You're freezing! Take off your wet pj's and wrap yourself in this blanket. Lie down on the comforter and try to go back to sleep while I change the bed. Mommy doesn't care at all. This is like special time for you and me."

I guide him to the comforter on the floor. He's still shaking, as if he'd been whipped. I kiss him, but he's staring at the ceiling.

"Close your eyes, sweetie," I whisper, as if I were the night nurse, "everything will be all right."

When he's asleep, I struggle to lift him back to his bed.

CLUE NUMBER SIX

The pieces fall faster than you can pick them up.

148 Bunk Beds

Last week I was so haunted by how haunted the house seemed, that we all spent the night over at Nina's. Bad idea. When I went to tuck Marcus in, he was writhing.

"What's wrong?" I ask, fearing appendicitis.

Silence.

"Marcus?"

More writhing.

Bending down under the upper bunk bed, I can just make out his face. Tears are streaming down into his silent mouth.

I kneel down to stroke his hair, but he rolls to the wall. Suddenly he's screaming, like an infant, like a grown-up, "I miss Dad."

I lie down next to him and listen to him wail.

Of course, there's nothing I can do.

As we cry in the dark, side by side, with the empty mattress above us, we could be in a tepee. Tribesmen would hear us and bring Wears-Scarves-in-Summer back. If not for me, then for my son. Because it doesn't take a wise man to know that it's far worse for him, that it's difficult for a boy's spirit to soar without his father.

In the morning, I softly pinch Marc to see if he's still breathing, still dreaming.

So far no one has died.

PART FOUR

A Casanova at twenty eats casserole at forty.

ODELET TO A GRAPE

He picks the smallest grape from the stem, a small reddish baby, and drops it into the cradle of her navel.

"What is your favorite fruit?" he asks, indicating the fruit he has arranged in a bowl on the night table.

Apples, mangoes, pears, and oranges nudge each other, while the banana drapes over them all.

A bunch of grapes warms in his large hands.

"Oh, I don't know," she says as he bends down to eat the sweet grape off her belly skin. "Maybe pomegranates, because the insides look like rubies."

"Or broken hearts," he says.

She is smiling. There are, she notes, no pomegranates in the real still life by the bed. She feels colors—red, yellow, orange—and a cold weight of the triangle of grapes he rests on her breast. He swirls them, like a paintbrush, over her torso, puts one in her mouth.

"I like grapes," she says, swallowing its liquid.

"Me too," he says, rolling another one down between her legs, "when they're inside you."

149 Catechism

"Fuck you, mutherfucker, you fucker!" I'm screaming as a truck tries to head-on-collision our car. To offset our lightly freckled, haloed appearance, we Catholic girls tend to swear like sailors on leave. I'm a good mom, though. I don't want my children to curse indiscriminately. Elender and Marcus repeat the catechism I've taught them. "Swears," they say, "are for near-death experiences in moving vehicles."

150 Cookie Recipe

Wait until they spread out to become themselves
Don't turn the oven light on and preview inside
Expand your patience as they brown
Move from the past (dough) to the future (sweet, crunchy dollop)
Believe that cookie dough is the strongest glue in the world
After love
Or grief

151 Statue Maker

I should have frozen them then, my little children.

"Mommy, come look, quick!"

I wake to their excited voices and Tobin lets me slip out of his embrace. Without grabbing anything to cover myself, I rush into their bedroom and see Elender and Marcus, age three and four, standing motionless and naked on top of encyclopedias.

"We're statues," they giggle, and the heavy books teeter as they jump off their pedestals onto the red wall-to-wall carpeting.

If only I could have frozen them as statues—like we did as children on our front lawns playing the neighborhood game statue-maker—kept them from every danger, including me and Tobin.

152 Frozen

After Tobin leaves for good, the days drip like water from the roof of a damp cavern forming stalactite sculpture. I walk slowly, as if chilled, getting to the freezing point.

Yet my feelings of love for him—a habit not yet chipped away—continue to stir and warm me.

I love my lost husband as I love the statue in the park. When I go for a walk in the rain, I know I'll come upon it, an unmoving man with hard cloak folds, giving a flowing illusion. There is always the urge to be held by this giant, to be static, as the weather changes and the park goes from dusk to dark.

I don't think I can live in the real world anymore.

153 Ash Scanners

The Phoenix is said to rise out of that fine black dust, with magic wings.

A mythical bird that never dies, she scans the landscape for distant places.

But I am weary of magic; it's what got me into this mess.

154 The Ways We Enable

From my bedroom window, I can see my neighbor's purple ash tree with its foliage that looks like desiccated bunches of grapes.

I keep insisting I love Tobin.

Clinging to that; it still seems enough.

All those years when he didn't look at me as I climbed in bed—his eyes like military scanners fixed on his newspaper *Die Zeit*—was my constant giving a way of not noticing him either?

The gourmet servings of myself wasted when all he had was the taste for ash.

155 **The Good Book**

The jacket is not dusty, its pages are not yellowed; there aren't any pressed flowers inside. It's a slim volume, no leather spine with gold embossing, and if there's wisdom contained, it's without the patina of age. Yet it's become my Bible. In fact, it is *my* Bible. I've started a journal to make the disarray of my life more coherent to myself.

The first page says:

slamDUNK DIVORCE for the Unathletic
upYOURS Books, a division of Division House, New York

I envision upYOURS Books as a small press in a loft printing self-help books, such as *You Are Fucked Up and Need Help, Dumb Fuck*, and *The Secret Everyone Needs to Know Before Walking Down the Aisle,* and *Ten Easy Signs That Your Relationship Is Over.* The titles and the logo that I draw—pages of a book spread open to look like butt cheeks—make me laugh. And I *need* to laugh.

To not overuse the D-word, I've made up every synonym for divorce I can imagine: *riftsville, splitsville, state-of-disunion,* among others. My personal over-the-top favorite: *The Disunited States of Agony.*

On a bad day, and there are many, I go to bed, get out my journal, and imagine myself unencumbered—or with a nanny taking my children to Central Park—in an arts and crafts–decorated apartment writing my quirky books under a deadline from Percy, the bearded Trotskyist owner of upYOURS.

I sketch a picture of myself, with bangs I don't have, making me slightly more New York–angular than I am. Underneath I write my bio:

Claire McCloud was born in the United States of married folk. She never quite grew up until her parents split up. After studying to become an unsuccessful artist and playwright, she worked as a soap carver and an insecurity guard. This is her first book.

CHAPTER ONE

On Dissolution and Disillusionment
Like death, there are stages you will go through when you dissolve your sacred union. Dissolution of marriage is a type of death. Only, if you have children, it doesn't end.

Yes, our parents had their world wars; our generation has divorce. As surely as they did, we are living with ghosts. I talk about my ex as if he haunts me, because he does.

Like any war, you can't jolly the breakup along, or slow it down, nor can you decide to end it precipitously, unless you have nuclear capabilities in the form of a Hiroshima cloud of money and the mountainous forgiveness of Mother Teresa.

Every separation has its own tone and rhythm that seems to be led by a mad conductor. She's not from our time zone, and she hasn't been paid, so she does things her way.

Each phase is longer, madder, and more haunting than the moon's, yet less predictable. During these stages, your words become eerie sounds, peculiar noises, loud thwaps. Those around you may seem frantic, like odd creatures trying to squeeze into a small circus tent—only the tent is your headache, pretty much the only constant these days.

These are not stages of development; they are stages of destruction. None of this will feel any good. Sorry.

156 Weed

I tried pot once and was high for nine months.

Every morning I looked out the window crying, "Oh, shit, the trees are still weird!"

I am one of those rare people who need their inhibitions, what few I possess, firmly in place.

Under the influence of marijuana, the legendary one and only time I smoked the stuff, I pointed out the rapist/killer on a campus we were visiting in Indiana where a girl had been raped and killed. "He's the one, he's the one," I repeated, totally flipping out, to my sister Catherine.

Years later, when he was convicted, we found out I was right.

That infamous time I was high for nine months. This, along with not enjoying one-night stands, discouraged me from partaking in the aftermath of the '60s revolution. I was on the tail end of the hippies, the baby boomers—the me-me-me and what-do-you-think-about-me generation. We have looked so hard and been affixed by so many labels, we cannot find ourselves anymore.

Still, I wish I had a gateway drug or even a drug that is on the other side of the gate. Just something to get me through this pain, through the image of Marcus crying all night long. And the possibility that Elen has not even begun to cry yet. She doesn't want to be a tributary in our river.

157 Entry

Alone in my bed.

Elen and Marc have done their homework. If they ask for help, I always say, "I already went through fourth grade." It doesn't matter what grade they are actually in.

I need time to write an entry in my journal for my *slamDUNK* guide to divorce:

COPING
If this were war, we'd all be dead.

I also need time to cry.

After a few hours making my face and the pages of my journal soggy, I continue to write:

This could be a powerless-point presentation
for getting a divorce degree summa cum maudlin:

STAGES, SYMPTOMS, AND UNASKED-FOR ADVICE
(not necessarily in order of appearance)

ANGER
Avoid knives and screwdrivers.

ANGUISH
Intensified if children are involved.

BITTERNESS
The taste of anvils in mouth when spitting.

CRYING JAGS
Can appear at any time and although hard to believe, are a form of healing.

DENIAL
Things—like getting back together and being happier than ever—will work out.

GETTING RID OF GRAY HAIR
Instead of looking like frumpy ex-wife, try to look like ex's new girlfriend.

GETTING RID OF GRAY MATTER
No bong tokes or acid tabs—brain cells are limited.

FEELING GUILTY
Every good deed will be punished.

FEELING OVERWHELMED
Be patient, can go on for years.

FEELING LIKE A FAILURE
May last until death or remarriage, whichever comes first.

FEELING SUICIDAL
Can continue until first fling or until flinging self over balcony.

MISERY
Suicide seems inexpensive.

PARALYSIS
Resistance to getting out of bed, may also include literal paralysis where limbs simply stop working.

SMALLIFYING
It's not such a big deal; stop complaining.

158 Consolation

More than half my bed is covered with open books—occupying roughly the same amount of space Tobin would have.

I skim and switch between them, settle into one all night long whenever I forget that beds are for resting, for sleeping, for making love. Reading is my substitute for sleep and my consolation prize for being alone.

159 Goethe Snacks

Marcus peers in my room. "What's for dinner, Mom?"

"Nothing, why?" I say.

Elender walks in, smiles, and sits on the bed. "You're always tired," she says.

"I know, guys, it's very tiring."

"Really, Mom," Marcus is tireless when it comes to his stomach, "what's for dinner?"

"I'll be whipping it up in a second," I muster. "Go memorize a chapter of Goethe's *Faust* and dinner will be ready."

"What's Goethe's *Faust*?" they ask.

Elender and Marcus leave my bedroom quickly, like children racing toward their mother, instead of away from her. I am fighting a sickness with no symptoms.

160 Jugular

"I'll get up soon and make dinner," I say, touching my neck.

"What're we having?" they chorus.

"Kids, I don't know. Let me rest for a minute."

My definition of motherhood: Your child slits your jugular, laps up every lickable drop of blood. Then with ruddy cheeks, he or she scoots off to college, saying to your inert form on the floor, "Thanks for everything."

161 Suburban Free Food Pantry

Yes, they have them. And yes, I've been there. As a matter of fact, I've sponged so many times that they told me never to come back. I've even flunked getting free food.

162 Shampoo

What causes a breakup? If all the shampoo and conditioner bottles are not lined up by brand name and facing out in the shower? It could be just that simple.

163 Goldfish

The lake is my meditation. Can't go a day without seeing that blessed mass of fresh water, our Great Lake Michigan.

My mother says, "The lake is our living room."

It's an inherited trait, this devotion to water.

I'm treading water as the children swim around me, playing the game we always play—baby dolphins. For the first time, I can't be the mother dolphin with her swift, protecting fins, and subterranean sounds singing out from her sleek form into the blue. All I can do is thrash in one place, treading the deep blues.

In these open waters, everything is new, but not in a good way. This newness is premature, unwanted.

I imagine the lake dry and, in its place, a prairie burning. *Oh, it's good for the new growth. I know, the scorched earth looks pretty austere, but the flora and fauna love that charcoal effect.* I should warm to this, but any newness now is wholly unfamiliar (hence the term *new*) and—like arriving on a charred, distant planet—disorienting.

Each day brings the slow-feeding torture of another first. The first time I sleep in the marital bed alone. The first time Tobin calls and asks to speak to "the children." (I know their names, motherfucker!) The first time he calls me *their mother* in public instead of *my wife.* Tighten the screws, put the hood over my face, and chop my head right off.

The first time out with another man fills the lake again, but brings turbulence.

I am out with our next-door neighbor, Gabe, who used to help me haul in furniture I was painting when it started to rain, even when my husband was at home. ("Sure, I'll help you bring it in . . . Hitler Jr. being an asshole again?" he'd whisper.) The first person we meet after squeezing our way into the appropriately named Gold Star Sardine Bar is Tobin! Gabe is truly just a friend, although from the way I'm dressed in a short black skirt with fishnet stockings, Tobin doesn't think so. His wink looks like the smirking of an eye, the stare of a fish.

The first time the children are picked up for visitation brings unexpected questions. What is the proper protocol? What would Miss (formerly Mrs.) Manners say? Do I say good-bye in another room to avoid Tobin's seeing me? Me seeing him? Are the children uncomfortable and do they worry we will fight? Do I run to the window and scratch at the glass like a demented, abandoned pet as they walk down the sidewalk? Beg them to have a good time, but not too good. (Oh, I hate myself.) Pray that they come back, that they'll want to come back, that they'll sleep well, that they won't get hurt, oh God.

I try to remain buoyant the first time they spend the night with him and call me crying, missing me.

"Daddy tried to be nice," Elen tells me later. "He said, 'I'm sorry I can't comfort you as well as your mother.' "

When I hear this, I am forced to remember, in a flood that feels like bloodletting, a few of his good points—his attentiveness to my piano playing, his goodness in bed.

It's getting difficult to think straight; I'm just cringing and cramping in wait of another first.

There's the flood of jealousy I feel when the children are looking forward to seeing their dad for the first time. Usually they are ambivalent, but they are going on a weekend trip with him and seem genuinely thrilled.

I pack my children's overnight bags with clothes and toys. I make them each a drawing. For Elen, a fairy castle with two little baby fairies saying, "Life is magical, so relax."

For Marcus, a lion climbing a tree with the words, "This is fun!"

I put cardboard around each so it won't get crumpled. Elender has started this tradition. She says, "I like to look at the drawing when I miss you."

After they are all packed, I remember something else, and walk into another room. By the time I look around, I've forgotten what I have to do.

Marcus tells me I have the attention span of a goldfish. I'll take it as a compliment.

I like goldfish. I used to watch them during the time I was recuperating from mononucleosis in high school. I marveled then at their ability to swiftly swim in any direction without smacking the sides of their bowl. Schools of fish can do the same thing, full stream ahead they travel, aware of their boundaries, their direction, turning, any second, on a razor's edge. Love is like that. But in our case, Tobin and I were pushed up against the glass, pulled apart by currents. No way to escape except up, out, and over.

164 Reentry

I feel calmer when I climb into bed and write *slamDUNK:*

DIVORCE FINISHING SCHOOL
(Etiquette for the Seriously Divorcing)

Don't get into red convertibles with strangers.

Don't introduce children to other men/women in your life.

Don't bring other men/women home to sleep in your bed.

Don't date. (You are far too vulnerable and insanely needy.)

Don't care if your soon-to-be-ex is dating. (He/she is making a fool out of him/herself by being vulnerable and needy.)

Do wear a scarlet *D,* for *divorcing,* on your chest to explain everything that is going wrong, including why you and your children are missing appointments and award ceremonies.

Obviously I wasn't able to follow these guidelines myself.

CLUE NUMBER SEVEN

You try to figure out what went wrong, but you fail even at that.

165 Blacksmith

> Oh a blacksmith courted me, there was no man better, he fairly won my heart, I wrote him a letter, with his hammer in his hand, he looked so clever, and if I were with my love, I'd live forever.
>
> —TRADITIONAL

We're court-ordered to sell our marital home—the town house. This is just another in a series of court orders culminating in the divorce decree which—I don't know now—will take place in two and a half years.

Elender, Marcus, and I will be pulling the move off pretty much on our own, with the help of hired burly men, and perhaps a little help from Nina's son, Alex.

At least we won't have to move the piano, because Tobin took me to court about the Bösendorfer, and he won. The grand has been muffled and packed off to Germany.

If my now-you-see-him-now-you-don't lover, Christopher, were in a now-you-see-him phase, he could have lent a martial arts level of lifting.

Instead he said, shortly before the move, "I need to purify myself." This, I don't need to remind myself, after spending a couple of nights in my bed. Ah, the drama of sexual bulimia.

I can't complain—but I will, frequently and bitterly—because he's lending me his truck. While he's scrubbing his soul (and other notable parts), I'll be lifting a huge mirror with Marcus that we will, to our horror, break, thereby beginning the cycle of the next tormented seven years. As if we hadn't already suspected it.

We drive, fully loaded, so to speak, to the new place. Elender and Marcus jump out, run to the front door.

"Guys, we have a lot of stuff to carry in," I say.

They look at me incredulously. Marcus melts down. "You mean," he sobs, "we have to unload it all?"

We are renting the second floor of a funky old building that was once a blacksmith shop in the wealthy suburb of Wilmette. Successful people all around. (Why am I here? I have to ask.) My neighbors include an ex–porn star who walks her six cats around the block most days.

The kitchen is homey but dangerous. The countertop near the sink is warped and ripped, so jagged, we will all have gashes. Yellowed bits of clear tape have been used to keep its edges from attacking us. But I need a thick industrial swatch to do the job. If I were a blacksmith, I would buy the right kind. Maybe I could borrow some from the cat woman. Although that might seem kinda kinky. Sadly, the days of borrowing anything from a neighbor, even flour or sugar, are over.

We are moving too far away for the children to continue in their parochial school. At least they finished out last year. To have them in their new public school district, I am paying double each month: the mortgage on our old house and the new rent. We have no money left for food, even if I could prepare it.

Oddly enough, this was the cheapest acceptable apartment I could find. And it's in a better neighborhood than our town house. So instead of becoming a single mom statistic and having my lifestyle go down after divorce, I've moved up to the North Shore, a chain of lakeside suburbs where some of the richest people in the United States live.

Our apartment has what they call *character*. Elender calls it "only one bathroom!"

But given the problem of having to be with each child when they go into any room, I am grateful for the smallification. *Très* non–North Shore!

I'm going against the grain every step of the way. To get into our place, we have to pass the original blacksmithing shed and climb up a steep inner staircase. There is no light on the stairs. I replaced the bulbs and they actually worked. For a day. The electrical wiring, like the wiring in my brain, must be fried, and the landlord can't fix it. Besides, I owe him rent and it's tricky to ask for anything.

Going up and down the stairs to our house is treacherous in the dark. When we come home at night, I tell Elen and Marc to feel the Braille of the walls. Soon we'll be blind Indians, able to climb mountains (and walls) without tripping.

I caution my children's friends, "Don't trip down the stairs and kill yourself or your parents won't let you come back."

In a rare spurt of energy, I line our sidewalk and stairs with tea lights.

"We've got a landing pad with a runway!" says Marcus.

But, for me, we're not landing. We're not taking off.

Every day is another stop at a campsite with more beans in tin cups and tired children waiting for their story by the fire.

166 Mother Courage

I've never had to show courage every day until now.

167 Motion Detector

I take a lot of comfort, when I'm not weeping in the basement, from writing:

FIVE WAYS TO COMFORT YOUR CHILDREN WHEN YOU MOVE

1. Invite their friends over for a pizza/help-us-pack party.
2. As a thank-you, give your children and their friends an envelope containing a two-dollar bill.
3. Make a large banner saying WELCOME HOME, KIDS to put on your new front door on moving day.
4. Before anything else, have the children set up their new rooms.
5. Before the boxes are unpacked, bake muffins and let the sweet fragrance fill up your new house.

168 New Sun

I wake in the new house, find yellow tiles on the counters, pieces of an old sun.

Elender hands me a note, *I am board.*

A week ago I found a crumpled-up piece of paper under my pillow saying in Marcus's bold, angry scrawl, *Fck you.*

I'm in his room now while he sleeps. Taping the edge of a frame so a photo of his dad doesn't keep sliding out, I look around. I notice his dad's phone number on top of his precious wooden box that contains coins and some rare baseball cards. I secure the number with tape, to make it more permanent.

Tidying my son's room, his sovereign place of keepsakes, I touch each object Marcus loves. I wouldn't treat his teddy bear badly. I wouldn't say anything against his friends, or favorite teacher, or a sports team he adores. He loves his dad even more! I double over, thinking how excruciating it must be for him. Never mind the soft panic I've been feeling for weeks now.

This is all very noble, but I have to be honest. Underneath the compassion is the ubiquitous subtext: May Tobin rot in hell.

In looking after our children, we are revealed over and over to be monsters.

169 Prairie Street Puppets

Little blacksmith house on the Prairie Street. It's our first house alone, without a man of the house. Laura Ingalls Wilder couldn't have done it better. Oh, wait, I forgot. Yes, she would have.

I really can't afford the rent.

Until my scheme to turn us into a family of voice-over actors sounds our way to more money, I'll have to think of something else. Inconvenient reality: I have a hard time thinking these days.

Somehow, I conjure a short-term plan based on odds and ends.

The rule is to not buy anything. To make do with what we have. Our house is ridiculously runneth-overing with art supplies, so it won't be difficult to find what we need.

After a few weeks, we have created five puppets:

Dunno, a red-haired sweet dope, who doesn't know anything, constructed with wire and painted sheets.

Fripp, his African girlfriend, made out of bits of African fabrics and cotton.

Gwendie, their beautiful daughter, who looks like a mulatto version of Elender, put together with old tights and silk. She has long wavy hair removed from a Barbie doll.

Bionda, a stray dog that speaks with a British accent, formed by twist-tying an old bathroom rug.

Vince, the prince who is smitten by Bionda. He is started from a decapitated Ken doll. His head is an old ball.

I attach the strings on all the puppets and Elen and Marc make them move.

"They look real, Mom," Marcus says.

"Who says they're not," I say.

It hurts just a little when we sell off our invented family for twenty-five dollars apiece.

170 Charity Bags

My children and I are well acquainted with any store that provides testers. Basically we beg by being brazen. "My, that's good. Do you have any other flavors? We'd love to try them all." Like good customers, we put the item in our shopping cart—only to take it out before we hit the checkout.

Poverty is the mother of ingenuity.

From my bed, I can hear the refrigerator door opening. Elender and Marcus must be in front of it again—the big white talisman of the American family with magnets attracting notes and photos to its exterior. Only hunger could seduce us into its cold.

The landlord, who is a generous, Jesuit-educated man, bought me a new refrigerator and often brings me loaves of fresh bread. I hope he doesn't know the true state of desperation we're in.

The refrigerator door is fully opened now, making the humming louder. A hushed click and the door is closed when they see there is only mustard and a can of whipped cream. How much do they mind?

I try to shop. But *try* implies failure, and that's what's going on here.

"Try and fail, try and fail, until you fail again," my mother advises.

She brings over bags of groceries. So does my father. Since their divorce, my parents live separately not too far from each other and not too far from me either. An advantage for my children, who adore them. Acquaintances and even enemies bring me things. I've been a vegetarian for twenty years and my daughter is allergic to milk, yet there, nestled in the brown-bagged produce, is hamburger meat and a gallon of milk. Can beggars be trendy lactose-intolerant vegan choosers? At a barbecue a few years ago, a friend asked my children if they wanted a hamburger.

"What's a hamburger?" they both chimed in.

If my friends or family members stay and make dinner with me, I'll venture into the kitchen. Otherwise, I play the piano for hours (again, my dad saved me and sent over the baby grand he's not using) or go to my bed. I want my notes to be food, my songs to nurture us all, but they are dark and starved of hope with words like, *"You said you love me forever, and now you say it isn't true. I was the geisha of your senses and now I'm a beggar without you."*

The charity bags sit on my counter, looking like the seven dwarves, each demanding something: To be put away. Today, all I could manage was to put fresh apples from my mom into a bowl on the table. I can't ask anyone, but when will I get over the difficulty of putting these gifts away? Each according to . . . Each in its proper receptacle . . . Where is that?

Panic keeps me away from kitchen knives and the stove. I think the children are realizing I make meals only if we have guests. I need distraction as much as ingredients.

Like any food that requires a specific cooking time, I can't rush these feelings, nor can I slow them, freeze them, or discard them.

Before the divorce, Elen and Marc put their after-school hands into little wooden bowls filled with cashews, raisins, sesame sticks, dried apples, and almonds. Tobin and I prepared elaborate salads for dinner. Arugula, romaine, and young spinach fashionably dressed with olive oil, lemon, garlic, and tamari. We had homemade soups for lunch. He specialized in the meat soups, like oxtail or chicken. I diced vegetables for mushroom barley, lentil, or leek soups. We art-directed the table with place mats and cloth napkins. When we went to Ravinia, the free-air music festival, Tobin insisted on carrying glass plates for our candlelit picnics. Our friends may have thought it pretentious, but it looked beautiful on the lawn as we listened to Mahler.

Now I resist preparing or eating any food we enjoyed together. I can't go to any grocery store or restaurant where I was with him.

There should be supermarkets that capitalize on divorce.

As I hide in bed and read a book about composers, a chapter about Scriabin—who, at age seventeen, wrote an amazing piece I'm working on—I can hear the kids crunching on apples. I no longer feel hungry, but I sense my children's hunger like a tidal wave coming over me. The refrigerator door opens and closes for the hundredth time.

171 Handouts

I go to the school district building to fill out forms for my children's free lunch, free bus, and a fee waiver—all for their new school. Because everybody's rich here, it's a done deal, not many questions asked. If I had moved to Chicago, I would have been just another single-mom face. Here in suburbia, I stand out, almost as if I were carrying a placard saying, I'M POOR. I'm living off the fat of the system, and it feels all right.

172 Off the Clock

Every clock in our new house tells a different time. Elender brings this to my attention. She laughs but is slightly distressed.

"Okay, which is the right time?" she asks.

I don't know what she is talking about until she goes around the house and reads to me each conflicting timekeeper. No wonder my poor Elender keeps her own alarm clock hidden, sets it, and gets herself up each morning.

Only occasionally does she sputter in protest.

"If I didn't get up in the morning, no one would be on time."

I can't imagine this is good for her, so I take to getting up earlier, for a while.

I decide to wake up at five in the morning on Wednesdays and Fridays. Elender and Marcus nod as I lay out my plan: We will set out our layers of warm clothes (it's the middle of a horrendous Chicago winter) before going to bed. Early in the morning, while it's still dark, we will head for the lake. There we will walk for an hour, enjoy the sunrise, the ice formations, play with the dogs along the frozen beach, contemplate our future while watching the silver spectacle of the morning sun on the water, walk back to the car, drive to a café for hot chocolate and croissants, and then go home for them to dress for school before the first bell.

This stolen time is not on anyone's clock. We have a life together as a family before the day has even started.

When Marcus tells Tobin, he is stunned. "Your mother? Claire? Up at five in the morning?"

173 Migration

Although I don't want to end up in the police blotter, the children and I walk many nights, even at midnight, along the lake.

After the lakefront is officially closed, we hide from police beacons like immigrants or nomadic folk or homeless people. At first we walk everywhere because Tobin took the car. Then we walk because we love it.

Any night can be an adventure. We've encountered deer, raccoon, skunk, and possum. We've watched rats scurrying under the rocks along the beach. We've seen the moon during every phase and talked about light and reflection on water. We've looked at the stars and discussed how some of them may have already died and we are just catching the last of their sparkle from light-years away.

As if we are Indians migrating, we traverse our small corner of the earth. Marcus and Elender are accustomed to walking with me because I didn't get a driver's license until a few years after we moved to the States. It was my personal, if futile, crusade against the all-pervasive automobile. Even as toddlers they marched along without complaint or strolled in their double carriage.

For me, it's the best medicine. As someone said, "There's no problem so great that you can't walk away from it."

174 The Going Gets Tough and the Tough Get Sleazier

Winding up from a much-needed meditation on how much I need to meditate, or, alternatively, medicate, I hear the bell ring. Not a soft, reverberating Zen tone, but the insistent, buzzer-happy finger of my son on our doorbell. The kids are back from visitation with their dad.

I answer the door, using it as a shield against my husband's with-another-woman eyes, and Elender and Marcus squirm past like giddy guppies. I know they have met his girlfriend.

"She's really nice and has two adorable dogs," they say.

I choke.

"If she's nice to you guys, then she's all right by me," I am able to say.

I know this sounds crazy, but I want to like her because she will be in charge of my kids. Please take good care of them, keep them safe, I vibe to her.

It took him a while to find a girlfriend, so I don't begrudge him, and I don't feel jealous as a mad hatter. The only thing hard to swallow is my children's involvement. Packing their bags every weekend is hard enough, especially since we had finally reached the luxurious stage of no longer having to schlep diapers, special foods for Elen's milk and egg allergy, bottles, extra clothing, and toys; but I do it and they're ready on time. Still, it irks me to think where and with whom they've been.

His girlfriend, his girlfriend rolls around my head like a hula-hoop with spikes until I swiftly catch it, remembering I am grateful to her too, even if she's a spawn of Satan, because *my* children have arrived home in one piece.

The first words out of my son's lollipop-smeared lips are about *her*. Like an aviator's scarf thrown back in the whirlwinds of a start-up propeller, when Marcus says *"she,"* it whips me.

There is nothing easy about my life right now except mother-love for my wonderful progeny. So, this is going to get trickier for *moi.*

"She's much younger than you, Mom. Prettier too, and nicer . . . and lots thinner," my son says.

"Oh, really, Marcus, how nice for your dad," I reply with a blithe tone, making a mental note not to sign the permission slip for his next field trip.

"No, she's not, Markie. She wears makeup, tons of it," says my daughter, who will still be in my will.

"Yeah, the bathroom was a shrine to makeup," says my prodigal son, returned.

"Believe me, Mom," continues Elen, "without all that makeup, she looks like a boiled rat."

Things are getting tougher, or I'm getting weaker, and secretly I'm glad the women around my children are getting sleazier, or I'm wearing less makeup.

The bitter pill wants dissolving, but it remains lodged in my throat, keeping me from saying, "So that's where your dad was last weekend when he never came to pick you up!"

I want to tear my pubic hair out when I remember Marcus last weekend as a clock vigilante, waiting for the hand to cross over any black number that would make the doorbell ring. Waiting for his dad to be standing there to free him from his cheery yet on-the-verge-of-weeping stakeout.

But he is their father, and I must never trash him. It would be like ripping out a chamber of my son's four-chambered heart. But oh, how tempting to say, "It would be too good for him to burn to death on Christmas Day before opening his presents—and forgetting to buy you yours!"

175 One-Handed Pull-up

Perfect beach day. Time for some enforced fun.

Grab the towels, find the cooler, put together some snacks—maybe even a picnic, and don't forget the kiddos.

Elen chases Marc up and down the shoreline. She's laughing; he's panting.

"Take off your shirt, Marc!" I yell.

As he pulls it over his head, I notice for the first time (triple-bad mom) that he has gotten fat.

On the way home, we stop off at a hardware store and I buy a pull-up bar for Marcus's bedroom doorway. I need to unfat him.

"I want one too," says Elen.

So I buy two pull-up bars.

It takes me longer than my IQ score would predict, but I figure out how to follow the directions and install Marcus's pull-up bar.

Later that evening, an acquaintance, Jimmy, whom I met through a choir I occasionally sing in, visits us.

"I've got a chin-up bar," says Marcus. "Do you want to see it?"

"Sure," Jimmy says, slowly walking up the stairs. It's been a long day for him, and I know he's going through a divorce as well.

We all follow him. When he sees the bar, he moves more quickly until his one hand grips it. Before our very eyes, he pulls himself up with one arm.

Marcus's eyes are almost as wide as his girth. "How do you do that?"

"I'm a triathlete."

"What's that?" Elen asks, her voice full of awe.

"It means," I say, "that he's three times more athletic than most people."

Jimmy laughs. "I actually climbed Mount Everest."

May his tribe increase.

"Wow!" both children exclaim.

"I'll show you pictures sometime."

"That would be great," I say, "but now you guys have to go to bed."

"It's late," he says. "I'll see you another time."

"Sure," I say, knowing the unpredictable departures I too am capable of these days.

"Get yourselves ready for bed," I say to the kids. "I'll be right back."

I walk him downstairs. "Thanks for showing us that cool pull-up."

He doesn't respond and walks out the door. Either he's missing his own children, or I forgot to brush my teeth for a few weeks.

As soon as the door closes, Elen and Marc run down the stairs, yelling in unison, "Mom! Are you sexually attracted to him?"

"What are you—? That is none of your business," I say. "Go to bed immediately."

"But," says Marcus, "he's soooo cool. He can do that one-armed thing."

"Yeah," says Elen. "Couldn't you try to like him, Mom?"

"To bed!" I yell.

In truth, any man, one-armed pulling up or not, would have a hard time muscling in between me and my kids. It would take quite a guy to penetrate our steroid-strong triangle. I'm not saying it's a good thing, but Elender, Marcus, and I are in a petri dish and anyone outside is just an observer.

When the house is quiet, I stand under Marcus's doorframe and try to lift myself with both arms. Even with a jump, I can't.

176 Wrong of Passage

Just waiting every moment of the day for the ritual called Crawling Under the Covers. Oh, the egocentricity of sleep. And writing in my journal. Me, me, me, and the heaviness I feel upon me. For a little levity, I continue *slamDUNK*:

RANTING
Bring earplugs when people are on cell phones to ex-spouses.

LOSING EVERYTHING
Hair, house keys, car keys, money, credit cards, clothing, wallets, contact lenses, bowls of potato chips, diaphragms, and, yes, your mind.

CATASTROPHIZING
I'll be homeless; I'm dying; no one loves me.

LOSING WEIGHT/GAINING WEIGHT
(Choose one)

FATALISM
I'm old and ugly anyway, so I might as well be divorced. (See also FEELING SUICIDAL)

CLINICAL LABELING
My ex is finding his inner asshole.

GRIM REALIZATION
Often accompanied by hyperventilation: I have to cook dinner!? The phone bill is past due. I need to wash my daughter's soccer uniform. I have to shovel the walkway. The front tire is flat. My son needs me to sign his late note. Where's a pen? I have to take a shower. I have to breathe.

DISORIENTATION
Can be experienced as actual dizziness. (See also LOSING EVERYTHING)

REMORSE
Can be intermittent, involuntary, or even short-lived.

FIXATION ON PRINTED MATTER
Read and repeat packaging labels as if they were horoscopes: If button is up, reject; discard unused portion immediately.

LOSS OF CONCENTRATION
I can't remember why I wrote this one.

SEARCHING FOR YOUR HIGHER GOOF
The wrong spouse.

SLEEPING CONSTANTLY/OR WANTING TO BE
Often coupled with insomnia.

INSTANT GRATIFICATION
Not soon enough.

MAIL AVOIDANCE
Knock before not opening.

MALE AVOIDANCE
Short phase, followed by tall men.
Or a long phase, followed by short men.

FEMALE AVERSION

FEELING HIDEOUSLY UGLY

FEELING AMAZINGLY ATTRACTIVE AND SEARINGLY SEXY
(Sadly, another short phase.)
(Or a long phase with short hair.)

AVARICE

DATING
(See FUCKING)

FUCKING
(See DATING)

REFUSING TO DATE SO MEN ASK INCESSANTLY
Unfailingly successful.

FORGIVENESS
Though not advised, this is commonly skipped over.

GRIEVING
A lifetime of grief for every time you say, "I do."

177 Innocents in Smithereens

Realizing there will be fallout from any war, I prepare myself in the few ways I know how. I read and write. I sleep and stay under the covers as much as possible. Luckily I have two children who can keep each other company. But I feel cowardly being in bed all the time.

Inspired by the journal I'm keeping, I ask Elender and Marcus, the undisputed innocents, to write their slant on things. To them, there are no finer lines of demarcation or finalization. It's all just divorce, their universe in smithereens.

"Other kids might go through their parents' divorce and need some advice," I say. "You can help them by writing down some stuff."

"Hey, Mom," says Elender. "That's very good."

This is some of what she wrote:

ELENDER AND THE DIVORICE

BY ELENDER MARIE MCCLOUD-KLEINHERZ

Hi my name is Elender. I am almost 9 years old. My parents are divorced. All the main fighting started when my brother was going to his soccer team party. My parents got in a fight while we were driving to it. I was 8 years old. My mom asked my dad who was going to pay for the food at the resturant the team party was at. My dad did not want to talk about it and jumped out of the car in the middle of traffic and stared to walk home. I was embarresed because they were yelling at the top of there lungs out on the street. I also felt very scared. My mom was so mad she took my brother who was 7 and droped him off next to my dad who was walking home. I was embarresed, sacred, and very confused at the same time. My mom and I went to the party and my dad and brother walked there.

I think the divorece *was not much of a shock. I saw it coming but it was sort of a shock because when my parents told me they were getting divorced I didn't feel much of anything I just continued my life. But now it's staring to hit me because it's goten though to me that my parents are not together and live in difrent houses. Now that's one of the most confusing things about divorce. I live in two houses. I know that I go to my dad's aptment every other weekend and on Tuesday from 7:00 p.m. till 8:00 p.m. But when my dad goes to Germany and when he can't see me on Tuesdays and all the other changes that might happen, I get so confused about where to go. A nother problum is that I have to pack clothes every time I go to my dad's house. It's very annoying.*

My dad has a problum with taking me to where I need to go like soccer games and father daughter stoff. Like, I belong to an indain princess tribe. It's a father daughter group that does activities together. Once when we were going to go camping together for the weekend it was the second to last tribe camp out and I was just getting over a fever. My dad told me I was to sick to go and didn't want to take me. But I was really fine. So when my mom agreed with him he stared to tell her I had to go I was so confused I didn't know where I was going. In the end I didn't go.

My Dad droped me off at my house and left my brother and I at home even though my mom was not home. He had to go to pack his clothes and stuff because he was leaving for Germany the next morning.

178 Cursive Innocence

Marcus writes in his wobbly cursive:

When my dad moved out of the house, I became very depressed. I was not my creeful happy self anymore. I was always late for school and usly sick. I asked my mom "Why did dad go away?" She said, "Well, if he didn't, we would fight a lot."

That's all he writes. Clearly, we have stunted him.

179 Seven Languages!

I met Quentin Perry at what was a very odd dinner party of medieval singers. Unlike the other members, he was not wearing tights. When I asked him why, he laughed his mellifluous laugh. "I run enough risks of getting killed every day."

From the moment we sat next to each other at that dinner, we were instant friends. He speaks the same three languages I speak, plus four more!

Everyone who meets Quentin tells me, "He's the most interesting person I've ever met." Probably his physical beauty has something to do with it, although at his age, that's almost overshadowed by his larger-than-life presence.

Tallish, with a concrete build, his face with its broad, high cheekbones could be, yes, Native American. But it's his eyes—light green—in his dark copper face that fascinate.

180 Lion

"Just because he's handsome, doesn't mean he's a good person."

"Just because you're older than me, doesn't mean you're wise."

"Except I am."

"I know."

My friend Quentin and I are having lunch, or as he says, "scarfing liquids and solids." It sounds like baby food. Exactly, he says. His idea of food is the farm food on which he was raised: a side of beef, freshly plucked chicken, real butter. Everything of quality and, most of all, quantity.

"Look at this pathetic nouvelle cuisine. If I hadn't brought my glasses, I couldn't *see* the food!"

"Don't you have diabetes or something?"

"Yes."

"Well, shouldn't you be careful?"

"Let's talk about you, my dear. You are, I'm told, going through an upheaval."

"You're handsome, and you're a good person," I say, hoping to divert him.

"And I'm gay, and you're straight. So what?"

"I think I'm pretty twisted."

Silence.

"This divorce business is worse than I ever imagined."

"Don't be ditsy. Remember, Tobin is a lion, not a kitten. I mean it."

"What do you mean?"

"He's a lion—he'll rip your head off, he'll harm your kids."

"They're his kids too."

"Don't defend him. Don't be on *his* side anymore. Be on *your* side starting now."

"Okay . . . ," I say, knowing he grew up deterring predators on a farm that plundered the livestock.

"Expect the worst. And expect to feel even worse."

"Thanks."

"Just part of the service."

When he's paid the bill, he hugs me in his strong, farm-handed arms that probably fought off packs of coyotes with a pitchfork. I'm sure he sees my tears.

"Don't be afraid," he says, showing me with a Supremes' stop-in-the-name-of-love gesture, how to keep Tobin at bay. "No matter how hideous it gets, you are still the protagonist in your own novel. It's always interesting to turn the page and find out what happens next."

181 Uniform Night

"Run! You are in danger of being physically harmed!" I scream.

"Child abuse!" yells Elender, running to her bedroom.

"Parent abuse!" I yell back, chasing Marcus.

I am trying to get ready to go out tonight if I can ever get out of this house.

I play the piano to calm down, then stand at Elender's closed door.

"You cannot forget the one rule in this house: *Never throw objects at someone's face.*"

"I don't care," comes through the door.

"You have to care," I say. "You would be sorry later if someone's eye was hurt."

"Besides, that's not the only rule," she says, sassier than a cat. *"Never put dishes with food or drink on the piano."*

"Always establish your own personal rituals," Marcus yells from his room.

"Okay," I say. "This is serious. You don't throw utensils at me. Or your brother. In anger. Ever. Period."

Silence.

"And you, Marcus," I say, because he's obviously listening, "don't grab food from your sister. Or anything. Period."

Silence.

"Marcus?"

"Yeah."

"I'm going out with our friend Quentin. I need to know that you guys are going to get along."

They both come out. I feel bad leaving them alone, but I don't ever have money for a babysitter. My parents, who are sometimes available for backup, are out of town.

I really feel I need to go because Quentin has arranged for me to play piano at the beginning of a political fund-raiser. And I'll be paid.

"Stay out late, Mom," Marcus says. "We want to see if we can handle it."

I hope this means they are leaving their fear of rooms behind.

"Okay. I won't be far. You can reach me on my pager or Quen's cell phone. You know the number."

Quentin and his lover are ordering drinks when I arrive and start to play "Someone to Walk Over Me," my S&M version of the old standard. I finish the set and as soon as a politician starts to talk, my pager goes off. Most likely Elen and Marc needing something. I go over to tell Quentin.

For a guy without kids, he's quick on the uptake. Without me asking, he hands me his cell phone saying, "Take it on the way home."

I call the kids.

"Mom," Elen says, "uh . . . Marcus answered the phone and it was this creepy guy."

"What? Why was he talking to him?" I ask, getting my coat on.

"That's what I said. He asked if we were home alone."

"Who was he?"

"I don't know. Marcus doesn't either."

"I'll be there in twenty minutes. I'll talk to you and Marcus as I'm driving home."

Once in the car, I phone home.

"Marcus?"

"Mom, I'm sorry I talked to him. But he kept asking questions."

"Honey, it's not your fault. But next time, don't talk to strangers on the phone."

"Okay," he says. "Mom, are you go—"

"Marcus? Honey?"

The phone goes dead.

I panic. Try to breathe. *You'll be there in fifteen minutes*, I comfort myself. I'm not sure if it's the phone that has run out of batteries or if something has happened to the kids.

I dial our neighborhood police station.

"Hi, I'm on my way home and my children are waiting for me, but they received a weird phone call."

"Do you want us to send someone over?"

"Um, yes. I'll be there any second myself, but I am a little worried." I give her our address.

"How old are your children?" she says, exhibiting a disturbing officious tone.

"Oh, seven and eight . . . almost nine. A . . . a friend was watching them." How easy it is to lie when a knife is to my heart.

"If they are home alone when the officers get there, they'll have to be taken into custody."

Double-edged sword–ish, Caucasian chalk circle–esque. I have called to protect my children and now risk having them taken away from me.

"I'll probably be back before they even get there," I say, noticeably hyperventilating and pressuring my foot on the gas pedal. Should I run red lights and get pulled over, or risk arriving too late as my children drive off in a squad car?

As I approach my house, I can already see the bright lights. I run inside. Luckily, it looks as if the three male police officers have only just walked in. Try to smile at them, I advise myself. Hugging Marcus tight, I think frantically, *Where's Elender; she's the one I need.* "Hi, I'm so glad you're here," I say. "I'll go get my daughter." Noticing her out of the corner of my eye starting to walk down, I tear up the stairs. "Hi, sweetie," I say, practically carrying her up to the landing, out of view of the officers. I put my finger to my mouth, bring her into my bedroom, soundlessly close the door.

"Elender," I whisper deep in her ear, "I *need you to do this for me* or the police will take you away from me. You have to lie *now* and say that Nina was looking after you." I am buzzing with so much fear, I can't see her reaction. I hug her as we walk downstairs. *Calm yourself,* I hear in my brain, *she'll be perfect.*

I say to the cops, "Well, thank you so much for coming. I was a bit worried. With that crazy phone—"

The burly one interrupts, "Uh, we'll need to talk to your daughter. She's the older one?"

"Yes," I say. "No problem. Honey, can you talk to the police officer?"

"Sure," she says, my brilliant little actress.

"Honey, how long did Mommy leave you two alone tonight?"

"Oh, we weren't alone," she says. "Nina was looking after us."

"Who's she?"

"Mom's friend."

"Where's she at now?"

Yawning, she says, ". . . she had to return a movie."

A+.

"We'll have to talk to her. Uh, ma'am, do you have her phone number?"

"Of course," I say, writing it down, knowing she's away for the weekend. Another officer calls.

"No answer."

They—all three—head for the door. Good sign.

"Have a good evening, ma'am," one says.

"Thank you so much for coming. I really appreciate it," I say, slowly following them out.

Once they are gone, I collapse on the couch. Marcus and Elender sit on either side of me. "Guys," I say, "I'm sorry. That was an experiment that didn't work."

"I'm sorry for talking to that guy," says Marcus.

"Sweetie," I say, hugging them close. "There's a lot of creeps out there. I'm just glad you're both okay. That's all I care about."

We never find out who he is. But the menacing call magnifies our sense of being without a protector. I won't leave them alone again. And when I'm with them, I'll ward off my feelings of vulnerability.

"Mom," Elen says. "It's Friday dance night."

She's right. Although it's late, Marcus blasts *The Bodyguard* soundtrack. We turn out the lights and put the customary candles in the middle of the floor and dance around them. We are still our own small tribe.

182 Unarmed

Even in my dreams, my mind chews on the past, like an old bone. But it hurts so much, it must be my bone.

"Oh my God!" I scream to no one as I awaken early in the morning. Intense pain.

If someone has shot me in the arm, I don't think it's very funny. I try to sit up, but my right arm won't move. No pins and needles: my arm and hand just dangle. The stabbing throb lets me know it's not asleep. My right arm has officially died.

In a cold sweat, I lie back, the air currents causing me excruciating pain. I try not to move.

In a few hours, Elen and Marc will be getting ready for school. A mom who is not me will have to drive them.

183 Rose Party

A couple of days into the arm trouble, I hear Elender and Marcus come home from school. They tiptoe into my room, walking as if in slo-mo. Sadly, they are aware that the air currents from their movement will make their mother wince. If I refrain from screaming, I won't refrighten them.

Elender stands stock-still and whispers, "What about my birthday?" She's about to turn nine. Which means she wants a theme party.

"How about a mausoleum party?" I could suggest. "That way everyone can lie down and not move for the entire party."

"I want a 'rose' party, Mom," she says, barely audible.

"A rose party sounds great, honey," I say.

Coming right up.

I am in bed on the third day my arm has not resurrected. Has not rolled back the stone. Time to summon my parents to my latest drama.

"Dad," I say, holding the phone with my left hand. "I'm in some kind of excruciating arm pain."

"I'll call your mom," he says.

"Uhh, I think I need to go to the hospital."

Knowing my reluctance to use Western medicine, Dad sounds surprised. "We'll be right over."

Five minutes later, Mom calls. "We're on our way."

Thinking of my kids asleep in the next room, I wonder who will stay with them if I die.

I need a right-hand man.

184 Morphine Offer

Okay, apparently I'm not dying.

Yet.

"We see about three people like you a year," the hospital doctor says. "It's a frozen shoulder . . ."

Brrr.

". . . and we generally prescribe morphine. It's worse than labor pains. Some say worse than kidney stones."

Preaching to the choir, Doc.

"There's no instant cure," he continues. "It'll probably go away in about a year."

And in a hundred, it won't make any difference at all.

185 Alternative Medicine for Arms Program

"It's not any better," I tell the doctor on the phone. "In fact, it's worse. I wake from the pain every night at exactly three in the morning."

"I'll refer you to a specialist," he says.

But I have no insurance, not having had enough money for Tobin's COBRA (the snake!) plan.

Luckily, my neighbor's husband is a shoulder specialist. "I can operate and make it work," he says. "But, off the record, I'd recommend alternative medicine. My wife has had a lot of success with it."

I try acupuncture, chiropractic care, Rolfing, massage, shiatsu, prayer, moxibustion, and swearing. Nothing really works. And I'm horribly in debt because of it.

I feel like Humpty Dumpty. Nothing can put me together again.

186 Frigid

Because of the loss of my limb, I lose the job I recently got managing a secondhand store. The fact that I didn't show up or call probably influenced their decision to fire me. I didn't call, because I didn't want my bosses to spread rumors that my shoulder is frigid.

Secretly, I don't believe the doctor. I think he just made up "frozen shoulder"—like some socialite once concocted a drink and called it a frozen daiquiri.

Obviously the doc doesn't want to tell me the truth.

That I'm dying.

187 Cause and Effect and More Causes

Because I lost my limb and my job, I'm unable to pay my rent, which causes more stress and makes my arm worse and renders me useless in any world.

188 Fixed

She's spooky, but she's the real thing.

"I can help you," she says to me in a bookstore. Either she's psychic or she noticed me fumbling to pay using only my left hand.

"My arm is dead, but painful," I say, noticing how tiny she is. How could those doll hands do anything?

"I see," she says, giving me her card. "It's not dead, just hiding from bad things."

She's Lia Rain, a healer, and she'll put me back together again.

Her massage is surgery. Without an incision, her skilled hands remove scar tissue. For hours she works on my whole body because, as she says, "Your arm is connected to it."

When she goes deep, I cry out, "Sadist!"

"This is the part of my work I like the best," she laughs. "You pulled back to punch, but you never released," she says, pushing into my armpit as if attempting to extract a demon. "We've gotta find the punch. It's somewhere. Maybe between these ribs." She prods until there's a space and miraculously, my right-hand fingers begin to move.

189 Cat Fight

"Lia, I woke this morning and my arm's working a little better. But what's really weird is that I have these strange . . . things . . . all over . . . that hurt. Like the stigmata."

I'm calling her as usual in the morning, as she requested.

"Do they look like cat scratches?" she asks quickly.

"Exactly. And they sting like a motherfucker."

"Excellent," she says, ignoring my profanity. "It's the fascia releasing."

I knew that.

"Okay," I say, "but why is it splitting open my skin in long gashes? I feel like something out of *Alien*."

"Your arm is better?"

"Yeah," I say.

"This is good. I'll show you a book on fascia release."

And I'll show you a book on cat fights.

It takes six months, twice a week, thousands of dollars my dad pays to Lia, but I'm definitely getting armed again.

190 CEO Girl

Just as lions were born free, my daughter was born successful. She could, even at this age, run a Fortune 500 company.

191 Expenditures

All products, except free samples, or things acquired from the Lost and Found, are too expensive. I am taxed beyond the government.

192 Castoffs

"I'm doing laundry, kids. Give me your whites."

No answer.

I go to Elender's room, where she, Marcus, and a friend, Sarah, are working on an elaborate, wild jungly-type puzzle on the floor.

"I'm doing laundry, guys. Give me your whites, give me your poor, give me your hungry. Oh, and give me your darks."

It's winter again in our blacksmith home, and I notice Elen is wearing a glove on one hand. For someone as sensible as she has always been, she's awfully dramatic.

"Cold, Elen?"

"Not really. I lost my other glove. Thought I'd try to find it . . . Couldn't . . ."

She's fitting pieces together as if it were surgery.

"Oh. We'll go to the Lost and Found tomorrow," I say.

They know the drill.

Any Lost and Found will do. School, the YMCA, community centers, retirement homes. We ask for whatever item we need, making our request generic enough for a full viewing of the items. Elen or Marcus show a goofy gleam of recognition when they see something they need or want, sometimes grabbing at it and overdoing to the point of looking demented.

I corroborate, saying to the desk clerk, "Gosh, they've been looking for that blue-and-white headband for months," or "That's where it's been. I've been wondering where that jacket was. Your grandmother will be so happy!"

Then I talk to the clerk about how "their grandparents buy them everything" as the children rifle through the goods.

So far, we have a collection of wool headbands, mittens, snow pants, boots, and fleece sweatshirts. I love handing out winter gear to children who visit us. It's fine if they never return it, because it's not ours to keep. As I tell my children, "We're like *The Borrowers Afloat*."

Keeping afloat, with the castoffs of our affluent neighbors. Everything I get for free is literally a lifesaver.

193 Little White Dogs

Her eloquence needs no preamble. Elender continues to show me more excerpts from the "divorice" journal she's keeping:

> *Another time when I went to my dad's house I had to go to two soccer games. Now these were my last games of the season. The first game was at the same time as a barbacue my dad's girlfriend was having. Her name is Mary I like her very much and I know she's not taking place of my mom. She has two cute little white dogs, I can pick them up. I love dogs. And I love her dogs. But I didn't get to go to my soccer game because we went to her barbacue. Also my dad asked me if my last game was very important to me. Of corse it was! My dad was invited to a Sunday brunch the time of my last soccer game. But I got to go to my soccer game. What a releaf! But my brother and I both had a party afterwards my brother got to go to his party. My dad took me to my party for fifteen minutes and made me leave. I had to get my trofie early. I had to go because it was time I was supost to be droped of at my mom's house. I trided to call her but she wasn't home. My friend's mom said she would take me home at the end of the party. But nooooo. My dad had to take me home. Guess what right when we left mom got to the party. My dad dropped me off at my house and left my brother and I at home even though my mom was not home. All the girls on my soccer team felt sorry for me and told my mom to bring me back. So I went back and had a blast even though a lot of people left allready.*

CLUE NUMBER EIGHT

You're trying to love, but all you do is lose it.

194 — Fairy

Actually, I do not believe in divorce. I do not believe that love, real love, the love we had (oh, did we?) can die. I do not believe in fairies, but I told my children I did. They asked me to describe the fairy I saw when I was five years old.

"Small enough to comfortably fit into a tulip. Blond hair with reddish sun streaks. Green dress made from leaves, tied at the waist with vine. Light pink wings with golden tips."

"Mom, I think you are mistaking a river fairy," says Elen, who knows from fairies. "The flower ones' dresses are made from petals."

Because I described it over and over, my fairy, hailing from lily pad or blossom, lives on. And on this very page, my once love, is doing the same.

I do believe in love.

I do believe in love.

I do believe in love.

195 — Lasso

When Elender and Marcus were toddlers, they had different tolerances for affection. Marc was what Tobin called a *Schmusehase,* which means a rabbit that cuddles all day long. Tobin called Elen *Quaselhund,* meaning chattering dog, our English equivalent of "chatterbox." I relished these German nicknames. It reminded me of high school, when I translated everything possible into Native Indian.

Although an affectionate child in other ways, Elen had to be practically lassoed to get a hug. She flitted about her environment, commenting, asking questions.

Marcus draped himself across any available parent at all times. As adorable as he might have been, the way he fell like a rag doll on top of Tobin in public was irritating.

Elender sat through any concert or play, straight-backed and raptly attentive; Marcus slouched, started to whine, and would climb into Tobin's lap.

No matter what Marcus did, he received no discipline from Tobin. This could have been a good thing, and some might have mistaken it for unconditional love, but I saw it up close and personal. It was called babying. I saw it as German patriarchal favoritisming. It struck me then that he didn't seem to baby Elen at all.

A few years after the divorce, in a restaurant on Mother's Day, Marcus will be yelling. "You hate Dad and you want me to hate him too."

"Get over it, Marc. That's the past," says Elen.

"Plus," I say, "I don't hate your dad, and I would never want you to hate your dad."

But it's just blah-blah to him and he continues to yell, "Yeah, right. You can't even talk to him."

Elen gets up. "You are embarrassing me," she says in a stage whisper. "I'm leaving."

I follow her out since she's not quite a teenager and I don't trust her outside in the big bad world yet. Maybe when she's thirty. And carries a Beretta.

I come back to Marcus, who's openly crying in public.

He's still the little boy in his dad's arms, making a public display of his boredom. No tears, Claire. This is your son's show.

I excuse myself to the washroom.

Looking into the bathroom mirror, I say, "Claire, be strong now. Let him talk. Let him get it off his chest. Anything it takes to make him healthy. After he knows you've listened, be silent. Then tell him something real."

"Marcus," I say when I return, without a hint of vulnerability, "let's go outside and you can tell me whatever you want."

We walk outside and Elen pretends she doesn't know us.

"You say nice things about our dad, sure," he says, "but you always have a certain tone of voice."

It would be hard to take on any day, but especially on Mother's Day when I'd like to pat myself on the back, tone of voice and all.

After he's finished, Elen comes over and delivers her little sting. "Way to go, Markie, a real happy Mother's Day."

We all walk, in silence, to the car.

When we are in front of our house, I tell Elen to go inside. "I need to talk to Marc for a few minutes."

"Oh yeah, make me feel guilty," Marc says.

"No, you're within your rights," I say. "Elen, we'll be in soon."

She walks up the sidewalk elegantly. Even at this awkward age, she's perfectly poised.

"Marcus," I say, "I understand what you've been saying. You've said a lot about how 'I' feel: how I felt about your dad, why we were divorced. What 'I' think, and so forth."

Marcus seems to be listening. Miracle.

"The only thing I want to say is this: You keep saying 'my dad, my dad.' I want you to understand that I know the man. His name is Tobin. He was my husband. I know him, maybe better than you and Elen ever will. I stood by him. I was proud of him. I loved him and I will always love him for making you two great kids."

No tears, no tears, I tell myself.

Think of the invisible lasso. This time, it's Marcus you have to pull close. Without touching him.

PART FIVE

Love is blind; divorce sees with a vengeance.

PERSEVERANCE

In the land of no longer, I rouse the girl I was. She is alone on a wheat-colored hill with her older sister's bicycle. She can't reach the seat, so she straddles the back fender. Metal heat sears her thighs; but nothing, not even an oversized bike, will keep her from learning to ride today. She tries again and again to find the balance of the wheel, falls again and again until the sun is leaving the day.

With legs and hands outstretched like a starfish, she rides down the hill, the hot sting of wind against her bloody knees. She is not someone's sister, not her mother's child, or someone's future wife.

She is four and a half years old, silhouetted against the hill, proud of her speed, thirsty, and aching to glide, to be just me.

196 **Cheese-sitting**

I look back at our earliest years—like someone peering through a drug-induced high, realizing how good it is and how crummy reality is—and am alarmed to see a few snakes among the rose petals. Not necessarily poisonous but distinctly cautionary.

I'm visiting Tobin in Germany to meet his parents. It's after the floorquake but before my dizzy departure. My mother is coming soon to visit us and her daughter's future in-laws. It's a peripheral trip before she focuses on Rémy in a hotel in Paris.

Apparently, my cleaning of the kitchen and laying on of the linens have defied the German *Ordnung* code. Tobin is standing over me, unable to quite put it into words. But that won't stop him. He finds a mop and bucket and pointedly reswirls invisible dirt on the floor. Then he smooths and retucks the bed linens. He changes the pillow slips to actually match the fitted sheet. Good point, really.

If he hadn't been hedging about a firm date for our marriage, his domestic ardor wouldn't have caused me to phone our friends Christa and Bernhardt and ask them to let me spend the weekend with them. If he hadn't met me on the Strassenbahn the day before and refused to talk to me during the trip because I had worn the "wrong outfit" to go dancing, I wouldn't be bailing.

As it happens, Christa and Bernhardt are going to be out of town anyway, so I can crash there.

Tobin stares as I pack a few things and then he says, "Where are you going?"

"To Christa's."

"Really."

"*Ja,*" I say.

"Okay . . . I'll drive you?"

"Fine."

Christa kisses me and Tobin, then ushers us into her place. She gives me a few instructions about the plants. Bernhardt hands me a pile of papers. Alarming. He's an artist in the kitchen, involved with a cooking cult that cultivates pigs to eat certain herbs so they won't have to be seasoned later. Double gag. Why don't they just mutate them into having no bones? Oh wait, that's what they sort of do to veal calves.

Anyway, Bernhardt is making cheese. It doesn't bear repeating how and where he obtained the original milk, but the instructions are encyclopedic. He briefs me. The top of the page is headed: Turning *(Drehen)*. I never dreamed turning a milky blob could be so complex. Each turn is done using fractions of the entire mass, and is completed every four hours. This is worse than having a dog. On page three, a reference to the full moon makes me wonder if we are concocting a potion. If the moon is full, I must refrain from turning the cheese up to twelve hours, depending on the coloration of the blob.

"Make sure," says Bernhardt, pointing specifically to page three, "you follow all the directions."

"I'll try."

"It's very important," he stresses.

And so is the Geneva convention, but it doesn't have as many pages.

Christa gives me a conspiratorial roll of the eyes.

"Danke," they both say, and shut the door behind them.

"Can I spend the night?" Tobin asks.

"Do you know when there's a full moon?" I ask.

"Why?" he asks. "Are you going to bite my neck?"

I can't help it; I already miss him, and I'll need help turning the cheese.

197 Personal Banker

But now, breakdown or no breakdown, I need to start thinking about providing for my children. I feel like a driver seeing a police car approaching and trying to act normal.

While the divorce is pending, I receive some money from Tobin, but it's only half what I need just to squeak by. Then he loses a large commission. There are less-than-charitable rumors that he did it on purpose to avoid paying child support. I don't want to go there. All I know is that the money flow dwindles to little driblets, and I'm running on almost empty. Later he'll move to Germany, where he'll send money even more erratically and never in the agreed-upon amount.

Talk of money gives me that inadequate feeling, and then a raging migraine.

If I were a different type of woman, I'd have quickly landed a job in a bank, perhaps as a personal banker. But since I'm me, I can only too easily picture my first day on the job.

CUSTOMER:	I think I have an overdraft, could you check my account?
ME:	Sure. Yes, you're a few hundred in the negative.

CUSTOMER:	Oh God! I don't know how I'll pay the rent.
ME:	Oh, that's easy. We're a bank. We have lots of money downstairs. Just go help yourself.
CUSTOMER:	Thanks. This is a bank that works!

The truth is I've been fired from almost every job—except modeling and any job connected with the art world—throughout my life. I tried waitressing once and was fired on the first day for drawing portraits of the customers on the back of their checks.

At one point during the years in limbo, before my divorce is final, concerned friends help me get a job at Northwestern University, slouching over some computer work. At that time, I don't own a computer nor have I ever actually touched one.

At the campus office, no matter how hard I try, I am utterly unable to concentrate on anything that is said to me. The only thing I can recall is socializing with some people during lunch breaks. Alone at my desk, I am in a stupor.

Although I'm sure I have been told and retold, I don't have the slightest clue what I am supposed to be doing. After a couple of weeks when I still haven't done even one keystroke of work, my boss takes me aside. She fires me in a friendly fashion: She pays me double to leave. Either she knows how emotionally disturbed I am or she is making sure I leave quickly without doing more damage.

I am frightened when people ask me, "What do you do?"

"I'm self-retired," I could say.

When people see my creative work, they go talent-scout-hysterical and exclaim, "It's criminal that your music, poetry, artwork isn't out there!" Usually they use the G-word. So what? Maybe I don't want my stuff out there. I mean, have you seen what's out there? I'm not denigrating other artists—although I've been known to—I'm referring to our culture's idea of worldly recognition. It's one vapid success story after another, hardworking Americans, particularly women who are the first generation to get the glaring green light to go for the green. To avoid the sin of sloth we must pull ourselves up by the thongstrap and become famous. Rich. Exhausted.

Of course, I'm exhausted too. It takes a lot of energy to engage in full-time underachievement.

In truth, I count my children as two jobs. I dare not tell this to any of my lawyer/surgeon turbo-mom friends, although, in my defense, they themselves have hired help and chauffeurs.

Speak to me, spirit of procreation and spirit of careers, tell me what to do. And I'll con-inertly (as opposed to pro-actively) do it.

After the Northwestern fiasco, I don't know how to cash in on my newfound leisure time. I find myself looking for a job, or so I tell people, including my father, who pays for my children to go to an expensive Northwestern summer camp. Actually, I go to Lighthouse Beach, next to the beach where my children are, and sleep the summer away in tall prairie grasses. Of course, *sleep* would be too lively a word; I am unconscious from mornings until afternoons, barely making it home as Elen and Marc jump off their camp bus. I am a sunscreen-slathered, bikini-bathing malingerer in hot sand and grass until one afternoon I wake to a stranger stroking my bare foot. I look at him and start opera-singing so he will know I am insane and therefore not attack me. Then I walk slowly away from him, clamber up a hill, and run to my car.

I don't know where to go.

198 **Personal Detective**

But I really must get a job. Said like a true addict trying to stop free-timing. I once imitated Roseanne Barr and Madonna for an industrial movie. "Hotels are an open door for anyone having a bad day," I said in Roseanne's brazen nasal. Madonna was more subdued, always verging on sexy, "I live for large, fluffy towels. I really do."

The producer was a friend. Now he is taking a break from producing to run his father's private investigation business. The office is only two blocks from our house.

"Can I work for you?" I ask him.

"Sure," he says, hiring me on the spot. "The best private detectives are actresses, performers like you. And I promise you, Claire, you won't have to go through other people's garbages in back alleys. Someone else will do that!"

Nice job description.

I'm on the phone doing a British accent to gain some info when the line beeps with another phone call. I switch to the other line. It's "me own flesh and blood."

Elender is sobbing. "Marcus . . ."

"What! What happened to Marcus?!" I scream.

"Marcus slammed my hand in the door . . . twice!" she whimpers.

"What? Do you realize I'm at work? And I can understand once, but twice, now that is stupid. Of you!"

I thought they would be fine home alone for a few hours, since I'm only two blocks away. I leave immediately and never go back.

A few months later, in the dead of winter, my detective boss/producer calls and asks me, "Can you do an on-camera spot?"

"Yes," I say, getting ready to disguise myself once again.

199 Vox

I'm thinking, "It would be nice to receive checks in the mail rather than bills." There must be a way. This percolates in my brain as I look over the frozen lake on my pre–crack of dawn strolls with my children.

Then it occurs to me: Quentin has done some voice-over, and he receives checks in the mail.

After a lunch meeting with him, I decide to make a demo. He coaches me through the development and production of my tape. After it's finished, I submit it to his agent, who represents the biggies like Margaret Travolta. Quentin warns me that the chances of the agent taking me on are "very slim."

A week slithers by.

Miraculously, the agent phones me and says, "The tape is great. You are just the creative person we are looking for."

I'm beginning to find my voice.

200 Knowing When to Leave

Friends are more than friends now; they are safe havens.

I hold on to sturdy objects in their houses like a drowning person gripping onto a lifesaver.

When friends ask me to stay for tea, I say yes a little too vibrantly.

I stay too long.

Or don't leave at all.

I become a family member.

201 Marcus

He needs his own chapter. Alas, his own book. He's the one I'm worried about. Forget Tobin, forget me, understand Elender, but remember, always remember Marcus, whose life is the boy's life—treacherous at best, but now plummeting and perhaps ruined. He writes with his left hand, which makes his handwriting eccentric and grown-uppy:

My Dad left our house and I started playing video games a lot.

202 Lachrymation

The electricity has been cut off—uncanny how quickly the bill will be paid tomorrow—and I'm writing *slamDUNK* by candlelight:

> You'll be hemorrhaging tears during this breakup. This is normal. You are not a robot. All of your childhood fears and feelings of abandonment will rush at you like water unleashed from a broken dam. Shedding tears will relieve pressure. Weeping is the job you must do (without pay), but avoid this work in front of your children. If this is impossible, tell them honestly, "Yes, Mommy is sad, but she'll feel better soon." (Or you'll find her strung up in the bathroom tomorrow morning.) Not to worry.

203 Turning Liabilities into Assets

A glass of soy milk on my night table and the electricity is paid up. I'm set for another *slamDUNK* session:

> GIVING UP
> Popular wisdom deifies those who never give up.
> But if Stalin and Hitler had done it before the killing started, the world would be a different place.
> Giving up can be necessary, even advisable during the termination of a marriage.
> No matter what you may rationalize, both sides are causing harm, doing wrong, and committing crimes against good karma. It is difficult to keep ahead of the negative feelings you will experience.
> Just giving up for a day or so can bring tremendous relief. Simply go to bed and do nothing. The luxury of escape will rejuvenate you until your next dive under the covers.

204 Tumbleweed

When I grew up, families seemed anchored to their particular home on a particular street. Like stars, I oriented myself by them: *Turn right at the Wilsons' house, left at the Schumans', go a couple more blocks past the Brinkers' and the Lowells'. You've gone too far if you get to the Taylors'.*

I knew where I was going because they stayed. The biggest news we heard was that someone was moving. Their father had taken a better job and they were moving to another state!

Now I seem to spend all my time moving.

Everyone moves, even stores—Hoos Drugstore on the corner seemed rooted for life, but poof, it's a corporate bagel deli that's rarely open.

From the time I met Tobin to the time my divorce is final, I will have moved more times than I can remember. My generation is the tumbleweed gang. Rolling to gather more speed, we find we can pick up and lose everything at the same time.

205 Timeframe

Meeting in Chicago: 1 life-changing night
Proposal of marriage: 28 what-took-you-so-long days
Length of engagement: 9 delicious months
Honeymoon: 5 fabulous, hungry days
Move to Germany, children's births: 4 sleepless years
Move to Chicago: 2 semisweet years and 1 bitter year
From filing to divorce decree: 3 sour years

Years together: 11
Good years: 4
Bad years: 8
Good and bad years overlapping: 2
Total time wasted: ?

206 What I Looked Like Then, What I Look Like Now

I didn't drive until I was thirty-three, so it took longer for my butt to start conforming to the seat of the car. At about forty-one, I noticed the difference: My ass cheeks looked like two little badly formed hamburgers.

Hamburger patties can define a woman. Ask my friend in California who complained about her mother: "She didn't care enough to even form the hamburgers she made for dinner."

I thought then that I would do better, but I don't even feed my children hamburgers.

I am actually almost short, but everyone thinks I'm gobs taller. I have long limbs, typical of those born under a full moon (Moon When the Limbs Stretch Their Stuff), and until forty-one or forty-two could be called "willowy." These days I'm just "weeping."

My older sister, Catherine, told me, "At forty, the knees will go." She was wrong—it hasn't happened yet (knock on Formica)—just as she was wrong about my children's honeymoon being over at age seven and eight, and wrong again about them drifting apart at ten and eleven. They are still like a little married couple, affectionate, locking arms when they walk. Of course they bicker occasionally (like a married couple), but they make up with a hug and entwine their feet as they sit on opposite sides of my daughter's bed doing homework.

Who knew hair would turn out to be almost as important as marriage. Or love. Or sex and death.

My hair was Rapunzel-like long from age twenty-two to forty-two. It is still thick and lustrous, although it dried out a bit when I started reducing the gray.

Now it is shoulder-length, a tricolored blond flag that waves tirelessly, signaling, *I'm still attractive; I coulda been a contenda. . . .*

When it was short and very blond, before I married, at least five people a day told me, "You look like Princess Di." When it grew long again, they said Meryl Streep. Before that, when I hennaed my hair, I was Diane Keaton, Vanessa Redgrave with a mix of Audrey Hepburn, and while living in Paris, I was often told I looked like "Jean-Ef-Kennedee." How's about I look like a woman, *n'est-ce pas*? Brigitte Bardot? Later, in Evanston, when my children were toddlers, and I pursued a music career, my photo sessions showed a kittenish, Bardot-ish me at the grand piano. Now some say I'm exactly Julianne Moore without the pancake-flat profile. That's okay by me, since I think she's a great actress. Keep up the comparisons, I say. Maybe someday, I'll actually look like myself.

207 Tits & Ass

When I was young, I couldn't fathom the American fixation on large ones. To me, they seemed like sandbags one would have to lug around. I can appreciate them now. I gawk and ruminate at amply endowed women. Wow, nice knockers. Where can I get me some of those?

When I was growing up in Evanston, our father would take our family of six children to the Playboy Club in Chicago. It was pleasant, actually, and I never felt the slightest need to emulate the heaving chests under the bunny garb. They were a curiosity. They were, well, Bunnies—from my underdeveloped point of view, cute and probably particularly fond of carrots.

Every boyfriend of mine seemed satisfied with my cute breasts. Maybe that's because my first boyfriend Clive was gay. Or maybe he just loved me.

My next major six-year relationship was with the young aforementioned British man I met at Oxford named Rick.

"The smaller the better, darling," he always said.

I roomed in a convent where, most evenings, I sneaked him in my bedroom. As the nuns made a bedroom check, he hid in the closet. He was brilliant and irresistible—his talkative shyness, his wit, his impeccable way of loving me. At the bottom of the closet near my shoes, I found a note from him: "Marry me. Or I'll grab the nun's foot."

For years we corresponded like an almost married couple, floating our feelings out over the thrashing ocean between us.

His best friend played guitar in a rock band called Ugly Rumours along with Tony Blair, the lead singer. Yes, Tony Blair. Apparently I met him hundreds of times at pubs and parties. They both still hang out with him. Good for you, Tony, old chap. You didn't choose a wife with big ones.

All my lovers have found my bum irresistible, as do most people, even now. It is extremely round, and people, even children, have the peculiar habit of grabbing it, squeezing it, and hitting it like a volleyball. Baffling, really. I don't go up to an appealing ass and mess with it. What up? When I turn around or go upstairs in front of someone (even women!), I feel the urge to put my hand on my rear to protect it. But I don't, because that seems ridiculous, and whack, they get me! But for most guys I know, the ass is an aside. Only the breasts are worthy of soliloquy.

After breast-feeding my two children, my breasts became a bit larger. I still didn't always need to wear a bra, though, which seemed a blessing. This fashion anomaly alone was enough to get me leered at in stores and parks. Similarly, my unshaven legs provoked consternation and lust.

A white man followed me as I double-strolled my children. "Let me give you my razor!" he screamed. A black man said softly as I passed by, "Ooooh, I wanna suck on it. I never seen a white woman with hair on her legs." Imagine me on the North Shore. Or don't. It feels like Italy anyway, with everyone grabbing for a piece of my ass.

When I was a preteen, I suffered under the great injustice that boys can go bare-chested and girls can't. I took my shirt off whenever possible to prove the world wrong. As a teenager, I would bare my chest on a dare from my friends and sit cross-legged with them on a busy street corner.

Hurray to those many women who scale mountains topless.

My breasts are the pages of a book opened in the middle.

208 Elevator Phobia

It starts innocuously, as most miseries do. Perhaps it began when the children started fearing empty rooms.

I find myself chewing over whether anywhere I have to go will have an elevator. I'm in danger of a panic attack just thinking about getting into the metal box alone.

As a matter of policy, I'm almost overfriendly to strangers in nonclaustrophobic situations. Enclose me in an elevator with anyone, though, and we become long-lost best friends.

"Nice weather they're having out there where there's weather," I fairly shout to my elevator buddies as I go to a job interview. "Do you work in this building?" I ask as I return from the disastrous interview. I don't care if they're ex-cons, or if they think I'm pushy—I have to engage.

If I hadn't gotten stuck in the elevator on floor seven of the court building on West Jackson in Chicago with twenty other sweating pre-divorcées, would I be normal? I wasn't before. (After that episode, I walk the seven flights to Domestic Court, telling the panting lawyer by my side I need the exercise.) Is that when my elevator-thang all started?

But I remember years earlier, before I was even married. I was on my way to a friend's apartment when the elevator stalled between floors and the building manager had to pull me out.

I suppose my ele-phobia has always been there, simmering, but as most things that used to trouble me just a little, it's much more difficult to handle these days.

Now when I'm alone, rising or falling in a vertical steel coffin, pressing buttons frantically and trying to quell my panic, I feel like Lazarus when the doors open and I walk out alive again.

But then I start to think about the next time I'll have to take an elevator. I fix on the darkness of the shaft. I would like to be on terra firma at all times. Because if there is a screeching crash, I'll be to blame and my children will ask, "Why did she get into that elevator?"

209 Rain Memory

> Western wind, when wilt thou blow
> The small rain down can rain?
> Christ, that my love were in my arms
> And I in my bed again!
> —ANONYMOUS

The first week after Tobin and I met.

When drops of rain touched our hair, we felt them as kisses. We ran until we slipped with soggy grocery bags. We shivered to get closer, and broke off wet chocolate into each other's mouths.

210 Hypno-wrappers

The wrappers of candy bars are hypnotic. One minute I'm thinking about the yellow-orange paper of a Butterfinger (they rule over Snickers), and seconds later, I am driving my car to a 7-Eleven, walking zombielike to the counter for the inevitable purchase of a king-sized one. I never buy the regular minuscule size, because if there's even an infinitesimal chance of an earthquake, the power may go out and the stores will all close.

211 A Gazillion Snickers Bars

Forgive me, I never read it, but I've heard about a magazine article called "The Snickers Diet." Apparently, the author chronicles herself falling in love and being so smitten, she can eat nothing but Snickers bars—five to ten a day—and losing a ton of weight within a week. Talk about junk food justice.

I'm losing weight at an alarming rate anyway, due to my food-preparation phobia, but I sometimes wonder if I take on the Snickers Diet, would I gain or lose since I'm falling *out of* rather than *in* love?

212 Wailing

This—my fucked-up life—is the whole orchestra. Sonorous and portending oboes blend into capricious flutes, tickling and giggling their way toward oblivion. Trumpets bully and clarinets warn. Accompanied by enduring string-wail, the cataclysmic kettledrums thump their way to a final reckoning.

But my life is still *music*.

213 Sweet Savior

Snickers, Butterfingers? Fuck that. For a real catastrophe, you've got to smallify. Readiness to run is key. I stock up on candy corn. Fill an entire shopping cart. Watch others stare. (They'll be doing it soon enough.)

214 Phone

The phone rings and I pick it up. Tobin's beautiful voice. But when he hears mine, his voice becomes cold. "Can I speak to the kids?"

"They're not here."

"Oh." Seems about to hang up.

"What's up?" My face flushes and my heart—oh, my heart—beats like a fiend.

"Wanted to change Wednesday night to Thursday."

"Fine. I'll—"

He hangs up.

My words are little ice picks.

215 Clocks

When Tobin left, he took every clock that worked.

I was late for everything, including dinner with Christopher (the Younger). When I finally arrived, he was already gone.

I can't even keep time.

216 Ninth Anniversary

The last anniversary we celebrated sticks in my throat. We barely made it to an Italian restaurant. Just before leaving for our reservation, Tobin raced out with the children to buy me roses.

During the meal, he unpacks several presents I had given him. After thanking me, he says, "You look sad."

"Not really."

"What?" he asks, but he looks away, as if shielding himself from the answer.

"You didn't get me anything?"

A long pause.

"The roses," he says.

And I start to cry.

We leave the restaurant and get in the white Mercedes.

As we're driving, my crying makes him angrier. He takes the whole bag with my card, drawings, and gifts and heaves it through the sunroof. I look back and see a child on a bicycle swerving to avoid it.

In silence, we enter our home.

After a few minutes, I go back outside and get in the car to try to find the bag.

It's a beautiful evening, weather-wise. The wind is warm and everyone is out enjoying the beginning of summer.

I remember thinking for the first time: This is the end of us.

217 What I Say

If I talk to anyone, I'm compelled to answer truthfully.

"I'm going through a divorce."

"Yes, I have children."

"They see their father every weekend."

"Oh, thanks, we'll get through it."

"We used to live in Germany."

"He's an artist—yes, we're both artists."

"You know Chicago Art Palace? He painted the mural inside."

"You're right, I guess that's what happens when two artists live together."

Or not.

218 Everywhere I Look Is the Past

Chicago Art Palace. The opening gala. The last nice time Tobin and I spent together. Live parrots adorn the trees in the atrium. Gold- and silver-painted semi-nude dancers gyrate to the noise of the crowds. Actors dressed as characters speak to you as if you too were in their story. The lavishness is reminiscent of the half-naked, gluttonous carnival party in Paris with Clive.

Tobin and I are entwined all night, dancing to the rhythm of jazz and rock bands, spinning closer to our beginning, middle, and end.

How could we have known that a few years later, we would dance separately in our seats, wearing the fuzz of the newly divorced? During our children's talent show, when Sheryl Crow's "All I Wanna Do" accompanies our children on stage, I can't help noticing Tobin and I are the only parents in the audience rocking out sitting down. Despite it all, we're still too hip to be squared, halved, or drawn and quartered.

It is sad to be connected by something so tenuous as a pop song. Strange to be moving to the same rhythm, knowing that we are sliding more offbeat. From the beginning, as if we were in a movie, music has soundtracked our relationship. We listened to Soft Cell's "Tainted Love" during our engagement. Mid-marriage, Tracy Chapman's "Fast Car" wailed from our stereo, and to commemorate our dissolution, Bonnie Raitt sang a soulful "I Can't Make You Love Me," which I reproduced, a cappella, in divorce court to the amazement of the clerk.

"Was that you singin'? I ain't never heard nobody sing nuthin' in divorce court," he said.

I write my own songs for our private soundtrack, starting with "Waldi," an instrumental tribute to my husband's birthplace, getting into more erotic terrain with "Geisha of Your Senses," and proceeding on to heavier subjects with "*Ce que tu veux et ce que je peux (c'est toujours contraire),*" "Blind Man," "You Said You'd Love Me Forever (And Now You Say It's Not True)" to the time just before the divorce decree, when I wrote the anthem "I Will Live to See a Better Day." Then I wrote "Old Glory," "What I Called You Then, What I Call You Now," and "Won't You Take Me with You (By the River Falls)."

During the many court appearances, I sing my most recent lyrics whenever the judge recesses. As his robe recedes, my voice gets louder like a stereo blasted high. As he returns to slam down his judgment, I lower my volume.

Tobin and his lawyer barely restrain themselves from rolling their eyes. I am giddy inside. No one can take that away.

Tobin looks like the good German burgher in a checked suit coat. (I would have divorced him earlier if he had ever worn that with me.) Her Incompetency—the name my fourth lawyer gives Tobin's lawyer—looks like a rodent, skinny and thin-haired. She looks down at her files, then smirks at me—an artist, and a housewife/mother.

My lawyer Kevin from the law firm I rename Hither, Thither, and Yon advises me to wear sunglasses to hide my tears. He says, "Female tears are a manipulation judges just hate." Still, behind the dark lenses, the tears slide down.

When the legal proceedings are boring or intolerably intense, as was the fight over the Bösendorfer piano, I write music in my head, tap the rhythm on the court bench, and stamp my foot lightly on the hallowed floors. Maybe they think I have Tourette's. The music drifts in, is heralded by vibrations from an anxious drum—my heart.

219 What I'd Like to Say

I wonder if other people share my occasional aversion to mundane reality?

Each day, I want to answer the questions about my marital status in whatever way I fancy.

"I'm happily married to a proctologist. I miss him so much. He's doing research in Ghana on village elders' butts."

"Yes, the children and I will see him during the Christmas holidays; we'll go on an African safari—can't wait."

Or:

"No, I've never been married."

"No children either, but I have a cat—does that count?"

"No, I live alone."

"I'm a nonpracticing nymphomaniac."

The truth casts its darkness and I walk the day elongated with memory's gnawing. If I could tell lies, I might start believing them. Maybe I could get over the truth, jump over my own shadow. *Über meinen Schatten springen.*

220 Rubble

I take many steps backwards.

Surveying the dissolute landscape of my marriage, I squint at the distant horizon where siblings and parents wave.

There is the real father now and the former young man who took the hands of small girls—my sisters and me—taught us to flip off the side of a living blue pool. The sun-warmed water splashes fear away.

There is the real mother who forms poetry out of the ocean to Paris, and there is the shell where we all started, hovering to hear the original sea hush.

There are my sisters, married, divorced, married again, with degrees, with children, with less than their due and rarely more, and the beautiful little naked girls who are us in the sprinkler on a humid August day in Chicago.

We are paper dolls, and I can clothe us for any remembered occasion. I can re-see the smiles, the trust, a child's easy happiness; but it is also a warning. This doesn't last. Nothing ever does. Images are all I have left: Now I must rescue them.

Father, Mother, sisters, brothers, you are all testimony to the present, yet part of a dusty tableau, serving as backdrop for the wreckage to come. If the past menaces, it's because we can't live it again.

There will be failures, deep ones, and laughter that abrades some of its pain. What surfaces is a buoyant feeling of "Look at me; I'm still here," and along with it, a recalled love that comforts my confused, conflicted heart.

Careful.
One look backwards brings suspicion.
Did it really happen that way?

PART SIX

A man in the bed is worth two at the gym.

CHASTE

Day after day after day after day.

No kisses for you, she tells herself.

Night after night after night after night after night.

No stroking for you, my dear.

No one, not even a randy stranger sidling up to you and outlining the contours of your breast with his palm (this didn't happen much before the divorce either), reaching up under your shirt to touch a nipple, holding your long hair like reins to lead you to the alley behind your children's school, to bend you over near the Dumpster with all the uneaten lunches brimming over, the stench reaching your nostrils as he grabs you from behind, and you look up at the cloudless sky and wonder who you are and who he is and how you got there—and if you'll be arrested.

No one furtively watching you during Mass while your children sing in the choir and that same no one eating you with his eyes until you leave the pew, walk into the stiff bushes circumscribing the courtyard rectory and wait until he pushes you against the cold stone slabs of the church until he is deeper inside you than any religious belief.

Nope, none of that.

No licking or fucking with your mouth, or looking into each other's eyes or the air above your body and his body, imagining nothing but what you see and feel in places where others have been, and will be again.

No, nothing anymore quite like having him hold your throat as he splits your legs apart with a nudge of his knee, and you silence the keening as his tip pushes into you, making the sound of a cherry skin popping from its seed.

No, no, nothing now like any of that for you, she whispers into her hands.

221 Faith

You can only predict averages, not individual events.
—QUANTUM PHYSICS

It has now officially been two years since I've been in a serious (think smiley face with a frown and furrowed eyebrows) relationship with a man.

Childlike as it seems, to the very last moment, I believe Tobin and I might still get back together. I don't want us to, but belief is stronger than volition or need. Unless faith is need-based.

And not all of us need faith.

222 Into Each Life a Little Litigation Must Fall

Like any normal person, I will readily admit my failings, when bludgeoned.

223 Perfection Recipe

First, always take a train. The train ride itself, with its rocking and smooth gliding, invariably gets one in fighting trim for an erotic rendezvous. Don't doubt the power of wearing a skirt when reaching up to put one's luggage on the rack above; the foreplay of a handsome stranger helping you guide it into place amidst all the masculine briefcases; the conductor leaning over to look down your blouse as he nips your ticket with his ticket-puncher; the slim body of a sailor as he sidles past in the narrow corridor; the businessman's elbow nudging yours as his smoke whizzes out the open train window. Your lover is waiting, but your adventure has already begun. Which man is at the end of the line is your choice, but the journey is full of variables. If you are observant and ready for adventure, you will reach your goal.

At age twenty while abroad, I discovered how to concoct the sweetest memories from a few ingredients. I arrive in Paris from Aix, where I've been studying. Rick, my British lover who looks like Bob Dylan (what was I thinking?), is flying in from London. The hotel is of the cheap-but-clean variety, where a chambermaid turns down the bed covers and gives you a knowing glance. How I'd like to have her role for a day! I wash, eschewing Napoléon's famous words to his Josephine in favor of my motto, "Always smell excellent everywhere."

Waiting for Rick to let himself in with the second key the erotically savvy concierge gives out to latecomers, I slip naked between the unfamiliar scent of the sheets. Already I know how good this is going to be.

224 Christopher

Rick was a long time ago, before the men who follow, before Tobin. I imagine them linking arms, forming a kumbaya circle, before I arrive to break it up.

It seemed almost impossible, given my psychotically strong feelings of loyalty, that anyone, even if a judge ordered it, could have come after my husband. But someone did. He first appeared during my happy years with Tobin.

"We've been married many times in past lives," he says spookily, touching my arm.

"Where are my alimony checks for the last century?"

A sad smile wafts across his face, and he offers me his hand as if it were a lotus blossom.

"I'm Christopher, and I know your name is Claire."

I'm the demo person at a health food store—my job du jour—and Christopher works in the produce section. For hours, I've been serving organic zucchini bread to the middle class.

As I'm cleaning up my demo station for the day, he offers to wash the dishes and pans I've used.

"No, thanks. I can do it," I say.

"Let me, seriously. So you can get home to your kids."

In a matter of weeks he's babysitting for my children, who are four and five at the time.

He brings me purple flowers.

"The color of our spirits," Christopher says.

"Why does Christopher bring you flowers?" my husband, Tobin, asks.

"I don't know," I answer.

I really don't.

A girl his same age, in the meat section, informs me that Christopher, age twenty-one, has a terrible crush on me.

"That's ridiculous; he's a puppy," I tell her.

When I demo Tofu Pups the next weekend, Christopher is no longer there. The meat girl tells me he's been sent away for a while.

"He's a badass," she says, giving me a knowing glance, as if I were their peer.

Years later, a few weeks after Tobin suggests we end our marriage, I take out the card Christopher gave me weeks ago when we met in Winnetka, by chance, in a five-and-dime. After warming it in my palm, I finally play a little number on the touch-tones of the phone.

He answers.

"There's a coffee shop in the city that serves organic chai," he says. "Your favorite."

We meet there the next day; his tight hug revives more than the chai. He has grown up, evidenced by his newfound humor.

"May divorce be with you," he says, shaking my hand.

He's still a *Star Wars* freak. He's also a martial arts student in the body of an angel—tall and graceful with a blond ponytail halfway down his back.

I explain my situation. His touch on my cheek is as light as breath.

"You are having trouble breathing," he says.

"How can you tell?"

"I do bodywork; I can help."

"Okay," I say, not entirely sure what bodywork is.

"Someday, I'll climb up the outer wall into your bedroom as soon as the Hun's asleep," he says, tightening the rubber band on his ponytail.

"Okay," I say, hoping but not thinking he's serious.

225 Dream Closet

Tobi, you invite me to your new house.

The children appear in the doorway, squirming and tapping their feet as we talk.

You give me a dress from your closet, bounty from a current girlfriend.

I thank you and try it on, floral silk on a salmon background.

"Beautiful, beautiful girl," you say in a tone bland as a cotton swab.

Why do I rip the dress off my body?

A voice drips from the ceiling.

"No guarantees, remember, no guarantees."

I fold into your arms, calm in your too Teutonic cool.

It seems better now.

226 Bodywork

A few days after the café, Christopher calls, asks if he can come over.

"I'm taking four girls to the opera and I need to change my clothes. I'd really like it if you'd come too," he says.

"Thanks, Christopher, that's very sweet, but you go with your friends."

"It'd be good for you to get out, Claire. We could go to a shop, somewhere in Lincoln Park, and I'll buy you a dress."

How does he know that's where my favorite boutique is?

"You're an angel," I say. "Really. But another time."

"But I can come over and change? It would save me an extra trip into the Loop."

"Okay," I say.

Ten minutes later, we're alone at my house. My sister has picked up my children for an overnight with their cousins at their sprawling cottage overlooking a ravine. Tobin is at work and, if my short-term memory serves, will not be home until four in the morning.

Christopher orders out Thai for us. He seems to know my favorite things without asking. Pad Thai, with extra lime, spring rolls with extra cilantro, no meat.

From his duffel bag, he pulls out a suit in a plastic dry cleaning bag, the receipt still stapled to it. He takes off his T-shirt.

"I'll . . . I'll let you get dressed," I say, and walk out of the room into the kitchen, where I clutch the edge of a table.

He follows me, half-naked, and towering above, strokes my hair, massages my scalp.

Out of what could have been silence if my heart hadn't sounded like a drum in a rock and roll band, I suddenly want to make amends.

"I have to tell you that I'm sorry for the way I treated you in the past. I was always sarcastic and you didn't deserve . . ."

He sits me down on the kitchen chair.

"Claire, you are so good."

He kneels. Help!

"Everything you touch is so . . . lovely. You make beauty all around, in your house, at the store, for your kids. . . . And Tobin, he expects it as nothing less than his due. Or he pisses on it. I never could understand you two together."

He gets up, walks to the other room and comes back, throwing a soccer ball at me. "I got this for your son; I thought he might need it."

I'm stunned. I'd been worrying all day about how to buy him one. Money seems as short as my breath these days.

"Thank you," I say as he leaves to meet with his friends. "You're amazing."

Very late that evening, I hear pebbles against my window. Peering out into a full-moon night, I see Christopher starting up the wall. Who else could it be? But it doesn't seem possible, and even with my excellent imagination, I really can't imagine myself in bed with anyone except my husband, who is sleeping on a cot across the hall.

There are ways, of course, to have sex without having sex. It's called multitasking. Christopher might call it a type of bodywork.

"You need bodywork," is what he says.

He would tell me: The lungs are being cleared, lymphatic system stimulated, the neck muscles released, and the hips aligned. When I push his hands away, he goes for my feet. Wonder of wonders, even the feet can be stroked into a therapeutic stance; different points on the arch corresponding to inner organs—the heart being one I thought was broken but that, according to the point on my sole, is beating splendidly.

Christopher whispers as he glides over my stomach.

"This is your prosperity window. I ask that you take in and receive the wealth that is yours. Everything will be better, Claire, Claire."

His index finger traces my hipbone.

It's amazing how numb and aroused one can be at the same time. I strain to reach his chest. Gently pushing me back on the pillow, he says, "Don't worry about me. I want you to be happy."

"Happy isn't imaginable; I'll just try 'better,'" I say.

"How can I make it better?" he asks, with his hand on my pubic bone.

And then inching down to a point that corresponds to a total cure, his thumb circles softly.

> CLUE NUMBER NINE
>
> *You want a new life, but you'll settle for a new sex life.*

227 Smell

The olfactory sense is the only sense that is connected to the hypothalamus. This in turn is responsible for memories. Using the thighbone's-connected-to-the-hipbone logic, when we smell, we remember. Proust can attest!

So can I.

I remember the smell of the first mouth I kissed at three years old. He called me his Garbage Can Queen because we had our trysts in the alley near the garbage can. It's amazing, but every time we talk on the phone, almost forty years later, I can call to mind his scent.

It's not Old Spice or lemon or Eau de Garbage. Some men just smell right. Sadly, Christopher smells wrong.

228 As I Lay Divorcing

The most gratifying thing about having a young stud, however vulgar and enticing that may sound, is that when Tobin, who smelled right, finds out about Christopher, he'll be deutschly annoyed.

And if he ever finds out Christopher was in my bed while he slept across the hall, he won't like it that my orgasms were stretching bridges to him all night long.

229 Cereal Monogamy

I find it beyond cute that American males make themselves 747-sized bowls of cereal at night when they are feeling peckish. They also typically make themselves two sandwiches! Adorable. Correct me if I'm wrong, but I don't think females do that.

Without even knowing the club he belongs to, Christopher gets up.

"Got any cereal?"

230 Heterophamy

The expression in German is *Hier lacht Freud.* "Here laughs Freud." A Freudian slip does not indicate that Freud was a cross-dresser, although from what I've learned about his questionable theories that ensured his place in history, who really knows?

Whenever I take up with a man, I will at some point call him Tobin. Most notably, when we are arguing. And Freud laughs.

231 Arranged, Coerced Marriage

Roughly a year after we begin our affair, Christopher and I are summoned to the home of my Indian friends, the Sharmas.

"What do you mean, they want to talk to me?" Christopher asks. "I thought they liked me."

"They do, that's why they are concerned."

"Concerned?" Christopher says from his yoga pillow.

I don't mention to Christopher that I have told my angelic friends Dev and Kalpana about him and they seem to think he's a weasel, although they used the Hindi word that sounded like *kadu,* which translates roughly into "pumpkinhead."

"They simply want to invite us over to talk," I say after a deep inhalation.

The candles are burning on my dresser, reflecting in the mirror.

"Okay," says Christopher, stretching, "I hope they don't expect me to marry you."

"Don't be silly," I say.

But I'm thinking, *Why not?*

We arrive at Dev and Kalpana's serenely white house the next Friday night. When I enter the living room, Dev introduces me to several men I have never met.

"This is our cousin Mr. Chawla, his son Ganesh. This is our uncle Mr. Patel, his father from India, and you know my son Kumar."

While Dev is always elegant and polite, this stiff formality is uncharacteristic.

He quickly seats Christopher and me. Taking a chair directly across from Christopher, he fixes on him with his intense dark eyes.

"I will be frank, Christopher. I like you, yes, but Claire is like a daughter to us. She is that dear to us. We care about you only as far as she is concerned. I have said to Claire many times, 'Claire, you have chosen this boy, isn't it? But he is taking such a long, long time.' We want to know when will be the wedding day. We cannot rest until we know when will be the happy day."

Christopher's rosy cheeks drain of all color. His back straightens from a yoga posture of Slouching Tiger to a contortion of Defending Dragon.

Before he can speak, I try something. "I am honored to be cherished by you."

Dev will not be distracted.

"Christopher, I have a proposal to make. I will lend you and Claire forty thousand dollars to buy a house if you will get married within the year."

"I am not yet divorced," I offer weakly.

"But you will soon be," he says, looking sternly at Christopher.

"I have always felt married to Claire," Christopher says. "Actually, I think we have been man and wife in many past lives."

"When will be the wedding day in this life?" If Dev were less cultivated, he would have slammed his hand on the table for emphasis.

After a strained dinner, we leave, telling them we will seriously think over his generous offer.

In the car, I am almost laughing.

"It's not funny, Claire."

I imitate Dev, a man I truly revere: "You have chosen this boy, I'm not kidding you, he must marry you!"

"Very funny."

"Well, it's obvious that I'm going to have to talk to him privately, and tell him that I don't plan on ever getting married again."

"Good luck."

A few days later, Christopher presents me with pearls and lilies and asks me, sort of, to marry him.

He says, "Will you be with me until you are . . . How old are you?"

"I'm thirty-eight. And you're twenty-five."

"Almost twenty-six," he says, giving me a sassy wink.

"Well," he says, trying on the pearls, "I think I look good in these."

"Just like Colette's Cheri."

"Who?"

"Never mind," I say. "Where did you get these pearls?"

"What, do you think I stole them?"

"No, they're just so exquisite."

"You deserve them."

"Thank you, Christopher," I say. "I'm kind of stunned."

"What for? You're my true love. I tell everyone that."

"You mean, your other girls?"
"There's no one else but you."

But I'm afraid the pumpkin carriage that brought me to Prince Christopher will soon whisk me away from him.

232 Radiant Son

My son's growing up, still pre-preteen, but like a teenager hooked up to some piece of electronic equipment at all times. I go to say good night and he's asleep with a borrowed laptop glowing on his thighs.

He's magic, my boy: a glimpse into the future where children, constantly irradiated, are even more luminous.

233 Because the Night Belongs to the Bitch

They come in the night.

Men.

A few young, a few old, with an internal map dotted with need, leading to the destination of me. And I don't even sleep with most of them. They say I am the warmest of women. Perhaps I'm fevering?

I've been living alone in the blacksmith house a few years.

"I bet no one has ever called you a bitch," one man says.

He's right.

But I've noticed bitches keep their men, lashing out at them when finding the slightest fault, demanding more and more until their man feels no longer worthy of licking any part of her, except her boot spur.

Why do men stay with the bitches and leave nice women like me?

An acquaintance of mine complained about her husband buying her a red BMW. "I told him I wanted a dusky color," she whined.

Why does she get a BMW and bitch about it and I get a zilch and happily wait for breadcrumbs and bird doo? I could muster some theories, but I'm too tired.

No one, except those who have been mentally ill, understands the need I have for sleep. If the Snooze Police would ask, "How much sleep do you need, Claire?" I'd have to say twenty-two hours a night and two hours for some heavy napping.

So far, I haven't admitted to anyone, even Christopher, how much I actually do sleep. Inventing things I accomplished in the morning doesn't seem like lying, just a way to avoid being committed by the men in white coats.

I don't date, but I do have gentlemen callers, and Christopher sometimes spends the night. I close my door so the children won't notice, and he leaves before they wake. They inform me a few years later, "We always knew."

To avoid being pathetic in the eyes of my children, I have dinner parties every Wednesday night. As soon as I am a woman on the loose (randy stray—as in cat or dog—or wiggling, like a tooth), I am no longer invited to any parties. Ever again.

But not to fret. I have a lot of men friends, some who are married and some who are not.

I love men. They are generous, helpful, uncomplicated, sweet, muscular, aromatic, and they lift heavy objects.

Christopher stayed the longest of them, albeit intermittently, but I dumped him when I found out he was sleeping with, not one, but three, other women.

True to the playing-hard-to-get theory, he kept trying to get me back. He left notes on my car, sent me packages of beautiful clothes from my favorite stores, and threatened to kill men who were in my life.

It's the same old thing.

Heidegger said it best: "We pursue that which retreats."

Hence the triumphal bitch.

234 Portrait of a Divorcée as a Young Pariah

I am socially no more.

235 More Innocents

From "Elender and the Divorice":

> *Because I thought the fighting was going to stop after my dad moved out but it didn't Christopher came and started fighting with my mom. I had to go through the whole thing again. Then they stoped fighting and my mom came up to my room and comferted me. My brother came in too. Christopher would not go out of our house. Christopher called my mom's dad and he called the police so the police came and made Christopher get out of the house. I really hated him for a while after that.*

236 Red Light

Miracles last; mirages don't.

But I certainly needed a miracle after Christopher was gone.

Walking on Lincoln Avenue in Chicago, with Nina, I see my miracle. Or is it mirage?

His face—craggy-Renaissance, prone to excruciating handsomeness or mild ugliness—looks New York to me. When his eyes catch mine, he seems to be waking from a suffering sleep. I could swear his body is sweating silver beads. Something ineffable passes between us. Does electric current from nearby phone lines singe us? Or does the heaviest quark release from cells deep in our bodies, causing the lightest of atomic angels to visit?

All I know is I follow him up the steep stairs of a theater to a narrow hall. Mailing lists and posters are on the wall. I can tell Nina is confused.

"Where are we going?" she asks.

"We need to relax, right here. Now," I say.

We sit in the fetid lobby chairs. The man I will love sits across from us. Our knees almost touch; gold filaments might be connecting us.

"Who are you?" I say, incising the silence.

His seriously stunning eyes look straight into mine.

"Red Sullivan."

"Nice to meet you. I'm me."

"I can certainly see that," he laughs.

Nina says she has a horrible headache. I force money on her to take a cab home and she gingerly clicks down the stairs into the street.

When I return to the lobby, it's empty because the play has started. I enter the darkened theater and miraculously find myself sitting next to Red. The play features one of his protégées, he tells me later. After the applause, he turns my way, as if he already knows me.

"Shall we go for a drink somewhere?" he asks.

In the bar, we talk about our pasts and invite each other back to the present all night long.

Red works with human rights groups. He specializes in international prisoner abuse and founded Say No to Torture (SNT).

The next day, Red uses the phone to find me.

"I won't be able to get through today without seeing you."

"Not a problem I can't solve," I buzz into the receiver.

We meet in Hyde Park and walk his dog to the Point.

"Don't you feel insignificant when you look at this huge lake?" I ask. "It's like an ocean."

"When I look at you, I think the lake seems insignificant," he says.

Talk about foreplay.

The phone is our chaperone. We talk through it, straining to get closer. I sleep, wait for the phone to ring, talk to him, talk, talk, and then sleep again. Red starts complaining, "I think of you so much, my colleagues think I'm on drugs."

"Your point?"

We laugh.

This phone "phrenzy" is, apparently, foreign to him.

"How do you have time to do anything else—read, eat, work?" he asks, wanting me to translate.

"Go to the bathroom? Do drugs?"

He laughs.

"I'm not putting a gun to your head, darling," I continue. "You called me, you know."

"I know. Don't get mad, Claire."

"I'm not. I love talking to you."

"I do too."

SNT is honoring him at a downtown gala dinner. I can't help thinking about Tobin and our Chicago Art Palace evening.

Sitting next to Red, I realize he is famous in these circles. I admire his gravitas most, but this evening he is fun and exciting.

His hand strokes my lower back.

His colleagues are discreetly scrutinizing me.

"My friend Tom said you're so beautiful that he feels dizzy."

"Probably Ménière's disease."

He smiles.

"I realized when I saw you tonight that you are in living color and the rest of the world is in black-and-white."

"But you're Red!"

"I am pale compared to you, my dear."

At the end of the evening, he kisses me good-bye.

"Thanks for coming," he says.

"Sorry it took so long."

He laughs.

"I love you, do you realize that?" he says.

It sounds a little like whining.

Red is in the process of divorcing too. We are frayed by the very thing that ties us together. In the middle of one of our embraces I mention that I may seem very freewheeling, but I do have one scruple: "I don't sleep with married men."

Two weeks later he appears at my doorstep, on my birthday. He holds up his hand for me to inspect. Through the screen door, I can see his ringless fourth finger. His divorce is as sure as death. We have two hours and twelve minutes until my party begins.

In the candlelight of my bedroom, it's as if meadow air from a peaceful country descends upon us.

My fifty-year-old friend Quentin said it best: "When you meet someone who is made for you, it's a change of solid to light."

237 Park of Lost Lovers

Morning forms after Red and I have spent the night together.

We rise at dawn to walk his dog in a frost-shining park. A couple passes by.

I insist on his arm, and we touch at the hip.

This is a satisfied moment, never to be repeated. As if we could keep walking forever.

The light is still coming down from the round places of the sky and slender shadows rise from the earth. Under our feet is the crisp shell of weakening winter days.

When I'll look back (and oh, I will), I'll see myself there, not knowing we won't be together in the spring. Not knowing then how this morning will come to nothing.

We walk a long time, without words, with no real sacrifice except my joy.

238 Punk in the Night

Red is gone now. A brilliant, beautiful man. Maybe it had something to do with his busy, charmed life. The night I slept over at his penthouse when Christopher almost came over and tried to kill him probably didn't help.

Red answers the phone in the middle of the night. Without saying a word, he hangs up and jumps out of bed. I follow him into the hall.

"Who was that?"

"The Christopher punk."

"No way."

"He says he's coming over," Red says calmly, grabbing a baseball bat from the closet.

He kisses me. "Don't be scared. I'll be back soon. Wait in bed."

I don't want to emasculate him by telling him that Christopher is into martial arts.

"Red," I say, "he's totally into . . . *Star Wars.*"

"He sounds young enough to be into *Sesame Street,*" he says. "Don't worry. I'm totally into finding you in my bed when I return."

The sight of the dignified defender of human rights walking into the street with a baseball bat is a bit ironic.

In a half hour, he's back.

"I don't think he's coming. Tell that little fucker never to call here again."

"I won't be talking to him again," I say, as one who has been fucked by the little fucker.

"Hard to believe he's the same age as my students," he says, taking off his shoes.

"I can't believe he had the nerve to call here!"

"Let's forget it, Claire, and go back to bed."

A few days later, Red calls from the airport, where he's headed for Romania.

"I wish I could see you. . . . Flight leaves in fifteen minutes. I'll be traveling most of the summer, but I'll write you a postcard."

"Red, are you . . ."

"No."

"How did you know what I meant?"

"I've got to go, sweetheart."

And he does.

He almost masks our mini-divorce by the postcards he sends from all over the world.

When he comes back, he doesn't let me know.
After a month, I have to call him. "You're home."
"Been here since August."
Silence, not golden.
"Oh," I say.
"Great to hear your voice," he says.
"You're awfully remote," I say.
"Really?" He has a playful tone.
"Yes."
"Well . . . I'm happy you called," he says.
"I think we should break up," I say.
He takes a little breath and says, "That's a first."
"You mean you do the breaking . . ."
"Yeah," he says. "That's usually the way."

But I believe the real reason I am let go is not Christopher or faraway places. It's my legs. The way he looks at them. He's what men of his generation call "a leg man." Although I used to have great legs, they are becoming more serviceable than elegant. I still wear miniskirts at the drop of my pants, but I probably shouldn't.

Later, when Red and I are "still friends" (*nature morte*—inert blobs of people on a platter being painted by a dilettante), I tell him that I thought we were going to be together. No, he says, he never thought so, but he is sure he loves me. I love him too. But Red is gone and now come the blues.

Once again, I tried to stir myself in with a man. I should have kept it plain, in the bedroom. It's what men and women do best together, what gives the most comfort, and we should simply stick to it, avoiding all other complications and distractions. When you mix in money and kids and family and laundry, the stroking stops delivering its bliss.

Guard against real life. It is not all that it's cracked up to be. It's more. In fact, it splinters everything.

239 ~ Questionable Goods and Bads

Shortly before I end it—the first time—with Christopher, and before I move to the blacksmith house, I have the surreal experience of finding articles of unknown origin living in my basement.

He certainly has given us many things: a VCR, a computer, paintings, and countless toys for the kids. He is awfully young to have enough disposable income to help us so much, I think. Yet, I never wonder if they could be hot until he gives me the pearls. Something buzzes in my brain and I wear them with discomfort.

Searching for the water heater, I notice boxes against the wall. What's this? Nothing I recognize. Pandora's? I look inside. Toasters, Lands' End sweaters and luggage, leather boots, jewelry, radios, CD players, Walkmans, lingerie in various sizes (none of them mine), and expensive lamps.

But I won't have a chance to confront him about this shocker. Plus I can't imagine him stealing—he's the son of two police officers.

A month later, I'm at the opera with Quentin and his partner, who, for security reasons, will remain nameless. During the intermission an ashtray blonde comes up to me and says, "I know who you are. I've been sleeping with Christopher for the past four years. All he ever does is talk about you and I'm sick of it. I think you should know that I'm not the only one, besides you, who shares his bed."

I run through the foyer, my heels echoing on the stone tiles until I find Quentin.

"What's wrong?" he asks. "You look like you saw a ghost."

"Sort of."

"Shall we take you home?"

"No, you guys go back in. I'll take a cab."

Once safely home, I fill a large garbage bag with everything Christopher has ever given me. The pearls are the last item I throw in, crowning the top of the pile. I lug the bag to my car and leave it on Christopher's staircase.

A few days later, he picks up the loot in my basement. He comes when I'm not there. I hear later that Christopher has dipped into the trust fund from his grandmother for me and my kids. I have to ask myself if I'm beginning to think the worst about men.

As if I were devil-worshipping, I find myself by chance, standing next to him in crowds. I barely speak to him, but he somehow finds my car in parking lots and leaves letters on my windshield.

One evening, shortly before Christmas, the children and I come home to a box on our front porch. Inside are dozens of wrapped presents. Elen and Marc say together, "Dad!" I hide the note that says: *Miss you guys. Love, Christopher.*

240 Hate to Date

Writing in my *slamDUNK* journal makes soloing in my bed more tolerable:

ON DATING

Most likely you are no longer young enough to be returning his/her varsity sweater.

That's why you are reading this handbook.

Dating is an activity best done in high school.

Eat dates, they are full of fiber.

You'll need a babysitter if you have children, and you'll feel like a babysitter if you don't.

Dating is an American custom that puts an inordinate amount of pressure on two strangers.

Try to meet people any other way than dating.

Have dinner parties.

Faint in stores.

Pretend you're blind and go into the wrong house on your block.

If you see a good prospect on the street, almost run him/her over with your car.

A bond forms when you say sorry to someone you've hurt, intentionally or unintentionally.

As they say, all pain, all gain.

241 New Breed

Men everywhere I look. Were there always so many of them before I began divorcing?

Has my little discovery about Christopher's other women made me a little desperate?

I attract polar opposites: Zen-like pillars of serene masculinity or suicidally creative not-quite-clinically-schizophrenic artists. Because I understand both these types of men, there must be something wrong with me.

I do break down and date. Once.

I am invited by Tim, a man I met on the phone, friend of a friend.

I say yes to him because I'm free. (Tobin has visitation and actually showed up on time.) Also he sounds cheery, and I don't want to wreck his mood.

Tim wants to pick me up in his marvelous car. Apparently he owns a plane and a boat too. I had a toaster before my divorce.

"I'll meet you at the club," I say to make it as little like a date as possible. And to avoid ending up in his freezer, cut up and twist-tied into baggies, in case he turns out to be a psycho.

"It's no trouble to pick you up," he says, audibly deflated.

"Thanks, but no. See you at eight."

A few hours later, I step from the cab and run in crisp February air to the gleaming mansion that houses the country club. Statues of Polynesian women at the entrance look out of context with the English Tudor. Must be a theme evening. Reminds me of faux-carnival and I think of Clive and Paris and how long ago that seems. And of the Chicago Art Palace gala.

I'm wearing my elegant hundred-year-old black dress from Baden-Baden with long sleeves and twenty small buttons at each wrist. I received it when Tobin's grandmother died and her estate was up for grabs. Tobi gathered her dresses for me and miraculously they fit as if they had been tailored for my body. I'm wearing my hair up with silver-and-pearl barrettes. If I had worn it down, it would have fallen below my shoulders, looking pre-Raphaelite or hippie-ish or just plain unacceptable for a woman of my certain age. At least in these circles.

I feel protected in the black combat boots I shined before leaving.

Maybe acceptability isn't such an issue for me after all. But at least I can run from Tim, if needed.

After checking my coat, I enter the ballroom, where I'm beamed into a world of wealthy men and women. I feel a ferocity in my eyes when I enter the room. I wonder if I have always been like this and is it attractive or repellent.

Something unnamed is roaring inside me. I sense I could leap walls with it.

Tim said he is tall with blond hair. Under a chandelier is a short man with white hair. He looks ruddy, desperate, and either like an elegant court jester or a shabby diplomat. I told him I was medium decaffeinated Irish with a Nordic twist. As he walks toward me, his eyes show relief. We European kiss.

His arm locks over mine, and he guides me, like a prisoner, to his friends. As Tim introduces me, I free myself. They are all talking about subjects that start with airplane adventures and end with money or boats or other machines or more money.

Compelled to excuse myself, I take off on my own, wandering the rooms filled with black- and white-clad people. Speak to anyone who looks interesting, I tell myself. A diminutive woman with dark, perfect hair stops me. "That's a great dress," she says.

"Thanks. It's from Germany."

Moving unimpeded through the room, I meet older women—women who appear strong, well-groomed, and powerful—capable of navigating the waves of male waters. They talk about summer homes in Bali, and I say, "That's great." And I mean it, and they keep going.

A few women are younger than me. I see one of them at a table with a stunning man. They remind me of what others saw when I was with my husband.

Standing near their table, her eyes meet mine. She has clear green-brown eyes—beautiful—and her hair is thick, shoulder-length, blondy-brown. The man's hand is on the upper part of her slim, muscular arm.

I am alone, not smoking, not fidgeting, merely standing near their table.

Her man has dark blue eyes. His hair is a deep brown, almost black, and is probably the longest male hair in the club. He sees her looking at me and joins her.

"Are you a member here?" he asks.

"No, but you must be," I say.

"Actually, I own it," she says.

He asks me to sit down, which I do, next to her.

"So, is this your husband?" I ask. "You look adorable together."

"No, we're just friends."

She is a new breed, unfettered and confident. She is Julia, the daughter of a prominent politician. Her detachment straightens my spine.

In one leonine motion, she stands up, exposing a strong golden back. "Let's go dance," she says to me.

I follow her undulating walk into the darker room, where everyone seems well-lubricated from drink and money and food and groping.

Julia and I are dancing as if in a trance, moving our hips in the same way, making a sphere of unassailable yet sensual calm.

Tim finds me on the dance floor and makes a big deal about having a good time next to two dancing girls. And maybe he is. He hops around us, trying to spin us both at the same time, and I wind away from him.

"I'm getting my coat," I say.

"I'll get it," he says.

"Thanks," I say, "but no. Stay and dance with Julia. She needs you."

I wave to her, blow a kiss, and Tim follows me out to the coatroom anyway.

"Would you like to go to a bar with me and my friends?" he asks.

"You're sweet," I say, "but I have to get home. I'm having a mad affair with my teenage pool boy."

"Isn't that a bit young?" he says.

"No," I say, "I'm very immature."

I drive home in a thickening storm, wondering where I've been, where I'm going.

242 Witchy Mom

"Can we break all the windows in the house?" asks Marcus.

"Sure," I answer.

"Would it be all right, Witchy Mom, if we scribbled on the walls with Magic Markers?" asks Elender.

"No problemo," I say.

This is an ongoing game the children never tire of. Invented and passed down to us by Nina, she calls it Witchy Mom, and the kids love it.

"Witchy Mom," asks Marcus, "could we put mud on the floors?"

"Why not?" I say. "That sounds like a good idea."

"Can I eat M&M's for dinner?" Elen asks.

"Of course," I say. "Nutritious and delicious."

The exchange could go on for hours, and I could fly to the moon on a broomstick, wave to them, my silhouette illuminated. But I end it, insisting we get back to the family rituals they, at times, resist: dinner-making, homework-doing, prayer-saying, and bed-going.

243 Failure to Die/Extreme Pizza/Pizza Resucitation

Every day, Mimi fails to die even though she would like to. The children have been taking lessons from her for several years. Recently, when I could no longer pay for them, she took me aside, peering at me with her small penetrating eyes and gripping my arm with her strong bony hands. "Claire, I vill never stop teaching your children. Not ever." They've been on scholarship for a few weeks already.

She prays to her Catholic God to let her leave this world. But he doesn't answer her. Maybe because she's really Jewish, having converted during World War II at the urging of her mother.

She has outlived everyone—her first husband is smoothed over by African sand dunes, having been shot down above the desert during World War II, and her second husband and son are in urns on top of the grand piano. When I offer to bring her Thanksgiving dinner she says, "Vat! And I should eat a varm meal in front of my husband and son—in front of their cold ashes?" Never mind.

Remarkably, she still teaches piano. A night nurse, paid for by a devoted student, makes it possible for her to live at home.

One evening, I receive a phone call from the nurse telling me that her charge is not doing well. In fact she's been given extreme unction by the priest. I rush to her house and her face is swollen. Having refused all food for a week, she is whittled down from thin to bone. More alarming, she doesn't talk.

I've brought pizza in and the nurse heats it up. After a few minutes we hear her from her silent, dying room. "It smells so good. You naughty. I must have. The pizza makes me vant to live!"

I secretly believe all individuals are morbidly paired with another person. When one dies, the other will die at the same, exact time. Even if it's across the ocean and they don't know anything about the other's death. That's why death sometimes seems arbitrary—a teenager getting flattened, like a cartoon character, by a falling piece of a plane, or a young executive dying of an aneurysm in her lover's arms. Their mortal "twin" has died and it is their time to go as well.

I'm sure my death partner is Mimi. For this reason and many others, I hope she continues, as Hungarian pianist/sage/apothecary, to dispense her dosages of music and wisdom.

244 Got Cash?

"I mean, look what you put down for your expenses. Honey, you're an attractive gal. You've gotta put down more than two hundred dollars a month for clothes. And magazines . . . You put down zero. A girl like you has got to look at a few magazines. Come on. I'm really sorry, sweetheart. I'd like to see you divorce someone richer. This really gets me mad!" says my fifth divorce lawyer, an elder statesman who is grandpaternal toward me.

"You picked the wrong guy to divorce."

"I actually picked him to marry."

"Yeah, yeah. But I wish you were divorcing someone else."

"Me too."

"There's just no money," he says, getting out the paperwork. "I mean, honey, my fees are gonna be more than his income."

Is it really worth it?

245 Higher Mathematics

My sister Chloë (fire crotch) called to tell me, "My husband had a dream about you. You were ravaged by sadness and he told you, 'Contemplate higher mathematics.'"

There may be a logic of failure, but no matter how hard I try to calculate emotion, I'm out of balance all the way to infinity.

PART SEVEN

Love is a memory of loss.

CIRCUS ACT

Wine-colored bedspread in his otherwise white room. Clamshells, serving as plates, on a small glass table at the foot of the bed.

Sitting naked on a canvas pillow, she scoops a last forkful from the shell.

"Here," he says, "I'll go wash it . . . you know . . . the roaches."

"Welcome to our fair city," she says.

She chooses a foil chocolate ball from a white bowl. Mozart's face crinkles as she opens it. "Mozartkugeln," *she thinks. He has already taught her some German, beginning with the sweetest things.*

He returns, kisses her on the top of the head.

"Watch," she says, standing up. She throws her arms forward like a dive and does a handstand. Her pelvis arches so that she is in perfect balance—thighs taut, feet pointing to the ceiling, her long hair brushing the ground.

"Wow," he says as the Montrose el train rumbles past, shaking the tiny apartment, rattling windows, buzzing the floor.

She falls to her feet, laughing. "The el ruined it," she says. "I can usually stay up longer."

"You are like a circus," he says.

"Just don't put me in a cage," she says. "I like my freedom."

"No one," he says, popping a Mozartkugel *into his mouth, "can take away your freedom."*

"Yes, they can," she says. "The one you love takes it away."

246 Indiscretion and Indigestion

We're eating at Nina's, a nice change from Blind and Deaf.

Like any architect's dining room, hers is small, efficient, and elegant. (She went from tent to rent.) The table is set with real silver (an heirloom from Russia?) and coral-colored candles. Everything else is black and white.

Marcus sits next to Nina's thirteen-year-old son, Alex.

"I'm going to the soccer World Cup with my dad," Alex says.

Nina turns pale. "That asshole will never take you," she says.

"Should you be saying that in front of Alex?" I whisper.

"He's used to it," says Nina.

"Well, he shouldn't be," I say.

247 Mandate

For my children's sake, I will not speak harshly about their dad, no matter what he does.

Even when he doesn't take them to their soccer awards banquet and they call me sobbing.

Even when he doesn't show up on time and they wait with packed duffel bags by the front door for hours, and he brings *me* to court for obstructing visitation. (The Big Lie always works: *Into the showers, all of you!*)

Even when a can of soup falls on Elender's nose as she's shopping with him at the supermarket and he tells her to "tough it out" (*toughen-sie outen!*) because he's too lazy to find her ice and later gives her a cold wine bottle to put on her nose in bed.

Even when he brings them to his tennis game and she falls on the bleachers and he doesn't take her to the hospital for stitches because he wants to finish his game.

For my children's sake, I won't say he's a cruel, heartless bastard when he takes them out on the frozen lakefront and mocks their fear of the ice by walking farther and farther out on the frozen water, leaving them sobbing on an icy rock and begging him, "Come back, Daddy." I don't tell them he's a sick fuck when they tell me, "He laughed while we cried."

Or when he inadvertently locks them out on the apartment roof pool and they pound the door until someone lets them back in.

Or when he gives his seven-year-old son a switchblade, I don't say sarcastically, "What a great gift idea," when my son runs into the house shouting, "Daddy gave me a switchblade and taught me a trick!"

Before I can say *Emergency Room,* he spreads his hand and swiftly stabs between finger spaces, missing until he impales his palm. I pull out the blade and his blood rhythmically spurts onto my white robe. I require direness to be calm.

"Marcus," I say slowly. "Let Mommy hold your hand in the air while she calls nine-one-one." Later, after he is bandaged, I'll look at the blood-soaked robe and faint.

Yes, I'll be careful what I say, but I will check them into reality. If they complain to me about their dad's behavior, I say, "Well, I know he loves you, but he's obviously not thinking very clearly."

Elen says, "He's not the type who cares if we're crying."

I don't need to say anything, because Marcus says, "Maybe he could go to school to learn how to be a better dad."

Marcus is full of hope. It may bring him immeasurable suffering, as it did to me.

248 Mystical Connection

I will not speak harshly about Tobin also for my own sake.

Because we once had a mystical connection. Similar to the one I felt for the Bösendorfer grand. During the time I lost the use of my right arm, it started losing ivory keys, as if shedding in sympathy. Sitting at the piano bench could give more comfort than being in his arms.

I will not speak harshly, because he and his family gave me the Bösendorfer, and he enjoyed listening to me playing and composing for hours at a time.

Because he was affectionate to me and the children.

Because he tried to be a good husband and father—until he left.

249 The Ice Floe

After the children tell me about their father's bizarre behavior on our frozen Lake Michigan, I think of Tobi on that ice floe. He floats farther and farther out, receding from all memory of warmth. He sets like an ice sculpture and blends into the background tundra, unmeltable.

250 Anesthetic

I don't want to, and I'm sure with his schedule he doesn't want me to, but I feel so sad late one night that I find myself dialing Quentin.

"Hello," he says, sounding awake.

Thank God.

"It's Claire. Sorry. You still up?"

"Barely, but I'm working," he says.

"Oh," I say, feeling a bit idiotic.

"What's up, my fair lady?"

"I can't take it anymore."

"Okay."

"I mean being alone."

"It can be rough," he says, having been there.

"Maybe I could be anesthetized until I get through this."

"And what about the kids?" he asks, as if I were being serious.

"I could freeze them too."

"Not a cool idea," he says.

"What?" I ask a little petulantly. "Do you want us to suffer?"

"No . . . and yes."

"What's that supposed to mean? I wouldn't want you to suffer."

"Yes, you would," he says. "It's our only hope."

251 Resolve

Sandi and Don are an older couple—they are regulars at my dinner parties. They were married, but are now divorced. Don is an ex–pro football player and Sandi is an ex-model. They are, in fact, both each other's live-in exes.

The day of their divorce twelve years ago, returning from court, Sandi dropped Don off at the train. He got out with his suitcase, walked a few steps to look at the schedule. She waited in the car. He came back to her car window. "What's for dinner tonight?" he asked, and got back into the car.

They have been living together ever since.

252 The Ways We Hurt Each Other

"I filed my nails," Nina tells me. "And put on red nail polish. To match the fake blood."

Years ago, before her own divorce, she was angry at her husband and had staged a fake suicide.

"But Sergej knew you would never . . . ," I say.

"Sure, he thought I wouldn't," she assured me. "But I made his heart go boom boom."

"You know, Nina," I say. "People get put away for less in this country."

"Of course," she says with her wide-vowelled accent.

From what I have pieced together from this and other conversations: Sergej came home, saw Nina on the ground in a pool of blood. Thought for two seconds she was dead. Foul play was the first thought, then suicide, no, not Nina, selfish Nina. A slower thought about their son Alex came. Thank God he's not home.

When he realized Nina was faking it, the lightning flash had already struck. He didn't care. For the split second he thought she might be really dead, he hadn't cared. At least not enough. He bent down to tickle her and her hands shot up to his face, her red nails digging into his cheek, catching on his stubble. He almost screamed.

Instead he called his lawyer and that day *he* filed.

CLUE NUMBER TEN

You become a legal action figure.

253 Gout Cure

My late-night conversation with Quentin is what initially made me decide to host a dinner party every single Wednesday night for many years.

Since I knew I was going to be suffering for the love I had lost, I planned to enjoy myself, at the very least, once a week. And my children were happier because I was happy on that day.

I believe dinner parties can cure many ailments, both emotional and physical, except perhaps gout—although with my vegetarian cuisine, even that may be ameliorated.

254 Firsthand/Secondhand

Every Wednesday, magically, I can cook!

I prepare easy, inexpensive courses starting with carrot soup, roasted eggplant with garlic and sun-dried tomatoes, and fresh dinosaur kale salad. Steaming pasta is always the main course. And copious amounts of sourdough bread and butter are at hand. Never trust a household without butter—yes, German *step-Mutti,* I have changed. I usually make a quick cake and homemade lemon ice cream. (Cream, lemon, and sugar in the freezer—stirred whenever you think about it, *et voilà!*)

I get in the habit of setting the table in the morning so I can savor it. Each place is unique with mismatched dishes and cutlery and cloth napkins acquired secondhand. Candles are everywhere.

Such meals are an expense, but worth all the work because I won't clean the house or buy food and make it unless I invite friends over.

Elen and Marc, my official testers, are sated before the party begins. They stay up only long enough to greet the guests and take their coats.

We're on dessert and Nina is singing a little. It's the wine. Quentin and his boss, Jay, are obviously charmed. Because of his line of work—sports casting—no one outside of his circle of close friends can know about his lifestyle or he'll get fired. Quentin relies on the fact that I'm sworn to secrecy. While he finds Nina entertaining, he also knows she's a gossip. And he doesn't consider her a close friend.

My special almond tea is being poured now. We're talking about films and TV. On and on about films. And TV.

"Anyone ever had a *firsthand* experience?" I ask. "I mean, a real-life adventure, like climbing a mountain or tending a sick baby ostrich?"

Some people laugh. Most notably Quentin. He knows how I feel about this subject. Although TV is his bread and butter, I'm feeding him tonight and he doesn't want to bite my hand.

Having come from a more repressive society, Nina thinks my resistance to pop culture is ridiculous.

"What about you, Claire?" says Nina sloppily. "*You* have a lot of experience. And people . . . your friends . . . tell you everything." She leans over to Quentin. "Claire tells me everything."

"That's good, 'cause she's got a lot going on," Quentin says.

"Oh, not about herself. But the secrets, the demons of others . . . ," she says, slurring her words.

"I'll get some water for her," I say to no one.

"You fascinate me, Quentin," she says, touching his arm. "You see a lot of our darling Claire, but I don't know, I wonder, I think you are *not* falling in love with her. Everyone else does. . . ."

"Of course I love her," says Quentin. "What's not to love, eh?"

"She brings out the secrets in others," Nina says, almost putting her head down on the table.

"Good for her," Quentin says, getting up from the table.

I can hear him coming over to me at the sink.

"I know what you're thinking, Quen," I whisper, "but I didn't tell her anything."

"I hope you didn't."

I rack my brain. I've told Nina so much—did I say, did I hint, did I?

Jay and Nina are toasting their glasses. She's teaching him a Russian drinking song. A few other guests are about to go home.

Nina gets louder. She yells over to us, "Claire, why don't you and Quen get married? Isn't that a good idea?"

I put my arm in Quentin's. "Sure. Why not right now? You can sing our song."

"Okay," she says, and starts to sing.

It's a beautiful song, and her voice is rich, but of course, it's in Russian, and the subtitle is she's pissed.

255 **Host**

After one of my Wednesday soirées, a food photographer, Dick, asks if he can stay for a while. Making sure he doesn't have any suitcases with him, I say sure.

The children are long in bed, all the other guests are gone, and I'm pretty tired, but I make us some of my famous tea—almond and vanilla teas brewed together, served with honey and soy milk.

We're sitting at my crummy kitchen table with a few candles sputtering their last waxy breath. Dick says, "Did anyone ever tell you that you are so . . ."

Beautiful?

He pauses for a moment and says, "Intimidating?"

"As in, carrying nuclear bombs in my bra?"

Nervous laugh. "No, I mean you seem to do everything. I mean . . . that dinner . . . your piano playing . . . singing. Is there anything you don't do?"

You mean like fucking virtual strangers like you?

"I don't quite follow you," I say.

"You seem very intelligent."

And that would be a liability?

"Dick," I say, "relax and drink your tea. I promise not to talk astrophysics even once."

He reaches to take the cup I've poured him and without warning, he's kissing me. His tongue feels distinctly like a Eucharistic host—dry, petrified, unleavened dough.

I turn my head away. I'd like to say that I can't partake of Communion because I'm divorcing—that used to be the rule for Catholics—but his tongue keeps coming after me.

In Catholic Mass these days, you are turned away from Communion only if you are a murderer. So I'll have to murder him, I think.

"Thanks for bringing all that ice cream, Dick," I say.

"Well, I guess no one ate it," he says. "Would you mind if I brought it back home with me?"

I think people who do this are icky. Bring the host or hostess a present and then take it back.

"Since you asked," I say, "my kids would really like it tomorrow."

"Oh, in that case," he says, "I'll leave them some."

All of it stays or someone will be physically harmed.

"Okey dokey," I say.

He goes to the bathroom. While he's there, I hide the ice cream outside in the bushes.

When he comes back, he reaches in the freezer. "I can't find it."

"I guess it must have been eaten by someone after all," I say.

Looking flustered and a bit drunk, Dick leaves.

I take the ice cream out of the bushes and consecrate myself with a heaping spoonful of it.

256 Whose Fault Is No Fault?

With my fountain pen moving on the journal paper, I map out new trade routes to my spicy problems:

WHOSE FAULT IS NO FAULT

FROM HER PERSPECTIVE
Things she did wrong: nothing
Things he did wrong: everything

FROM HIS PERSPECTIVE
Things she did wrong: everything
Things he did wrong: nothing

257 What I Call Him Now, What I Called Him Then

My ex.
My love.

258 Soccer Mom

grocery section

I bounce to the grocery store, wishing I dressed weirdly enough for someone to have to guess my gender. It's my week for "team snack."

My son has admonished me. "Don't get the healthy stuff, Mom. Other kids don't have our taste buds."

teen section

I watch some teens push through the automatic doors—the girls, wearing lipstick dark as coal dust, smoke and swear as if profanity were a skill paid for by the minute; the boys sauntering carefully so their gargantuan boxer-revealing pants don't fall off to expose their less-than-gargantuan members. Their clothes look blown up, cut to fit models on billboards. My God, their needs are huge. So are mine.

northern section

I wish I could strut cool like them, not just wear outfits to counter the mom I am. What are Mom clothes? Go to the North Shore. The more north you go, the more conservative. If I walk through the southern suburb of Evanston after rolling out of bed in sweatpants and a T-shirt, no one bats an eye. But I would be fashion-arrested in the frigid northern territory of Winnetka (Whine-etka), where women are inclined to wear a particular style—turtlenecks or chiffon blouses that tie in a bow at the neck. I call it I-don't-have-a-vagina clothing. Now there's a great designer label.

junk food section

I wander through the aisles looking for junk food and juice boxes for the team.

"Is this junky enough?" I ask myself, not turning to Marcus for advice, because I have dropped him off at the soccer game.

tat section

At least I strive to be hip when I take my kids to soccer, in cut-off jeans and a white cotton T-shirt over a black bra. In an attempt to transform myself from a Boomer to a Gen-Xer, I rub a fake tattoo of butterflies and Japanese calligraphy between my scarcely visible cleavage. People comment, "It must be painful to get a tattoo there." I could tell them about pain.

I'm in and out of the store with plenty of time before halftime, by my standard, to go home and change my outfit. Recently I reattire a lot, my ensembles getting more outrageous each time. I race to pull on an army fatigue-type zippered jumpsuit above-the-knee thingy that I wear over a cream-colored lace body stocking. I zip it down for maximum décolletage and also to ensure the body stocking theme is discernible.

cheering section

After the chocolate chip cookies and Coke are distributed to my son's nervous smile of relief—Mom came through—I look across to see Tobin standing on the rival team's side. To stay far from me, he cheers his son from enemy territory, claps when he touches the ball. I guess the enemy is less an enemy than I am. Comforting.

dissection

Elender, whose game comes later, whispers to me. "Mom, I love your outfit. You look awesome. I bet Dad feels sad."

How does she know these things, and why are we giving her this taste of fracture so early? What the hell is wrong with us?

I wish I could turn really weird—smoking, swearing, and wearing pants that threaten to fall off. I wish someone hunky would help me take care of my children, watch their soccer skills, and cook meals while I make a fashion statement in a straitjacket. I wish I could unstrap from divorce.

259 Lingerie Passé

I don't wear underwear most of the time. (Okay, with a short skirt I do.) I don't even pretend it's proper or cultivated of me. Nor do I think it kosher to wear a coat over the sweatsuit or pajamas I wore to bed, when I drive the children to school. But it does save time.

After age thirty, if you don't have perfectly amazing underwear, it's better not to wear any. With no money to spend on myself, I have only a few pairs of perfectly amazing underwear or PAU: flower-print Hanes, and a frog-patterned French-cut brief from Victoria's Secret. I threw most of my PAU away after Tobi stopped talking to me. Then bought a few pairs after I remet Christopher.

My favorite bra is a strange two-toned snowy blue-and-pink racer-back. The shiny black one with gold stars all over is a close number second. But since I'm so exhausted, I don't get the hand-washing done, leaving their silk soiled.

When my beautiful mother was going through her divorce, she wore a tattered black bra. Later she confessed it was from Rémy and that was why she wore it until it fell in shreds from her breasts. But not knowing the dire romance of it at the time, her shabbiness made me want to slit my ankles and bleed slowly into the nearest tub. I took a job in a spiffy clothes store, bought my mother undergarments and clothing on sale, but she quickly ran up a five-thousand-dollar house bill there and never paid it. A divorcing woman is fashion-tricky. If illicit love affairs and divorce don't fuck up a wardrobe, look for poor taste to blame.

Like my mother's, my wardrobe is sparse. A few black dresses hang like wilted lettuce in my closet. Please invite me if there's a funeral.

A while ago, I filled huge bags with the Top 40 clothes Tobi loved on my body, gave them to my children's babysitters, mostly Northwestern students.

"Are you sure, Mrs. McCloud-Kleinherz?" they asked as they inched out the door with their bounty of greatest hits.

I wanted to undress my time with Tobi.

260 **Broken**

I call Quentin from my bed. It's Mother's Day weekend.

"Tobin broke into my kitchen Friday night. I can't live here until it's fixed. The wall. The door. I can't live here. The kids are—"

"Let's not get into it, but what is his problem?"

I'm crying.

"Claire, stop your crying. Things are gonna get better. Just not for a long time."

"I knew you'd say that."

"Then why did you call?"

"Because I knew you'd say it."

"Now you're talking."

Six months later I phone him with the same urgency.

"I don't know what to do," I say. "I just got child support for eighty dollars instead of two thousand."

"Did you call your lawyer?"

"Yeah." I can't breathe very well.

"Did you call Tobin?"

"Yeah, he hung up on me."

"Do you need money?"

"I don't know what to do. I've got rent, bills . . ."

"Claire, don't worry. I'll give you the money."

"Oh no, that's not why I called. I just had to tell someone."

"I've got the money, Claire, and it's got your name on it."

"I can't pay you back."

"I know. That's what's good about working in TV. I've got some extra and it's going to you."

In twenty minutes, he comes to my front door and hands me a check for four thousand.

I can breathe.

261 Absinthe

"I'll stay for the weekend so you can go to your seminar," I say to Nina. It's a good feeling to be the one who's helping someone else for a change.

"That would be great. The cats hate to be alone and Alex, well, he's hardly here; but if you could keep an eye on him," Nina says.

"No problem," I say. "God knows we can't stay home this weekend with all the repairs."

"What a bastard!" she says, taking a drag on one of the rare cigarettes she allows herself. "Doesn't he think of how breaking down the house would affect his kids?!"

"It's not the first time," I say. "But the kids were there."

"Why does he do this?" she asks.

"Maybe because they didn't want to let him in."

"He can't go in your house," she says.

"He said he thought the kids were in danger," I say.

"So he has to break the door down again?"

"He told the judge I leave them alone all the time."

"Fucker. He's better than a lawyer," she says. "What does he want?"

"I think he's desperate to break *me* down 'cause he can't."

"Well, I hate not being here for Mother's Day," she says, giving me a quick hug. "But I'll be back that evening at least."

On Sunday, the kids and I celebrate Mother's Day at Nina's with Alex. They walk into the living room with huge price tags around their necks. Alex looks slightly embarrassed, but Marcus is happy to have another guy taking part.

"Alex's mom is going to have to buy him when she gets back," says Marcus, bringing his neck close so I can read the tag. It says: *One million dollars. Obedient boy who thinks his Mom is cool, pretty, and nice. Happy Mother's Day!* I laugh. Elender's is similar but a bit more effusive. Alex's says: *Priceless, and so are you Mom. You rock.*

I go to sleep wondering when the priceless Nina will arrive. Elen and Marc are fast asleep in a tiny bedroom down the hall with the luxury of cats in their bed.

In the middle of the night, I wake with the eerie feeling of someone looking down at me. It's Nina.

"Hi, you're back," I say, starting to feel relief.

But her expression seems intense, and the words that come next are totally unexpected.

"Your breasts are so firm, like a young girl's," she says.

"Thanks, they're a hundred percent real," I say, knocking on the left one.

"Can I get in with you?" she whispers.

I am suddenly alert.

Silence.

I'd like to oblige and say, "Sure," but, having been offered this a few times before, I know it's enticing like absinthe's opaline green—dangerous in anything but the smallest doses.

I take her hand, more to ensure she stays at bay.

"Nina," I say. "If you weren't so beautiful, you'd take this as an insult. But I know you'll understand."

Silence.

"How was your seminar?"

She gets a little formal on me. "Not bad at all," she says, releasing my hand. "How's my son?"

"Alex came home both nights pretty early," I say. "He's a good boy. He even played with Marcus."

Silence.

Great Russian icon in the sky save us!

"Sorry to wake you," Nina says as she walks out of the room.

"Have a good sleep," I say, feebly, doubting that either of us will.

262 **Awkward**

If she had asked me to go hunting with her? I would have said no too. I could picture her with a handlebar mustache—she'd still be gorgeous—as she holds a long rifle in her hands so that it rests diagonally across her spare body. Maybe a couple of dead raccoon hang off the barrel. She wears a stiff buckskin vest and her boots are covered in mud.

She'd have that same intense, proprietary look on her face. *These are coon I killed with my own two hands. (The bullets helped a little too!)* And she'd wait for my look of admiration that comes easily. Mother, architect, *and* hunter and she still keeps her mascara from smearing. While we get the fire started, she'd talk about the places she's been, smelling wild prairie flowers, glimpsing deer and their young, and even catching signs of wolves. Naturally she assumes that I'd want to go there with her at daybreak.

She and the other Russians I know are a generous people. It could seem ungracious to say, "I don't like the hunt."

But Nina doesn't hunt animals. She hunted me the night her loneliness was, for once, like mine.

I think over our many times together—pouring green tea, talking as she smokes, stroking her cats until I sneeze, looking at the blueprints she expertly draws up—and I see those rituals were not strong enough to muffle desire, the kind of desire that turns wild and runs in fear of being shot down.

263 Stronger Person

Elender continues to let herself know how she feels in "Elender and the Divorice":

> *I really wish my parents would get back together. I know they can't live with each other but I wish they could and would like to. I mean not to fight and get along really well and get remarried. That would be wonderful. Or if they were friends at least, because they can't even get along as friends. But someday I wish they could just call each other up just to say hi and what's going on. I think maybe someday they will be able to do that. I sure hope so. I think the Divorce has made me a stronger person. I think I can deal with things a little better. Before my parents got divorced I thought hardly anybody got divorced. But now it seems like half of the world is divorced, or getting divorced it's a sad thing. If your parents get divorced I think your parents should tell you about what will happen ahead of time. Because if they don't you will be shocked, Because luckly my parents told me so I knew I would have two homes and all that stoff. Also if your parents fight it's much better to have a brother or sister because my brother and I comferted each other and hudled next each other when my parents were fighting he made me feel much better. When your mom or dad are grumpy or yelling at you it's just the divorce to much presher and stoff it's not you.*

264 Divorce Court Chicago Slaughterhouse–Style

You may not appear in front of the same judge who slapped you with a fine for a moving violation six months earlier—this actually happened to my best friend. You may not notice your ancient judge falling asleep as you testify—this happened to another friend. You may or may not hear your judge reprimand you, saying, "It's very nice that you are an . . . uh . . . artist, however, I suggest you change your lifestyle because the brunt of these children's expenditures will be on you"—that's what the judge said to me. But you will have to remain standing as you watch the gavel descend on its path, sure as a butcher's knife, hear words that will drain the blood from your already lifeless body, and be dragged off and cauterized by legal explanations from your lawyer, who will then suction any remaining resources from your bank account, property, or family.

The coward dies a thousand deaths, they say, but the person in the process of a divorce dies each time in court. Medical science cannot explain it, but vital organs shut down while filling out legal documents. Court proceedings reduce most laypeople's brains to the equivalent of lard or, if the person is very health-conscious (as in my case), soy margarine. Why are some divorces short and others epic? Why do some people get everything and some nothing? Why do some men leave with nothing but the shirt on their back and others strip the house down to the phone on the kitchen wall and then come back for the phone? Are there people who relish years of divorcing?

Like most people, I felt as if I were being laid out on a chopping block. My divorce took two and a half years of hacking.

265 Hammer & the Nail

All my previous five lawyers, including a woman, have tried to hammer it into me: Joint custody is the way to go.

"It's just semantics. Let him have his pride."

"But he's not a joint custody kind of guy." I say. "If he were, then we'd be a joint custody couple. I'd be thrilled if he would see them more and take them to their events!"

"It doesn't matter these days; most people just get joint."

"Is that joint pains? Or do you mean ganja?"

"You're funny."

"No helpy wifey, no jointy."

To them I am a tiny nail on the wall that even a sledgehammer cannot flatten.

My sixth and final lawyer, Justin, tries to tell me the same thing.

"So if it's just words," I say, "and words don't mean anything, let's just put the little words *sole custody* next to my name, and no one will be the wiser."

He says I have a point; we'll go for sole.

Maybe he said, we'll go for broke. That's the way it turned out. For me. And Tobin.

266 Divorce Oscar

Speech to the Academy when my story is made into a movie—starring Julianne Moore, of course:

> *Thanks to all of you, and thanks to my mother, who is divorced. I always wanted to be just like you, Mom. And thank you to my ex-husband, with whom I am not yet on speaking terms, for giving me a story worth telling and the venom I needed to be able to unsheathe the book that is now a movie. Oh, and thanks to God, who is always there, steering us to take our clothes off with the most inappropriate people and either get pussy-whipped, butt-fucked, or both. And, after all that, married to boot. And* (music starts coming on to drown out my voice) *thanks to the sacrament of marriage that sanctified making my wonderful children. Thank you. Please hold the applause until the last alimony check is signed.*

267 Ex-Rated

Yes, the men they come and go.

After the dinner parties, some of them just stay for good. On the couch. And when their socks smell, they have to go home. Or to the Laundromat.

I buy filigree lingerie, tiny enough to fit a homunculus, hang it on the walls near my bed, tell men during the dinner party, "Go look in my bedroom." If I can't be with a man, I can be everyman's fantasy.

I read Prufrock to distract myself, but I cannot forget the love song of Tobin.

268 Phantom Spouse Syndrome

I am haunted by an uncontrollable urge to wear the most stunning lingerie, but no one will ever see it.

269 Requirements

Yet another entry for *slamDUNK:*

> Here's the thing about a mountain top: It requires climbing.
> Here's the thing about love: It requires falling.

270 More Sonnets

I buy a tiny black-and-white TV and lay down the tube law.

"You can watch a half an hour of TV if you memorize a Shakespeare sonnet."

It's my form of child abuse.

Shall I compare thee to a summer's day, thou art more lovely and more temperate, I find all over the house in Elen's handwriting.

Marc's handwriting says, *Shall I compare thee to a summer's butt, thou art more stupid and more ugly*.

Elen and Marc have grown up without TV. Of course, they are addicts over at their friends' and cousins' houses. But at least I'm not supplying.

Parents in the neighborhood ask to rent out my children. "They know how to play," they say, "and they're so polite."

But I don't tell anyone this: My children are my poems. Should something dire or beautiful happen, I want them to have the right words in their mouths.

271 Wild Spot

My scheme to receive checks in the mail rather than just bills is finally working.

Luckily, I'm the kind of mom who doesn't mind yanking the kids out of school. It's a family tradition, really. I remember begging my mom to let me go to school. "But Mom," I'd say, trying to inch out the door. "I have a test!" She would rather we sip tea with her and talk about ontological fears, which we did on many of our truant days.

I have created a family business for Marcus, Elen, and me: voice-over for TV and radio commercials. It does require my children auditioning during school hours, but they always manage good grades, so I'm okay with that, and the school seems to be going along with my plan.

I've nabbed a few TV and radio spots. Marcus has been hired for a jingle. But it's Elender who's becoming successful. She is chosen after almost every audition. One of her commercials becomes a "wild spot," the financial equivalent of the G-spot, so it will be airing and moaning and paying us off for months. It's not a fortune, but she'll be making enough to pay for ballet and acting lessons, and we can start paying Mimi again for piano lessons. We'll also hit the firsthand clothing store a few times. I'd like to put it in the bank and let it accumulate for their college, but, as my lawyer Justin says, "What can you do when there's never enough money to go around?"

272 Factories

"Learning how things are made is more interesting than watching television," I tell my children. They seem game, so we tour our area. Naturally the chocolate factory is our first stop. Back in the day, one could take home samples.

"Due to legal issues, tours are no longer allowed," says an officious female chocolate-maker.

"Don't worry. If my kids are hit by a blob of chocolate, we won't sue. We'll eat it, no prob!"

Elender and Marcus giggle.

"Ask for the manager," whispers Elen. Obviously, she's seen me in action before—undaunted by authority and flaunting it.

"Could we see the manager?" I ask.

"I am the manager," she says.

So what.

"Can we talk to the owner?"

"He won't be back today. He'll tell you the same thing."

My children are not used to seeing me defeated by bureaucracy.

To cheer us all up, we buy an assortment of chocolates at the factory store. So much for talking my way into snagging stuff for free.

273 The Merry Red Herring

Photos are vivid in my mind.

In a photo of Christmas long past, making preparations with two little believers in Santa Claus, I am kneeling near the tree in a black velvet dress from my husband's deceased grandmother. My hair is one long glossy ponytail. The children, in sailor clothes, smile like stars on our *Tannenbaum*.

Tobin is taking the picture. My eyes and nose are red from crying. Of course, this happens every Christmas. It's the edge of the photograph that you can't see: He has ridiculed my traditions by insisting on his, and after all, this is *Heilige Abend,* Christmas Eve.

Everything goes according to his plans.

To the children's astonishment, and mine too, we light the candles on the tree. The smell of Tobin's family's traditional herring salad catches in my throat. He hugs us all together.

"Ach, wie schön," he says, and Marcus kisses him.

I notice a wax flicker out of the corner of my eye. The tree is on fire. Tobin leaps to extinguish the needles' orange tips now igniting. Poised near the smoldering, he tries to save us with a clap of his hands. I aim the water bucket. Give him exactly one second to do his worst. And then I drench him.

274 **Sediment**

I see it at the bottom of Turkish coffee. Is it concentrate or the dregs? The distillate of the dregs? Or the essence of what was contained and is now disappeared?

Quentin likes to read them, the coffee grounds, and is remarkably serious about it. He says being serious is a whole lot of fun. He changed my life when he explained to me about the phrase *I don't care.*

"All I know, Claire, is that when people start saying, 'I don't care, it doesn't matter, it's no big deal,' it starts to add up. And all of a sudden things don't matter, and they stop caring."

"I just meant it as a figure of speech," I say.

"Be careful."

Quentin gives advice in a nonthreatening way; that's why I remember it.

I feel so close to Quentin that touching him, although I do, is almost irrelevant.

I assume this is what all people should feel for each other. The essential sediment.

When we sink to the bottom, like Quentin and I and many others have done, we discover empathy.

275 Sentiment

I feel, therefore, I marry. Said Descartes on his wedding day.

276 Mugs

Elender and Marcus catch the bus on our corner for band at six thirty in the morning, when it's still virtually dark. They told me the bus driver asked who I was. I am the only mom who waits with them at the bus stop.

I clear out a tiny closet in the blacksmith house so I can look through a tiny window and watch them getting on the bus without humiliating them.

Before they leave every morning, I hand them each a mug of hot chocolate.

Later, I go down, find the two mugs on the ground where my children used to be, and take them back inside.

277 Lipstick

Always wear lipstick. People treat you better.

Augmenting my mom's advice, I said to Nina, when we were still married women, "Always wear lipstick when fighting with your husband."

278 More Uniforms at Night

A few months before the final divorce decree, the children are long in bed and I have been settled in at the piano, working on an instrumental for several hours. The silence of late evening intensifies the doorbell's ring. I wonder who it could be, and Anita Ward's song "Ring My Bell" discos in my brain. I rush down the few steps leading to the blacksmith shed on one side, the front door on the other. Before I open the door, I hear the male voice say, "Police." My heart gives a surge of power and alarm.

Not wanting to open the door, but not wanting them to ring again and wake the children, I say, "Who is it?"

"Police. Open up, ma'am."

If you don't call me ma'am, I might.

I crack open the door. Sure enough, it's two young cops. "You Mrs. McCloud-Kleinherz?"

"Yes," I say, realizing they are about my age or younger. "You can call me Claire. Did something happen?"

The blond one says, "Uh, ma'am, you missed a court appearance. We're supposed to take you into custody."

"Me?" I say in disbelief.

"Sorry," says the dark-haired one. "You're going through a divorce?"

"Yes . . . ," I say, not comprehending.

"And," he continues, "you were supposed to have been in court on Wednesday."

"You mean yesterday?" I ask. "There's some mistake. My court date is tomorrow morning."

"Well, miss," he says, pointing to some paperwork. "We have it here."

Noticing the *miss,* I decide to deal with him from now on.

Looking down near his index finger, I realize I have my dates mixed up. Damn my handmade calendars.

Sweeping back my hair from falling over his document, I try to smile. "Oh, my God," I say. "I made my own calendar, and I seriously think I messed up the dates. Let me show you."

I run up the stairs like a friend getting a coat and hat to go to the movies. I un-thumbtack the large poster board from the wall and run downstairs again. Even though it's not cold yet, I invite them to "step in for a second." And I mean for a second.

Fling hair, fling hair. "My two children—I have a boy and a girl—are both sleeping, or I'd offer you coffee or something."

"Not a problem," says Cop Dark Hair.

"See," I say, holding up the calendar. "I have the dates wrong on this. I can't believe how stupid I am."

Luckily I've been running up and down stairs, so my out-of-breath delivery has another explanation other than the real one. I am more frightened than if they were wolves at my door.

Cop Blond Hair looks at his watch and says, "If you answer and say you are who we are looking for, we have to take you to the station overnight."

I feel sweat forming on my spine, but I shiver. "Well, I couldn't leave my little children." Brush hair back with fingers.

The two cops shift their holsters.

"I'm going through a horrible divorce and so I'm here alone, obviously." I look down to show them respect, submission, anything they need to let me stay here with my kids. Then I look up at the dark-haired cop, all damsel-in distressed, which I am, without a doubt. No fairy tale, no joke: I am fully at their mercy.

"Normally," says Cop Dark Hair, "we'd have to take you in. But we'll just say you didn't answer the door."

"Oh, that's great!" I effuse. "You are so sweet. But if I hadn't, I wouldn't have met you two."

Even Cop Blond Hair laughs a little.

"Good night, miss," they say, stepping through the doorframe into the suburban night air.

"Good night. Thank you for your help," I say, as if they had come at my request. "I really appreciate it."

I climb the stairs and crawl to the window to make sure they drive away.

Too shaken to play, I sit at the piano, close the keyboard cover and rest on it until morning.

279 Lady Luck

Next day. Quentin is the first person I call.

"Honey, it's lucky you are young and pretty," he says.

Unlucky that I'm on my own.

What he could say but doesn't is: Lucky you're white and you live in Wilmette.

280 Bodily Attachment

Then I call the courthouse. "I'm in between lawyers," I beige-lie to the clerk. I don't say I'm broke and have finally, after going through five lawyers, found one who seems to actually care about me. "And apparently I missed a court date."

"What's your name?"

"It's a doozy, so I'll spell it. *M . . . C . . .*"

"Court appearance date?"

After she checks her computer, she says, "There's a bodily attachment on you."

"What does that mean?"

"It says you owe ninety dollars and then they'll lift the bodily attachment."

"So, I should come in and pay it?"

"Uh, I guess," she says. "If I were you, I'd get a lawyer to come in and pay it."

"If I had one."

"Well, miss," she says. "It's up to you."

I don't want to bother my lawyer Justin, because he just got back from vacation—the minute he left, everything went to hell—and has helped me a lot already.

The next morning, I take the train to the building and am directed to a large room with many employees milling about or at their desks. I check in at the main counter.

"I'm here to pay a fine to lift . . . a bodily attachment," I say. I should have known something was up by the way all the people in the entire room seemed to freeze. The main clerk looks astonished and says sarcastically, "You are, are you?" After taking my name—if only I hadn't given it to her—she gets on the phone. "We need two officers up here. Got a bodily attachment."

Everyone is staring at me. I fiddle at my purse, clutching for my wallet to pay the fine. Although I look as dangerous as Little Mary Sunshine, in a matter of seconds two officers lunge at me, tell me to sit in the chair, and handcuff me to it. My cheeks are burning. I have no idea what is going on. I can barely speak.

"What? I was told to come and pay a fine."

The officer standing over me says, "You are under arrest until we process you."

The main desk clerk finishes typing something, hands it to him. He uncuffs me from the chair and for a second I think I'm going to be free. But he yells, "Hands behind your back." And slaps on the cuffs. He and the other officer lead me out of the room. Pushing me into the hallway, he shouts, "Prisoner coming!"

The glands in my throat are swelling, and I have lost peripheral vision. "Where are we going?" I ask in full panic. The other, younger officer says, "You have to pay in the basement office." We seem to be heading for an elevator. It occurs to me that I am handcuffed with two men, going into an enclosed area. I may vomit. No one is around. No one can help me. In the elevator, I ask if they have my purse. The young one says, "Don't worry." But I'm far beyond worrying.

The elevator releases us into a dingy office with a scrawny female police officer. I try to ask her what is going on, but she gives me a look of contempt. Another male officer comes in the room and starts going through my purse, commenting on every item. "Kleenex. Lipstick. Cracked mirror. Cheap leather wallet." I'm already crying, although no one is noticing. "Could I just pay my fine, please?" The woman officer, showing her ragged teeth, says, "Look, you can be quiet or this might take a very long time."

Miraculously, the officer rifling through my purse is tiring of his little game, having found nothing of interest. He uncuffs me and lets me take out the money and give it to him. "After you are processed," he says, "you have to go to Courtroom Fifty-six and ask the judge to lift the bodily attachment."

"Yes, Officer," I say.

He hands me a piece of paper and they accompany me again in the elevator to my courtroom.

When the judge calls me to the front, he says, "And what, miss, do you do for a living?"

You mean when I'm not getting fired from every job?

"I'm a piano teacher," I say, keeping it simple.

"I can't believe we put children in the care of a person like you."

I guess this just isn't my day.

The two officers take me to yet another room, where I receive another piece of paper and then I am free to go.

CLUE NUMBER ELEVEN

You can't get what you want, because what you want doesn't want you.

PART EIGHT

Young love feels like heaven; old love pulls us from hell.

PICNIC REUNION

A lettuce-green hill rises from the edge of German forests.
Marcus and Elender tuck the small envelope of their hands into my grip.
Capable of something new, we walk to the top.

Elender rolls like a spinning bird, to the bottom.
Marcus, with a glint of question, follows her down.
I dive-roll into slanted light. Trees and sky ride
a merry-go-round until I stop short of my laughing,
little children.

Love, unmistakable as blown-glass, holds us there.

Counterbalancing, they pull each other up, their thighs golden.

I nudge them toward dark trees, where Tobin waves.
Opening the picnic basket, I surrender an embroidered white cloth
to the wind, smooth it over grass and sit.

Halfway between me and their father,
they look at him in the distance, then back at me,
hungry and unafraid, asking leave to peek at
who they will become.

281 More Light Years in the Dark

> The world is filled, and filled with the Absolute. To see this is to be made free.
>
> —Teilhard de Chardin

Early on we argued about science. The theme was always the same.

I believed at the time that there was something faster than the speed of light.

Tobin believed there wasn't.

We spent years trying to prove our point to each other.

I told Tobin enlightenment was instantaneous, faster than any speed, even that of light.

He said *Blödsinn* ("nonsense"), no physical law could be denied, especially the absolute of light speed. Hours of analogies, explanations, and frustration followed.

He ridiculed me when I finally hypothesized, "Love is the fastest speed in the universe." I didn't dare say that prayer was also pretty darn swift!

Years after our divorce, I am ecstatic—an article in *The New York Times* concludes there is something faster than the speed of light.

Now that physics has clearly sided with me, I want to call Tobin and reignite the quarrel. But if love—even buried, trampled and decomposing—is the fastest speed, I don't need a phone to enlighten him.

282 Keeping Track

A strong wind couldn't have done it faster. My life is blowing away. I've lost Tobin, Christopher, Red.

Dev and Kalpana are impatient for me to stop being single. Family and acquaintances are wary. That leaves only Nina, Quentin, my children, and my ancient Hungarian piano teacher. She knows about loss.

Her first husband was presumed dead, shot down in World War II when his plane was flying over Africa. She made a pilgrimage to the Pietà replica at Saint Servitas to sit vigil with Mary holding her limp dead son. She asked the statue, "How can you stand it?" She prayed on the rosary like she played the piano, going over and over. But he never came home. His body was never recovered.

After a few years, it began to sink in. Her husband, a beautiful man, not unlike my Tobin, wasn't returning.

When the Germans bombed Budapest and the air raid sirens went off, instead of going to a bomb shelter, she ran out into the street. "I was trying to get killed," she told me during a lesson. "To be reunited with him."

In the midst of a particularly heavy bombing, one of her male students carried her to safety and later convinced her to marry him. They fled to the United States during the Hungarian Revolution. There, she continued teaching piano, building a bunker of Bartók, Bach, and Beethoven.

Mimi is a constant reminder that life goes on—even when we want to give up.

283 Credit

There are sad people in all the places you can dream of. Tonight I am one of them.

In the supermarket, I feel too sick at heart to find the food I need. Instead, I put flowers in the cart. They are long, wild beings.

As usual, I am afraid to meet someone I know at the checkout. I never know if my check will be accepted. Once, during my marriage, I had a credit card.

With a kind of sick longing, I watch as the woman in front of me pulls out her shiny leather wallet with plastic compartments housing more cards than teeth in my head.

284 Shiny Seeds

The children are both overnight at friends', and I'm home alone, looking at the mess I've made. Bottles of gold paint, brushes in glass jars, pieces of fabric, needles and thread, tiny brown seeds all over the place.

I was sewing eye pillows, painting on their silk and filling them with flax, lavender, and mint. I made a beautiful tag with their name on it: SLEEPAROUNDS. They'll be sold in a few stores. The final court date for my divorce is approaching. I try to keep my hands busy on the piano or sewing.

285 Listen

Whenever I'm lost, I pick up *slamDUNK* and my pen points me somewhere.

SOME OF THE MOST WONDERFUL THINGS YOU CAN SAY TO SOMEONE YOU LOVE

Let me listen.
With you, I become a connoisseur in love's best restaurants.
Let me listen.
You intoxicate me with the golden liquor of your skin.
Let me listen.
I want to spend every moment with you, like my life's savings.
Let me listen.
I want to know everything about you, like a private detective.
I'm listening.

286 Holding Patterns

I open my hand and it is open, not for a man, but for my children. I need them as much as they need me. But I'm not able to make our lives really work.

Even with the voice-overs and occasional on-cameras, I still can't figure out how to sustain myself. It shouldn't be that hard, I tell myself. I should just consider myself a very large gerbil needing thirty thousand times more newspaper, exercise, and food. But let's not forget my children—two large gerbils eating as much as four grown men, who need orthodontia and designer backpacks.

Some bills on my desk are in the final screaming stage of NOW or JAIL! Others are accusatory or pleading with me, some are not even raising their envelopic voices, because I'm too scared to open them, and the most current ones require phone calls where I will be put on hold for several lifetimes. The shorter my tolerance gets for answering machine greetings, the longer they force me to stay on hold.

Holding patterns. Elender and I walk home in the evening from a concert at Northwestern University. I take her small hand and we cross a park in the dark.

"When you hold my hand, Mom," she says, "I'm not afraid of anything."

"I'm so happy, sweetie," I say matter-of-factly. "That's what moms are for."

In the dark, she won't know that I am broken down with hope that I might be doing something right.

287 Insistence

At a party I'm throwing, I've been plied with drinks, and I don't drink. But I do. A male acquaintance is insisting that I "act happy."

He wants to make me happy, he says. He plans to take me to Mexico. When I tell him I don't date, he insists that Mexico is a trip, not a date. More laughter from me, from him. Okay, at least he must take me out for dinner. I tell him this is not possible. But why, he asks. This is not right, he says. I smile and say the words again: I don't date. Is there any way he can see me alone? No, I don't think so, I say. I'll pour you a drink, he says. Thank you, I say, you are the best. No, you are the best. No, you.

288 **Picky**

"Yeah, I'm picky! Aren't you?"

"But he's rich!"

"But he's a jerk."

"Just marry him for a while. Marriages don't last anyway!"

"So I've heard."

"Besides, he's gorgeous."

"I hadn't noticed."

"Claire, really!"

"I honestly didn't. His face was obscured by his big asshole-ness."

This is a typical dinner party postmortem between me and my female friends, one of whom has set me up with an unattached male friend. I told her, "No blind dates"—unless they bring their Seeing-Eye dog, because I *know* I like dogs—"but you can bring him to one of my dinner parties." Which she did tonight. And my napkin ring had a better personality than he did.

After four years on my own, everyone, except Quentin, thinks I'm overly picky. "Claire," he says, "you don't need a man; you need a committee."

I like living on my own enough—minus the nocturnal sobbing—that I won't give it up for just anyone. I don't care if he is gorgeous (I've had that) or successful (sure, that'd be cool); the only nonnegotiable is that he has to be kind. And after that he just needs to be perfect in every other way.

289 — Adding Is Subtracting

Some Women Actually Write Ads to Find a Man

Some Men Actually Write Ads to Find a Woman

Ads Are Evil and Will Steal Your Soul Faster Than a Photograph

There Is Something Seriously Wrong with Our Culture

But Don't Mind Me

I have never read the personal ads before, but now I find myself sneaking a look every now and then. Most men ask for the same easily filled qualities in a woman: *You are sexy and look good in jeans* and *an evening dress.* Whoopee! Once, I ran across an ad that was intriguing and I felt like a trench-coated pervert in the bushes. But I dialed the number anyway. To my shock, I heard the familiar voice of a man I already knew and was decidedly not interested in.

I don't need to take out any ads, because I have a better method. I simply tell men: "I don't date." Any week is sure to bring a slew of phone calls from men trying to change my mind. But I don't like the idea of a man with his fat wallet in the back pocket picking me up in his car.

My female friends ask me, "Why do you always have so many handsome men at your dinner parties?"

Because of my butt, I want to say.

"Where do you find them?"

Up my butt and around the corner!

290 — Heart Rooms

It takes a long time to learn how to live without someone, and once you learn, it can be a beautiful and noble thing. But it takes only a moment to let someone into your heart. The sad thing is that when they go away, being alone is not so beautiful anymore.

I tell myself: This isn't your *real* life. This isn't the real Claire. She would have a nice man beside her and he would be a true partner in all things and her children wouldn't be suffering and missing their dad.

But then I say: Wake up, Claire. This *is* your life. Your life without someone. Your life alone. You have been shut out of that happy-with-someone realm. Face it, you are now officially locked in all the rooms of your own heart.

291 Curves

"Elen and Marc need another taste of country living," Quentin told me.

Obviously, he sees how lonely I am.

A few years ago, the first time we visited Quentin's farm in Indiana, my seven- and eight-year-olds learned how to drive a VW Bug with stick shift.

This time we will invade his weekend getaway with his lover.

As we're leaving the suburbs, Quentin calls from the farm to tell us, "The same neighbor with the Bug says you can ride his motorcycle."

"Will it be a big motorcycle, Mom?" Marc asks.

"Bigger than a breadbox, for sure," I say, squinting at the highway signs to find the right turn-off. My glasses broke, and I don't have insurance to get new ones.

"You always say that," says Elen.

She's not a teenager yet and she's already sick of me.

A few trucks whiz by and honk, scaring the wistfulness out of me.

I've heard that women in cars do the darnedest things—exposing and pleasuring themselves on the highway, to the Peeping Tom delight of lonely truckers. Ridiculous but arousing.

Sorry, boys, I may be a sexual being, but these days, I'm not being sexual.

292 One Thing

"Glad you made it," says Quentin.

His lover, Brad, takes Elen and Marc by the hand to show them a dog who was hit by a car, not once, but twice. She's under a tree recuperating.

"How long can you guys stay?" I ask, knowing he'll have to get back to the city.

"A few hours," says Quentin. "Just wanted to overlap enough to see how you're doing. And I want to get in a good chess game with Marcus. That kid's pretty amazing."

"Yeah, the kids are doing great, I guess. Everything else is status quo—hellish beyond belief," I say. "Any timely advice?"

"I don't know, Claire," he says. "You seem to be doing all right on your own."

"That's exactly it," I say. "On my own."

"I think it always helps when I'm overwhelmed to keep at least one thing in order. Just one thing in my life that runs smoothly, that's totally on track," he says. "Know what I mean?"

"Nothing's on track in my life."

"Pick something, hijack it, and fly it right."

"Okay," I say, wondering what that one thing should be—maybe the kids.

As if he read my mind, Quentin says, "Oh and don't pick Elen and Marc. I know they're your masterpieces. But pick something separate from them—your own thing."

He calls outside to Brad and the children, "Hey, Marcus, how about beating me at a game of chess?"

I bring the backpacks in from the car, and wonder if "one thing" is too much or not enough.

293 Documents

"They seem to be lost. You'll have to fill them out again," says my sixth lawyer, Justin (my fifth lawyer lasted a whole day), informing me he has lost twelve pages of documents.

I am deeply frightened by documents. Filling them out once almost undid me. I know a better person would have a solution. She would tell me, "Largify them and fill them in with crayons." So I take the blank documents to Kinky's, what I call the friendly neighborhood copier store, and enlarge them to OBESE.

I fill out the sections with thick crayons. It's almost fun. I can picture future lawyers in front of the court with a large pointer, indicating a magenta monthly asset. It will make things so much easier.

I arrive in court and greet my lawyer. The judge floats in and we all rise.

My lawyer asks discreetly, "Do you have the documents?"

"Yes," I say.

"Give them to me," he says.

I start unfolding them.

My lawyer looks more and more alarmed as I continue unfolding. "Why are they so . . . big?" he whispers.

We can feel the judge watching us.

"I biggified them," I say.

He grabs them and stuffs them under the table. "Never mind, we'll do this later," he says.

Luckily, Justin has a good sense of humor. "Claire," he says, "next time you feel compelled to 'biggify' something, take a nap!"

294 Attention

Quentin likes to sum up my mystique. "Claire, you radiate a vitality that some silly people take as an invitation to have sex."

Why then, I wonder, am I silly enough to take them up on it?

He says that I *am* an attention disorder.

Some people call what I have charisma. I call it lack of underwear.

Mimi reassures me. "Claire," she says, "you are from a catalog, such a vooman, made to order."

I'm a male-order disorder.

So why am I still alone?

295 Smash Potato

Ninety-four-year-old Mimi will be sexy till the day she dies. And maybe even after. Her take on interchanges between the sexes is always amusing and often instructive.

She offers advice whether requested or not, and unlike professionals, is a stranger to the notion of client–patient confidentiality.

She tells me the intimate details about the lives of her students. I'm sure she tells them all about me. I honestly don't understand how she knows anything about me, because I can barely get a word in razor blade–wise.

Lighting up a cigarette in her famous brass holder, she discourses on the human foibles of which she, fortunately, is exempt. "She is a crazy. Vat does she vant. Like all vooman, she vant to be a vife. Her boyfriend is a good vone, vith money. I like him. A good man. A vonderful man. Such a helpful man and a beautiful face, ya. But she doesn't know nothing. She talks and talks to him about the ring. Vat, is he a jeweler or a pirate? Asks him question like a parrot, venn vee vill get married? Venn vee go to the church? He doesn't vant to see her anymore, and who could blame. So I told her venn she brought Thanksgiving dinner to me. Such a good girl. Vas a very good turkey vith all things American, smash potato, cranapple, corn that pigs eat in my country, pumpkin pie. Ya. I told her, 'Don't to mention vone more vord about marriage. No matter vat. Not vone vord. I promise you, he vill come to you. Not? Vell, she obeys me perfectly, and short after, he brings the shiny ring and bows down to her, and asks her to be his vife."

The advice: Rings are life-or-death trinkets, and marriage is a blessing to give thanks for.

Although Mimi is the breadwinner, she pays lip service to every stereotype about the sexes. "Men are smarter," she says regularly.

Even at his first piano lesson, my son already loved her.

296 Candy Corn

I bite off each field of color, alternating where I start—at the white tip or at the more solid yellow base, then eat into the orange middle. It's psychedelic, seeing how many angles I can taste.

My stash is growing. I now have enough candy corn for my progeny and their grandchildren, who may turn out to be dulcetarians—eating only sweets.

297 When I Die

When I die, I want friends to find out I was a *lot* stranger than they suspected. I want them to look under windowsills and find hidden keys to hidden rooms where, upon entering, they exclaim, "Golly, I didn't know she collected dried squid!"

298 Typical Day in May

Start morning with psychotic/stalker/neighbor who looks like Creature from the Black Lagoon ringing bell at 6:30 A.M.

"Can you teach me piano?" he says through the locked screen door.

Thought I was still sleeping.

Sadly, wasn't.

Then court with four lawyers: three suing me, one suing Tobin.

Come home. Still don't receive child support check.

Go to bank, where I am big-time overdrawn for benefit of bank that takes more money I don't have in overdraft fees.

Inexplicably for hypervigilant mom like me, don't know exactly where kids are.

Find them outside in park.

Talk to suicidal friend.

When children are in house, toast sourdough bread, slather with butter, steam huge amount of asparagus we eat with fingers from communal bowl.

Progeny does homework; I go to bed.

Can't get up. Must. Kiss kids good night.

Rise to do laundry in basement—oxymoron—must move washer/dryer into attic.

Children yell down they can't get to sleep.

Look at pile of clothes in hamper and feel cryable.

299 He Gives Me His *Arbeit Macht Frei* Smile

For some reason (think martyrish lack of money), during all the time we've been married in Chicago, I've never bought myself a winter coat.

I come to court in the middle of a snowstorm wearing Tobin's white greatcoat.

He gives me his *Arbeit macht frei* smile and says, "Give it back."

"I need it for the trip home."

"Take it off."

Both lawyers tell us, "Quit bickering."

I warm to the fight.

300 I Take Full Responsibility for My Irresponsibility

The rest of the world is going through this with me. Some visibly wince as I approach. Others simply accept the scent of malaise I now emanate. My relatives give off a signal, though almost imperceptible under their help and compassion: *You have screwed up big-time. Welcome to the club.* The member list is vast.

"You should run for mayor," my friends remark.

It's true, I know a scary number of people, and I know their stories too.

Many have said, "I don't know why I'm telling you this; I've never told anyone this before."

I may be irresponsible, but I'm not untrustworthy.

301 The Man on the Cell Phone in the Painkiller Aisle

"Marsha, I told you if you talk about him, I'm going to hang up. Oh, really. And I didn't give you two dogs and a huge . . . Marsha, you never had to work. That was strictly your doing. I don't give a damn about him. Uh-huh . . . If that's true, Marsha, why don't you send him over to my house so he can touch what the dogs did on my front lawn. Yeah, let's see if it turns to gold. You sound like you have a good deal there. Uh-huh. And don't forget me! Giving you our house! Are you kidding? Is that so, Marsh? Well, then give it back. I'd be glad to live there again, with our two dogs. Stole? I stole them? Didn't our lawyers have something to do with who got what? Oh, yeah! I take better care of those guys than . . . What? I'm hanging up, Marsha. Marsha. I'm going to hang up if you talk about that. Stop shouting! I am not. Marsha, okay, I'm hanging up. Marsha . . . Marsha. Did you hang up on me? Marsha? Marsha!"

Cell phones are the new cigarettes. We all get poisoned by secondhand talk.

302 Opaque

Time is an opaque eye
peering through the darkness
where memories burst through
bright as stars.

303 — Slap

A painfully bright star: Shortly before Tobin says we should end our marriage, he slaps me across the face in front of Marcus. Good, I think, at least I've got a witness. An evil, self-serving thought. But thank God, he'll know.

Tobin and I are in therapy in earnest.

And he says he still loves me.

The word *still* leaves a red sting.

304 — Another Slap

Blindingly painful: the day Tobin moves out with a van, the day the children help him pack up his belongings (and some of mine). The day I'm screwing a twenty-five-year-old man down the street and return to find the house turned upside down and inside out from Tobin tugging at any last vestiges of feeling he had had for me. On that day when the children write with broken plaster on the sidewalk, I slap Tobin across the face. From the corner of my eye, I see Marcus recoil, as if I had hit him too. And in that suspended moment, I know this will come back to haunt me. This is what Marcus will remember when he opens his hand and sees white dust in it.

305 — Twisted

The truth is a long and twisted road
and monumental things
start to dissappear
as you look back.

306 Those Who Hang On

Nina keeps telling me about all the vicious conversations she has with her ex-husband, Sergej.

She is like many who can't quell the static between themselves and their ex-spouse. Even though her marriage is long dead, she constantly resurrects old wounds and tries to find men who will listen to her ranting. When she does, they don't stay long. So she reaches out to Sergej by phoning him and screaming at him. She would like a new life, but who wants her?

After Tobin told me it was time to end our marriage, I didn't beg him to stay; I didn't ask him to explain.

Explanations will not bring us hope; only mystery does that.

307 For God's Sake, This Is Not the Time to Drink

Do not become best buddies with alcohol. Not now. Any other time, honest. Just not now.

308 Nonadmission

I can't admit this to anyone: I don't feel any better ever.

309 Piano Homicide

In everyone's divorce, there are certain objects that take on monumental significance. They house the pain we feel. In ours, it was the Bösendorfer grand piano. Its loss crushed me.

To the judge, it was just another possession to be dealt with. And he dealt it out of my hands.

The Bösendorfer had belonged to Tobin's grandfather, a renowned pianist who played Bach in Baden-Baden for his friends—famous writers, poets, and artists of the day—to cure them of spiritual malaise. Mimi says Bach's music is "an ideal marriage, a conversation where two voices are equally important, contrapuntal instead of main melody with lesser accompaniment."

When the Baden-Baden estate was dissolved, no one claimed the Bösendorfer. Tobin played guitar. He never learned to play piano. His sister remembers the piano teacher's dog nipping at her ankles during lessons.

Tobin's father said to me, "You can have it. You play beautifully."

In court, Tobin says, "The Bösendorfer is a family heirloom."

"So are your children," replies my lawyer Justin.

And they also play the piano.

Justin and I and Tobin don't understand yet how hard they'll take it. Crying at night, Marcus will say to me, "We're used to you playing piano as we fall asleep." Elen will wear black for weeks and refuse to set foot in the empty room.

The day the piano leaves—that's the real divorce—I open it up one last time. With the end of a match, I burn into the soundboard the inscription:

The soul of this piano belongs forever to Claire McCloud and her children, Marcus and Elender McCloud

I fill the inside of the piano with dead flowers.

Before I seal it forever, like a coffin, I hold a knife to carve another phrase I want Tobin to understand. Although only five consonants, five vowels, the work is painstaking. And it's in Cheyenne, a language—like poetry—that almost no one knows anymore.

"It's only a wooden thing," I say to myself as they cover it and wheel it out. Kneeling in the silent void, I chalk a grand piano shape on the wood floor, marking where music had been made.

310 The Riviera, Postcards From

I remember when I still had the beautiful black beast. The Bösendorfer.

I'm playing the piano, my children are fighting, bills are piling up like offerings to an angry god, and the mail comes, delivering postcards from my children's father, who is writing from the Mediterranean. It is still snowing where we live, his once-family, and I beg another god to give me the strength to bless him, my once-husband, for all the happiness he gave me, wherever he is, even if it's the south of France. To bestow on him, in his absence, some gratitude for the long back rubs with scented oils, the kisses, the gifts, the food platters carried to my bed at night, the children from him, the smiles my way, his large hands that could cure, and create, and make beautiful, his love, imperfect like mine, the wisdom he gave without being wise, and even the generosity he could show.

And let us not forget the time, oh gods! All eleven years of it while our babies grew and his art too, and the distance between us stretched as far as Chicago from Tübingen, even though we were in the same bedroom.

Let me anoint his brow for being in my life, the mere fact of it, and let me administer to his need, if he has any, for comfort during these trials. Let me send him forgiveness like a strong beacon through the darkness of his animosity. Give me the presence of mind to seek peace. For us both. Allow me, oh gods, the magnanimity to pour love like a river on withering lands, like sunlight into caves.

And then, oh Lord, grant me permission to curse him effectively and rain down upon him sevenfold misfortune for all his remaining days so that he may barely live to regret the reckless squandering of the family who adored him in the temple of his own unmaking.

Forgiveness is nice, but it's hard to keep a good curse down.

311 Piano as a Girl's Best Friend

It brought us together. Like a classical jukebox, my fingers pressed keys to play Tobin's favorites: Beethoven, Chopin, Liszt, Brahms, Schubert, and, most of all, Bach.

At night, I left our warm bed to compose my own songs. Now I wonder whether it came between us. My shifting of allegiance started before the children were born, after we saw *Christiane F.* I slipped out of Tobin's sleeping embrace because a melody inspired by David Bowie's soundtrack looped in my head from ear to ear. All night long, sitting in the dark at its sleek blackness, my foot pressing the soft pedal, I whispered tones in the dark with my fingers barely denting the ivory.

My nocturnal visitations to the Bösendorfer grand became more frequent once the babies arrived. I had little time to practice or compose during the daytime, at least until they grew older. While everyone slept, I conversed with the piano, which harmonized my thoughts and feelings better than anyone could—even a best friend.

When the birds began their own songs, I nestled back in with Tobin for a while, but the ache to return to the bench was strong and I couldn't settle myself to sleep.

My only narcotic is playing the piano.

FINAL DEADLY CLUES

She stops feeling protected by him.

He stops feeling needed by her.

312 Overly Nice Gets Overly Nothing

It may seem heretical, but I should have relinquished my religious training in legal settings. Catholicism accentuates niceness.

In the courtroom, I should have shuttered my softheartedness.

Selfish as they are, according to my good lawyer Justin, Tobin's points about our children and our belongings and everything else seem to make a Tobin kind of sense to me.

Justin tough-loves me. "Claire. Get real. Are you on his side or your own side? And the kids?"

"I'm on my side, I think. The kids have their own."

"Okay. *Don't* be on his side," he says, closing his briefcase. "He's doing well being on his own side, selfish prick. Don't give him any help."

He was right, I had signed on in church to be his helpmate and was still helping him help himself.

Court rules are radically different from rules of courtship. Of everyday life. Of a spiritual life. A sense of common decency toward your spouse could skewer your chances of being treated decently by the judge.

In court, it's most important to remember: Every good deed will be punished. No ands ifs or buts, shapely or otherwise.

After getting a guiltful on the phone from Tobin, I call Justin. "I don't care anymore, honestly," I say. "He can keep everything."

Guilt can make nicey-nicey, and then spousy-spousy will not only watch you fry, but will chop you up and bread you. A crispy sacrifice to the gods.

"You can't do that, Claire," says Justin. "The judge says he has to give your half back."

"I don't want to take anything from him," I say.

"Well, I do," says Justin.

"You do?"

"Mmm-hmmm," he says, as if reading the morning paper. "I'll go and pick up your stuff."

"You will?" I ask, remembering how bad he felt about my "bodily attachment."

"Yeah, I'll go next week."

"You will?" I repeat.

"Yep. Just give me a letter saying it's okay, and we'll get this thing going."

Justin actually shows up at Tobin's and re-removes my half of our possessions from his apartment.

It's really pretty straightforward: Whoever is the wickedest and has the most money wins. (Unless you have a lawyer like mine.)

313 Dr. Kevorkian

Asking a lawyer to help you sever your marriage is comparable to asking Dr. Kevorkian to assist in your death. I imagine myself in the Munch painting screaming.

314 Better to Betray or Be Betrayed?

There must be a biblical reference that would make all of this more tolerable. Wouldn't it have been easier on all of us if Jesus hadn't set such a high standard? If he had said: "Thanks, Dad, but I will not drink of this bitter cup. I can't take any more suffering."

After Tobin (A.T.) leaves and before Christopher (B.C.) arrives on the scene, our Job phase begins, wherein afflictions are rained down upon us. Marcus gets lice, then Elender. I catch them too. We pour gasoline on our heads, but it doesn't work. We try a particularly noxious medication. It doesn't work until a third application. Then I am visited with scabies and the kids catch it from me. We burn the red spots with bleach and put circles of garlic around our torsos to keep it from spreading.

We're becoming such an attractive family.

Then I contract giardia again. I figure I must be dying, so I don't tell anyone. I want to exit with minimal fuss. But after losing a concentration-camp amount of weight, I visit a doctor. She prescribes tablets that taste like rat poison.

Jesus gave us the example of the worst thing for a human being: betrayal. He modeled it for us so that we might live and divorceth.

But what about those who do the betraying and the guilt they feel? There were times during my epic divorce when I thought Judas got off light.

Though I was long out of the habit, I prayed.

"Please, God," I said, fingering a necklace instead of a rosary, "let this be as bad as it gets."

But the next day something much worse happens.

Purely by coincidence, I see Tobin's Mercedes parked on a side street downtown. I get out of my small Honda by crawling over the passenger seat—the rusted driver door doesn't open. First I key the white paint job and write obscenities in red lipstick. (Double Oh God!) I recrawl into my car, back up behind the well-crafted German machine, and repeatedly smash into it. It's totally wrong, totally illegal, and totally satisfying.

315 High-Impact Gelato

My most cherished haunts are taking on an unfamiliar cast. I rename places. The Unicorn Café in Evanston becomes Hormone Café. Blind Faith Café is Blind and Deaf. Kinko's is Kinky's. The frozen-yogurt stand in the Old Orchard Shopping Mall is High-Impact Gelato. Nothing is recognizable.

When I go home, I walk past the hickory in front of the blacksmith house and it reaches out with spindly branches, causing me to hurry inside.

316 For $9.99, He Could Be in Your Home Today

When you don't live with a man, you start looking at men differently. You see them from a distance, like a horse whisperer who watches horses from miles away and can interpret their every gesture. I feel I could tame or comfort any man.

Early in the morning, I screw . . . scrutinize them in cafés while they order, beleaguered by coffee choices and their new, fashionable names:

Pansy chamomile
Poofter peppermint
Pussy espresso
Sissy cinnamon cider
What a wimp café au lait

Unlike women, who delight in cutesy tongue twister beverages, men sullenly point or make the clerk say the name and then grunt. You gotta love these guys. (I do.)

I stand near just about any unshaven Buck and long to be his Buckette. To be a couple ordering coffee after a night of kissing, fucking, or even snoring. Hell, I'm happy to burn my lips, sipping in the vicinity of a man.

317 **Fatherland**

The night before their flight, I have the children well packed.

Tobin assured them he would never have to move back to Germany. But assurances fly away from us now and he does too.

It's a shame for the children, but it doesn't really make a difference for me. The moment Tobin moved across the hall four and a half years ago, we were in separate countries.

"I have a really good feeling that you will have a wonderful, wonderful time visiting your dad," I say. "Hamburg is a cool place. You are not allowed to miss me, okay?"

"What if we do?" they both ask.

"Not allowed," I say. "Of course, I can miss you, but I want you two to have fun!"

"Can you draw me a special picture in case I do?" asks Elen.

"Me too," says Marc, "and give me one of your scarves or something."

"Me too," says Elen. "Your stuff smells like you and it'll help me go to sleep."

"All righty," I say, "two silk scarves coming up. Now, go to sleep so I can work on the drawings."

As I kiss Elender good night, Marcus asks, "What if the plane crashes?"

"Then you'll be dead and I'll be sad."

"Thanks a lot, Mom," Marcus says. "What if the plane really crashes? Or what if you die while we're in Germany?"

"Then I'll be dead and you'll be sad, but you'll get over it and have a good life."

I'm not so afraid of dying anymore, having already done some.

When they arrive in Hamburg with their Lufthansa sky chaperone, their dad is nowhere to be seen. Marcus is beside himself. To comfort him as he cries, Elen says, "Don't worry; Dad's just late as usual." Which ended up being true.

Tobin only died, thank God for Marcus, in our son's head.

318 Vow

Some memories burn brighter with time, like an eternal flame flaring up in a sudden surge of wind.

The white Mercedes rolls like an airplane on the landing strip of our driveway.

Tobin is late. Again.

Untypical for a punctual German; typical for nonresiding dads.

Elender and Marcus, already packed for an hour, rush to the front door.

Marcus is the first one out.

"Hi, I missed you," he says, bounding like a puppy until he reaches his dad.

I'm watching through the round porthole of the front door window of the town house. I may still drown.

Tobin steps around him, as if his son is a piece of luggage.

Marcus holds out his arms.

Tobin keeps his distance.

"You aren't going with me. I have special time with Elen."

The anguish on Marc's face makes him look adult. I restrain myself in my sinking house; this is his time with them.

"What? Markie's not coming?" Elen asks, stilled on the porch.

Tobin doesn't answer, motions to Elen.

She moves in slo-mo, all the while looking back at her brother.

Tobin follows her to the sidewalk, nudging her toward the car.

I abandon ship and open the front door.

I take Marcus's hand, which seems limp, and pull him inside. "Marc, stay here, sweetie, I'll be right back."

I run to the car with such speed that I surprise Tobin, am able to open the car door and get in. I give Elen an emergency look. "Go in the house for a minute, sweetheart. Daddy and Mommy have to talk."

She opens the back car door and moves as if swept by a fast current. Before Tobin can say anything, she's inside with Marcus.

I take the arm of Tobin's six-foot-four body and twist it (yes, Christopher taught me) until it hurts. I hiss quietly:

"Wenn du mir weh tust, das kann ich wohl verstehen—ich bin erwachsen—aber wenn du grausam bist gegen die Kinder, dann wirst du eine Kraft von mir herausbringen, wie eine Löwin fur ihre Kleinen, über die du gar keine Kontrolle hast, und ich schwöre dir, du wirst es bereuen."

His eyes are a spooked horse's as he hears me in his mother tongue, which sounds even worse, but the English would be unnerving enough: "When you hurt me, I can understand—I'm an adult—but when you are cruel to the children, you will awaken in me a strength, like that of a lioness for her young, over which you have no control, and I swear to you, you will live to regret it."

319 Honey, I'm Not Home

On most days there is not a lot of danger that anything will go right. Friends assure me that life is a paradise and we are all gods. Like a homeless person, I feel angered.

One shattered day, my chariot, the rusted Honda Prelude, is in the repair shop. The one-eyed mechanic asks me out on a date, and although I have nothing against Cyclops, I decline. I've had enough quantity misery, and am now looking for quality.

My dentist says I need a root canal, and then I stop by Nina's house to learn she has breast cancer. The only man who interests me hasn't called in weeks. My ex-husband is supposed to pick up the children at their baseball diamond for visitation, but he doesn't show up. The children are in the dark, freezing rain, and another parent takes them home. I find out later that he wasn't there because he was in Key West with his girlfriend. I pick up my car, try to be friendly to the repair man, and drive onto the icy street. I watch accidents along the lakefront and go home to no one.

The worst thing about raising children alone: There's no honey-I'm-homer at the end of any day.

The worst thing about being alone: To know we can't really live without love, and yet another St. Valentine's Day has come and gone, and we are still waiting to open our hearts.

320 Progression

1. Things I stole before the divorce: *Nothing*
2. Things I stole during the divorce: *Math calculator for my daughter, toilet paper, time at the Kinky's computer, cookies for my children's lunch box, a silk formal, soap, towels*

What's the statute of limitations on crimes of desperation?

321 Stone

Springlike evening in the middle of a long winter. My children and I, on thawing bicycles, approach a brightly lit Baha'i temple. A warm wind blows me a moment of hope. Gliding by the moon-white stone, I send out: *Let there be an adult in my life. Make him a sage for Marcus and a friend for Elender. Let him be the king of a small country.*

I don't care where the country is; I would pack up and live there. In a sanctuary like Dev and Kalpana's house filled with aromas of home-cooked dahl, pakora, and gulab jamun, where Elender says, "It's like time just stands still."

I crave peace. Even a tomb might do. But if they rolled away the stone, three days later, there would be no body. I would have become the stone itself.

I'd like to be a stone, no ups and downs. Just exist.

322 Lake

Driving back from dropping Elen and Marc at church for choir practice, I watch a man and a woman, at the beach with their dog. Bathed in new-day light, near the lifeguard chair, he takes off his sweatshirt, the woman by his side, their dog running to the water. I can only call it masculine, the way he folds it, without folding, hanging it over his shoulder. I ache a physical ache to see him take his shirt off like that. His woman climbs the lifeguard chair, squints her eyes to try to ward me off.

323 How Things Disappear

Last night I dreamed I carried Tobin through sand dunes. I held him like a child, his long legs wrapped around my stomach. I carried him far because he said he didn't know where to go.

Once he got down to help me find water and noticed my footprints still showed the way. Later I looked back and saw they were gone.

324 In All Fairness

In all fairness to Tobi, when he went to a men's group at the beginning of our marriage, and they all talked about their hidden pleasures, he told me he felt kind of mild because all he wanted to say, and all he said was, "I love, absolutely love, making love to my wife."

That day he used three *loves* in his sentence, yet we can't count on each other now. He called me his universal genius. "She's all I need," he said, "My twenty-four-hour Laurie Anderson." Like her music, our love was brighter than neon, experimental, but we failed.

I have a hard time saying it now, but I adored him. Everything about him, except his unkindness. Which turned out to be a bigger deal than I thought. A love-breaker.

325 Catch and Release

The river of communication is blocked—broken boats gone aground, logs and dead trees colliding, piling, cutting off water flow.

I can recall that same river where every thought we shared sparkled as it floated downstream.

How did it go wrong? Endless discussions haven't answered this sufficiently for me. We were young, that's all—saplings at the river's edge, our roots trying to take hold.

"Mom, what's the hardest language in the world?" Elender asked recently.

"The language of love." Without thinking, the answer comes.

I wanted its corollary—failure to love—to be easy. I wanted to spare us all, to feel smug as I executed the perfect divorce, honoring the children and both parents. Not a *breakup* of a family but a *reconfiguration.* Like the Big Dipper splitting apart and becoming two fine little dippers, brightly shining, still intact, and eternally scooping up their part of the darkness.

I was certain I could pull it off with grace and dignity while my friends avenged themselves in court. But there is nothing dignified about breaking a vow—a vow I had made with all my fledgling heart. From the moment the divorce decree is final, I'll be living with my own treachery. And I swear, I'll be more careful, in the future, what promises I make to others.

326 Tobin's Dream

He wakes to see her in the beautiful room.
She is wearing orange as bright as a candle.
She leans over him to breathe kisses on his body.
The kisses resound with pain echoing pleasure.
Soon everything will be wrong.

327 The Sorrow & the Need

I'm a stricken traditionalist. I believe in family and marriage.

There will always be a deep woman's unwisdom that waits for her husband's return. Crazy Penelope. Her room lined with hundreds of hourglasses—sand sifting through their tiny transparent waists, accumulating to each different level—while she stitches a real time that exists only to measure grief.

I wander my house, doing nothing, wondering why I can't settle into sleep. Why? Because I'm waiting for him.

Yes, it's as fatal as love. Because it is love.

Now we are a traditional American family—the divorced couple with two children.

328 Intimate Penalties

It's snowing wet clumps of white that stick to our coats like burrs, and the wind is picking up. Tobin brushes the snow off my hair and pulls up my hood to cover my head. His warm hands hold my face and our eyes almost meet before I see that the snowflakes are tinged with orange. My first thought is, must be lights from an ambulance, but the silence is so thick, you can hear the orange snow landing on the ground.

My second thought is more complicated and comes from a cloud snowing psychobabble, but seems to be true for me at the time: Yes, love is magic, but it is also pure deception. Love is the ultimate cover-up, blanketing every disappointment and betrayal. At least my brand of love, a non-bitch form of it, the kind that men, like Tobin, learn to run from because they, like untamed animals, need to play hard ball.

I reach under Tobin's coat to pull him closer, and my fingers touch his naked skin. The orange snowflakes are forming into balls. Fear and love make me catch them before they dissolve at our feet. Tobin's coat is in shreds and falls off his body. He stands there naked before me, and then he disappears.

329 The Last Courting

Again and again,
the day of the decree
comes over me:
The shiny floors of the judgment room.
This is release, I tell myself.
Release that should feel right.
My lawyer Justin says
"This is the last door and
I will help you through it."

"Thank you," I say.
For once, I understand:
when breath is gone
lungs do not lift,
and my heart
will no longer love.

330 The Undoing

"I don't."
"I don't."

Under fluorescent lights, we stand before a judge.
Instead of bridesmaids, we have lawyers by our sides.
We say nothing. Not "I do." Not "I don't."
The perfect un-ceremony.

Ten years ago, we stood before an altar and looked into each other's eyes.
There was so much we didn't see.

331 — Cut

If I cut a slice out of my past—time mutilation—there is always, will always be *the now,* when I am left incontrovertibly alone.

No matter how many times I relive the scene in front of the judge, I feel my heart open and opened.

In the courtroom, when it's all over, I'm confused. As if coming out of anesthetic.

"Are we divorced?" I ask.

Tobin is the only one to answer. "Yes, we are."

His voice—the one I had loved like my babies—bursts like champagne.

The ethereal cord between us has been cut.

The operation was successful.

332 — Alchemy Amoroso

Tobin said I knew how to love properly. Did I? Did he? I thought so, but I was wrong. I didn't thrive. It seemed to me he did, for many years. Was I blind?

When I realized he wasn't thriving, I wanted us to end. Why couldn't I have ended it for myself? Loving him was more satisfying than being loved. Grave mistake?

Is it twisted, even demented, to secretly champion your husband's escape? To silently cheer him on as he evades you and the children?

My friends can't understand how I don't hate you, Tobin.

Well, I loved you, even to the end.

But that was not enough to save us.

Quentin says, "Sure, sure, your ex has good points, but he must die."

I want you free, Tobin. Runnnnnn! Take everything you need to *get free* of us. Do not look back at your salty family. Leave this house of pain, where words are an evil spell and every teardrop poison in a fairy tale gone berserk.

I spur you on because I know you will never return.

Did you try to stay? Maybe. Did you think of your children above yourself? Only you can answer that. Did we do the best we could? I'm not so sure.

Flee! Fly through the slamming doors of our days.

Speed away from you and me; we do not need to be.

We are alpha and omega, the first and last to go when the party is over, and the children, in their party hats, ask, "Where's Daddy? Why can't you and Daddy be *real* Valentines?"

"Daddy will always be your Daddy. Daddy will never leave you," I'll say.

But I'll mean, "Daddy saved himself, darlings. Daddy is free."

333 After the Rain

I thought there would be no more songs. But nothing is as it appears. Beautiful rooms were beautiful only because he was in them, making me suffer, making love, making us home.

These lyrics came to me in the middle of the night. I had to get up and go to the piano to write the music.

After the rain has fallen down,
there is a place that I belong.

There is a reason to carry on.

It has no meaning until it happens to you,
after the rain has fallen down.

It has no meaning until you know,
Feel the wind blow
So
After the rain has fallen down,
there is a place that I belong.

There is a place,
I don't know where,
but it is there,
after the rain has fallen down.

334 Rise

How can one hide from that which never sets?
—HERACLITUS

At dawn, I walk through the still-dark rooms of my blacksmith house and stand in front of misted windows. I touch my index finger to the cold glass and start to write:

I almost saw him in the darkness. I thought he was my savior, but he was only John the Baptist, announcing the possibility of true love.
Because he saved me, I thought I owed him my soul.
But many people save us.

I wipe the window clean, wait for mist to cover the surface again, and then, as the sun eases into my own beautiful rooms, I continue writing:

I have an odd faith that, despite this scourge, perhaps because of it, I may find someone else, and we will save each other.

335 Storm, Leaf, Window

I look out the window and it's not winter yet.
Maybe things aren't as bleak as I thought.
There is only one thing that matters.

Love is the gathering storm.

Love is the eye of the storm, the end of the storm, and the storm itself.

Love recognizes us before we know ourselves.

It's the reason we mistreat each other. The reason we leave. Every time, we're shown that love is stronger than we are.

Love is the first thing we know.

The first time I saw a tree and felt its polka-dot light on the air around me; the first time I saw Tobin shake his hair from his eyes; the first time I touched Elender as she began to breathe on my naked skin; the first time Marcus—already broken—was placed in my arms.

And, of course, love will be the last thing. The thing that lasts.

The last leaf in autumn that clings to a branch and then falls with a whimsical zigzag. Crushed under my foot, I hear the crackled hush, but I still say love is here on this path.

Love is the only story I can follow.

Coda

The lake is icy turquoise brushed with palest sage. No waves. Almost as smooth as a mirror, stretching out into our unreflected future.

The air is colding down even as Marcus, Elender, and I stand on the pier looking out onto our own mini-Laurentide.

What they are thinking, I can't imagine. If I could speak now, without breaking, I would ask them. Their silence makes them seem too old to be children.

As if I need something more bracing than the iciness all around us, I inhale the air's frost straight to my heart. I take off one glove, bend down to pick up a crystally ball of ice.

I wonder many things.

Is it possible for parents to get into heaven? Will we need a plenary indulgence for all the harm we've done? And, after long years of marriage and divorce and estrangement, will we be like war criminals, too old to be punished for our crimes?

Will we find comfort in realizing that just because a marriage didn't last doesn't mean it wasn't a success?

"Look kids," I say, opening my hand. Half a thought tells me I'm not warm enough to have melted the ball. But my numb hand is empty, without even a trace of snow.

If I squint out far enough, I think I can catch a glimpse of Tobin on the horizon, encamped on a chunk of ice. If I could ask one thing of him?

Send me a signal every so often, like tribal smoke, telling me you're okay.

Then I can turn my back on this thickening lake and take our children home.

What I'll say to them?

Elender. Marcus. Because of you, I have managed. For today.

To myself?

I'll find the nearest piano. Somehow my fingers will sound out harmonies to a new song. It will be almost familiar, even triumphal. As the chords resolve, I'll recognize myself in the tune. Just sitting there playing a Cheyenne melody.

Aotzi No-otz.

Postlude

Cognac-colored candles, red velvet wallpaper, thick linen tablecloths, and Italian waiters who'd rather flirt than bring roasted pepper platters to your table. I take it all in. This is the future of our history.

Elender and Marcus will be in their late teens. I can almost see it—they're virtually grown-ups. Look, Tobin, we didn't stunt them with the poison we unloaded on them. They are dressed up, sitting with you, their dad, having dinner, drinking wine. Maybe it's in Germany. Most likely, it'll be in the States.

Earlier, Marcus will have called me on his cell phone. "Mom, Dad's in town. Where should we take him for dinner?"

"Alfredo's. He'll love it. Mafia atmosphere."

All Europeans love Chicago's mob underbelly.

"Cool. Thanks."

"Love you, Marc."

I'll be driving by that particular suburb where they are eating. My car will be broken but drivable, unable to go into reverse—a fitting metaphor, because I don't look back anymore—so I'll have to plan carefully where I'm going to park.

I want to make Elen's diary wish come true: *Someday I wish they could just call each other up just to say hi and what's going on.*

It's the very most I can do.

I'll find a space where I don't have to parallel park and walk to the ruby neon ALFREDO sign. I'll be dressed in black, either for mourning or New York chic, and wearing a temporary tattoo between my breasts. It's a colorful mandala from a religion I don't follow.

During the only-forward drive here, I'll have planned my entrance and my conversation: *You'll stick to the pleasant,* I will coach myself. *The people you know in common. His parents, his sister. After ten years—God, it's been ten years since you've seen him—give him nothing to hate. Twelve years since you've seen him in front of the children. Let them see you two talking like civil human beings who loved each other enough to make them. Be perfect.*

I'll open the door to the restaurant. I'll walk up the stairs to the red-velvet dining room. I'll take a deep breath at the entrance.

Love—yes, even former love—makes us brave as an Indian before a massacre.

Tobin will see me first. He'll take a breath and say to Elen, "I think that's your mom."

My family will look frightened, but I'll walk to the table.

Tobi, Tobin, I'll think, *you haven't aged well.*

Will I have?

"Tobin," I'll say, sweet and direct. "I heard you were in town, and I wanted to see you. I thought I'd break the ice so it won't be awkward later with weddings and funerals and . . ."

"Well, that's very nice," he'll say, caught off guard, almost smiling.

"I don't want to intrude. I know you are here with the kids, but I just wanted to say hi." Maybe we'll switch into German.

"Das ist aber nett," he'll say again. "Why don't you sit down?"

"Danke," I'll say, noticing my children sitting on either side of him, staring at us, unable to speak.

"Would you like a drink?" he'll ask, riveted by my tattoo, wanting to ask, but not asking, what it means. I'll notice that he's still attracted to me in the same old way—a physical longing mixed with a fascination and mistrust of all things American.

"Sure," I'll say. "But I can't stay long."

Steering us clear of anything controversial, I'll ask about our old friends, and he'll tell me who's gotten married, and the few who've gotten divorced.

Elender and Marcus will look frozen.

Tobin will sip his wine and take another furtive look between my breasts. Later Elen will tell me, "Dad asked whether your tattoo was permanent."

"So," I'll say. "I hear you are doing well."

"From who?" he'll ask. "I'm doing horribly."

"I mean, Marcus tells me you are very fit. Biking up mountains."

"Oh *ja,* that," he'll say. "Physically, maybe. But otherwise, I'm doing badly."

"That's a shame," I'll say, "because when you were with me, you were doing a lot of great things."

"When I was with you," he'll say, "I did a lot better."

Naturally.

There will be a silence, and the children will shift in their chairs. I'll look at Tobin and notice that his shoulders are grasshopper-thin; next to his heart is a pack of cigarettes.

I'll indicate the children and say to Tobin, "Well, we can be proud of these two. Elen and Marc. They've turned out great."

"Yes, I'm very proud of *these* two," he'll say, because by this time he'll be divorcing his second American wife, who has two small children.

I'll get up quickly, trying to say, "I hear your other children are adorable," but my voice will catch.

Elen will say with her serene, modulated voice, "Oh, Mom, don't cry."

"It's all right, sweetie," I'll manage as I walk around the table.

On sudden impulse, I'll kiss Tobin on the cheek, I'm sure of this part. I'll have just enough time to kiss Elen and Marc before the tears fall faster.

I won't look back as I walk down the stairs to the street and find where I'm parked.

As my car goes forward—it's the only way I can go now—I'll think what a good thing it was, our lost family sitting together at one table. Even for an instant.

Gott sei Dank, I made it work.